I0550059

The Snow Thief

Copyright © 2024 Alexandra Louise

All rights reserved

Cover design by: Alexandra Louise

*To all those who need more reasons to read fantasy, here are three:*

1. *The real world sucks.*
2. *Oh, wait. I guess that's it.*

# The Snow Thief

# 1

It was then that a single snowflake fell from the heavens and for the first time in a hundred years, things were about to change. It sailed through the night sky as if some invisible thread, a bond that could not be broken, was pulling it where it needed to go. Something called for it, and kept tugging it closer and closer until it reached its final resting place and that once perfect, as if formed by the gods themselves as a representation of their unique perfection, tiny little snowflake melted away into nothingness and burned an icy mark into the tip of his nose. That night, the dragon woke from his blissful slumber to a change in the winds coming his way.

****

The general hush that encompassed her surroundings was once again where Eira's attention dragged while she was supposed to be focussing on the exam papers being lightly tapped by her penned hand. It was the last one of the semester and she could not wait to be done. However, that anticipation was failing to push her through the last few questions that seemed to drag on as if being read over and over again in her head by some unknown voice. She did not know how long she had zoned out before the professor at the front of the room called out that there were twenty minutes left in the exam.

She redirected her attention to the exam paper and read the last question again: *What was your favourite part of the course? How about it being over.* She refrained from writing that down. Eira had never understood why professors insisted on putting questions like that on the final exam, in some sort of effort to make the exam seem less stressful to students, or perhaps as a friendly way to give extra marks. If that was the case, why not just make the exam worth less? It seemed like a waste of her and every other poor student's time, and the time of whoever was marking the exam. No matter what you write there you get bonus marks, so she quickly thought of something that made it seem like she was paying attention all semester, and scribbled it down. Then she folded the question and answer booklets closed rubbing back along the dents in the spines she had made in them earlier to keep them open, grabbed her backpack sitting on the floor beside her, and walked to the front of the class. She smiled at the professor and handed in the exam. He glanced at the clock and jotted down the time on the front of the exam, then turned to the pile of papers beside him.

"Very good work, Eira," he said as he handed over the marked paper she had turned in a week before. She took the paper and saw the giant ninety-two written in the quintessential red ink every teacher has a stockpile of. "You really have a knack for this stuff. Have you thought more about the field experience trip this spring? It would be the experience of a lifetime, getting to spend three weeks in a medieval castle and learn all about the history of the land and where this mythology originated."

Truth be told, she was just taking this class for easy marks and to keep up the requirements of the study part of her work/study visa. She had heard from others it was an easy credit class. She had no interest in the history of mythology. "It does sound like fun, but I'm not sure if spending three weeks in a castle is really for me," she responded.

"Well, the deadline to apply is not for a few weeks. Think it over, and have a good holiday."

Adelaide was a beautiful place to not be found. Eira was not from Australia. She had grown up in a small town in another country entirely; a much colder country. There was nothing to do or see there growing up so as soon as she was able she got out, never looking back. She took out a map, closed her eyes, and pointed a finger thrusting it against the map. To be honest, she only landed on Adelaide after about the fourth try. The first three weren't far enough away and she wanted to go somewhere she thought no one could find her. She hadn't lived outside of Adelaide all her life, only from the time she was about three until she turned eighteen when she knew it was time for her to start her own adventures. And something was pulling her out of that godforsaken place. Her family didn't mind. It was just her aunt left. Her parents died when she was young and so her aunt was left to raise her in the small cottage on the outskirts of the smallest town known to man—at least that's what it felt like to Eira. There was one of everything there: one grocery store, one gas station, one restaurant, and one automotive repair shop where her aunt worked. She was a mechanic there and the bane of every man in town's existence. What more did you need really? But anytime her aunt took her into the city, her whole world lit up as if some force was pulling her out of that small town and that force only got stronger as she grew older.

It was a brisk day in the city. Eira made her way across the campus and headed out through the large wrought-iron gates at the entrance of the university. Admittedly, she was distracted by many things, the most recent being the fifty-seven percent she had received on her philosophy final. She was hoping the exam had gone better but was mostly annoyed she even had to take philosophy in the first place. She didn't quite understand the point of it. While she seemed to have a knack for history, it was about the only class she seemed to be doing well in lately. Ahead of her was the same crosswalk she crossed every day for the last three years, at the same intersection at the same time. Eira had always made sure to have classes ending at three o'clock to be able to get to work on time.

Holding her backpack in front of her, she rummaged through it and was placing the marked paper she had just received from her professor inside when she stepped off the curb. If she had done so a second earlier or a second later, the outcome may have been different. Just as her foot touched the asphalt, a blaring horn blasted in her ears causing her whole body to jump and flinch backward. She looked up and witnessed a bus whizzing by and realized someone had pulled her out of the way. She had dropped her backpack and its contents had cascaded across the sidewalk. Perfect. A couple of books and her water bottle now lay on the sidewalk. She turned to thank the person who had saved her, but there was no one there. Twirling in place, Eira scanned the street and saw someone walking a dog and a couple walking down the street in the distance, but none of them could have been the one to pull her out of the way of the bus. She was the only person standing there, alone on the curb. She knelt down and quickly scooped up her belongings.

"I think I'm going crazy," she said by way of greeting when she arrived at work a half hour later. It was a small local pub she had been working at since she moved to Adelaide; which was where she met Nell. Nell was the only real friend she had made in the three years being there; a fiery soul who was not afraid to do what she felt like and didn't care who was watching. The complete opposite of Eira. She burst in on Eira's first day, soaking wet from her auburn hair to her bright red rain boots, and got into a heated argument with the manager about being late. She addressed him with a particularly Aussie curse word and the two had words until he finally gave up, knowing full well he was not going to win that battle. When the argument was over she noticed Eira standing there, smiled and said with her Aussie flair, 'I'm just glad it started raining when it did, otherwise, I would've had to be on time', and they've been friends ever since.

"What are you talking about?" asked Nell from behind the bar counter. She was slicing a lime and placing the pieces into a clear container. Eira moved around behind the counter and removed her coat placing it on the hook in the corner.

"I was walking down the street today and when I got to the curb I almost got hit by a bus."

"What! You right?" gasped Nell halting her slicing movements.

"Yeah. Except that's not the weirdest part. I stepped off the curb without noticing the bus coming and before I knew it I was pulled out of the way by someone, but when I turned around there was no one there. Even the people on the street looked as if they didn't notice anything."

"That *is* weird. Maybe you imagined it," she pointed a paring knife at Eira. "Maybe you just stepped off the curb and jumped back from the bus but it happened so fast that you thought someone must have pulled you out of the way," she went back to slicing.

"No, I swear I felt someone's hands on my arms."

"Maybe you have a stalker. Oh, or a ghost?"

"A ghost that *saves* me from being killed?"

"Well, it could be a friendly ghost." Eira didn't respond, just pulled her eyebrows upwards. "Well, I don't know what to tell you but, changing the subject, exams are over! How did yours go? I'm pretty sure I failed mine."

"I think it was alright," she replied and then proceeded to tell Nell about the final question on the exam she had just written.

"I hate that type of question," said Nell, "I usually write that the course is over," she smiled. "Anyway...celebration time!" She grabbed a shot glass from the bar and a bottle of cinnamon whiskey from the shelf.

"Nell, we're working."

"Well, *I* am, but technically you don't start for another six minutes." She poured the shot and handed it over, "You haven't even clocked in yet."

Eira took the glass with a mischievous smirk and looked around quickly to make sure Peter, their boss or anyone else wasn't watching. Then she realized they were, in fact, the only two in there besides a couple sitting way in the back that had no chance of seeing her immoral behaviour. Eira downed the shot and shook her head, "You're awful."

"Yeah, but you love me."

She then washed the glass, hurried to the back, and clocked in. When she came back out, she grabbed an apron hanging behind the bar and tied it swiftly around her waist.

"So, what are we going to do for your birthday?" Nell asked.

Eira stared at her with an expression that indicated Nell should know her well enough by now to know that she didn't want to do anything for her birthday. Birthdays were never a big deal to her. Eira's aunt made sure to always have a cake and a gift every year, and even a few of her friends over, but it was never anything monumental like some people like to make the occasion. For Eira, every birthday, every year that went by seemingly faster than the last was just bringing her closer to a future she didn't want. To be able to stay young and carefree for eternity would be the way she'd prefer to go.

"I don't want to do anything," Eira answered.

"Oh come on. Not even a little party? We can just do it here with only a couple of people."

"A couple of people always turn into twenty people I don't even know. So thanks, but no thanks."

"Okay, well I guess you still have a few days to decide."

Except that the next few days went by so quickly, Eira barely had a handle on what was happening. Her days were blurred into mostly work and nothing out of the ordinary happened since the day she almost died from impact by bus. Her birthday was just around the corner and she had finally convinced Nell not to do anything— although she still suspected something was going to happen. She knew Nell too well to know she'd just let sleeping dogs lie. Even if she agreed to nothing big, there was usually something small in store anyway and the few birthdays Eira had with her, she had come to like the familiarity of knowing her friend always wanted to do something nice. She just hadn't figured out what this year had in store for her yet.

The *what*, came the evening of Eira's birthday with a loud knock at her apartment door. She opened it to see Nell holding a lit birthday cake with, she assumed, twenty-one candles; she didn't have time to thoroughly count them. Not the best decision she thought, having a lit cake in the hallway, so she promptly blew out the candles and let Nell inside.

"Did you make a wish at least?" Nell asked.

"Yes." The same thing she wishes for every year: to be left alone and have the life she always dreamed of.

"Good—because I *will* light them again."

They cut into the cake and laughed for hours talking about this and that. Mostly about Nell's fascination with this new guy named Paul who just started working at the pub. The evening soon morphed into the night, and they were sufficiently sloshed on the margaritas Nell insisted on making even though Eira didn't have margarita mix or tequila. She pretty much only had ice and lemonade, so it was slushy lemonade with vodka. Nell was asleep on the couch while Eira, who had not had as many slushy *vodkanades*, started her nightly ritual of watching television in bed before drifting off to sleep. A bad habit—yes, but a comforting one. Her only company now was a small silver tabby named Pix. She had adopted Pix when she first arrived in Adelaide. She was just a tiny eight-week-old kitten who seemed to decide as soon as she laid eyes on Eira that she was the one for her, and she was not going to let Eira leave without bringing her home with her. She leaped right onto Eira's lap at the adoption centre and looked up at her with her big loving eyes, claiming Eira as her own. They had been together ever since—through the good times and the bad, she was always the one Eira could talk to and work out her problems with. As pathetic as it sounds, talking to a cat, sometimes you don't need someone to respond, you just need to be heard and Pix was always ready to listen.

"Well, Pix," Eira sighed as she picked up the cat from where she had made herself comfortable on the bed and pulled down the sheets to climb inside. Eira held the sheets open and the little cat scurried right next to her and snuggled into the warmth of her body. She pulled her laptop over and opened it up looking for something suitable to watch. She finally settled on watching *White Christmas,* a favourite of hers during the holiday season, especially the part where Bing Crosby and Danny Kaye dress as women. "Another birthday come and gone. I wonder what sort of adventures are in store for us this year?" The little cat looked up at Eira and yawned. "I know, you're not much for adventures and I've put all of that behind me. But, you never know, we could just have one of our own."

Again, she did not respond, didn't even look up this time, just shut her eyes and crawled deeper into the covers as if to say, *I'm bored with you now, I'm going to sleep.*

The nightmare was back that night. The one that had plagued Eira on and off for the last few months leading up to her birthday. Like some dreaded omen. She kept seeing him, the one who took her life away from her. A dark, shadowy figure always looming overhead.

*I'm coming for you,* a voice hissed. *You can't hide forever, girl. You can't keep running from your fate. You know it comes down to just you and I.*

Eira gasped awake moments before her alarm sounded and a small paw was pressing itself against her cheek. She got herself out of bed and was led to the kitchen by Pix who started howling beside her empty food dish. She glanced over to see Nell still sufficiently passed out on the couch.

When Nell finally awoke, she dragged herself off the couch groaning with the effects of the night before very present across her face. "Coffee," was all she murmured, so they headed to their usual spot down the street to try to revive themselves—mostly Nell—before work.

The local coffee shop was decked out with various holiday trinkets and the aroma of gingerbread wafted through as the two sat at a small table in the corner watching the various people strolling past the window doing their last-minute Christmas shopping. While Eira enjoyed her new life here, there was a small part of her that missed the snow during Christmas time. The holidays just didn't quite seem the same. Snow and Christmas just seemed to go together so perfectly, but perhaps that was just the way she was brought up. Eira never knew anything different, while Nell hated the stuff. The thought of freezing your butt off every time you walked to your car didn't appeal to her, and Eira couldn't blame her. The one bonus though, is there are very few creatures that can kill you. Australia was beautiful and Eira didn't regret her choice, but it was the land of a thousand and one things that can kill you and most of them would not survive in a colder climate.

"Ugh," Eira said sitting down at the table, pulling her phone from her back pocket, and placing it face up beside the steaming mug of holiday spirit. "Sometimes I wish it would snow. It just doesn't feel like Christmas without it."

"You and your snow," smiled Nell. "Hey, so I never asked you but...how did things go with that guy?"

"What guy?" She asked through a mouthful of cranberry white chocolate scone; a personal favourite.

"You know—that guy?" She stared at Nell without any idea who she was talking about but Nell persevered anyway, "You know, the one with..." she raised her hands and hovered them over her head, "the hair."

"Oh, well now I know exactly who you're talking about," Eira replied, her words dripping with sarcasm.

"No, seriously. You met him at that bookstore?"

"Oh, that guy. I went out with him like two months ago."

"Yeah," she smiled optimistically, "how did it go?"

"Well considering I had no idea who you were talking about—not well."

"Awe, that's too bad."

"Not really. He was nice and all but, not who I picture myself with. I want a real man. You know, the kind that still believes in chivalry and stuff. Anyway..." she placed another bite of scone into her mouth with her fingers and rubbed the crumbs off onto the plate. Partly to stall before saying what she was about to and partly because she was hungry, "I actually sort of got back together with...Trey."

Nell nearly spat out her coffee, "Trey! Why?"

"What's wrong with him? He's... nice," Eira defended, half-heartedly.

"Sure in an 'I'm too dense to actually have a solid relationship' kind of way."

"He's not that bad, and he cares about me."

"Didn't he cheat on you?"

"That was a misunderstanding. It was more of a Ross and Rachel thing," Eira clarified.

"Don't even get me started on that! And to quote Rachel's mother, 'Once a cheater, always a cheater.' Anyway, he spends more time at the gym than with you. Does he even have an actual job, or is it just picking up heavy things and putting them down? But, I digress, whatever makes my Eira happy." She touched a patronizingly gentle hand to Eira's cheek in an overbearing yet loving motherly way, "Also, I don't think they really exist anymore," she added.

"What doesn't?"

"Chivalrous men." Then she took a breath before continuing into what would be yet another rant that Eira was all too familiar with. "Men have gotten lazy. They don't want to be chivalrous so they settle for the girl who doesn't care about stuff like that or they fool her into thinking that they are when they're really not."

"Are you alright?" Eira asked. "You seem more cynical than usual. Anyway, I know my prince charming is out there somewhere. He just hasn't found me yet, but that doesn't mean I shouldn't give a guy a chance in the meantime."

"Nah, he's just good in bed. Just admit it," Nell sipped her coffee.

"I didn't say that."

"Your face did."

Eira smiled and sipped from her mug that had now cooled enough to make the creamy rich liquid bearable enough to swallow. She then looked at her phone and set the cup down, "Shit, we should get going or we'll be late."

"What? To find your prince?"

"No, for Cinderella duty. This princess still has to work."

"Yeah." Nell rose from her chair, grabbed the purse hanging on the back, and slung it around her neck and under her arm. "You should spend more time in forests," she added as she pulled her hair out of the strap. "The girl always meets the prince in the forest."

Eira paused for a second thinking about the truth in that, then bringing out that sarcasm again replied, "Yeah, I'll get right on that."

Work dragged on as the sun set on the city. Eira was almost finished serving drinks and food to the various patrons. She stared blankly at the clock above the bar trying to read the time, but every time she did she would zone out just long enough to have to start all over again.

"Hey!" She jumped in response to Nell in her ear. "There's a guy over there in the corner looking for you." Eira turned slightly but couldn't make out who it was from where she was standing. She placed the tray she was holding under her arm on the counter and headed over to the part of the bar Nell had directed her to. She scanned the room looking for anyone she knew, but no one's gaze caught her attention—until. A figure leaning against his chair at a small table tucked away in the corner.

Eira stopped and blinked, looking again. He wasn't looking at her, *thank God*. He had his head down, looking at the drink menu on the table. She debated running. She could slip out so easily no one would see and Nell would surely have her back with Peter if he came after her later for skipping out on her shift a couple of hours early. But would she even stay here, in this city? Or should she pack up and leave? He had obviously found her, meaning they knew where she was. Could she even run again and hide? When the immense beating of her heart faded from her ears and the sounds of the pub around her once again pulled her back to reality, she took a breath and headed over to the table.

"What are you doing here?" Eira gritted through her teeth. He looked up and gave her that devilish smile she hadn't seen in years.

"Nice to see you too," he said with all the ease of old friends meeting again.

"I said," Eira didn't want to play games, "what are you doing here?"

"I came to get you. What do you think I'm here for?"

"I'm not going back."

"You have to, you know you have to. You knew this day would come, Eira. Seriously, don't be so selfish."

"Selfish?" she said a little too loud and started to notice the people around them perk up their ears at their conversation. She hushed her voice again and leaned into the table, "I'm not the one being selfish. Have you ever thought that all of you are the selfish ones, just expecting me to be who you want me to be?" She turned to walk away.

"Please, Eira." His tone changed solemn, "You know there's no one else."

"Find someone."

Eira left the table and was heading back to the bar when she felt a tug at her arm, "You can't run, Eira. And sooner or later you'll be pulled back. It's the way it was always going to be." He let go of her arm and turned to leave, "Oh, and happy birthday." She watched as he slid out the door into the street.

"Who was that?" asked Nell. "He's handsome."

"What—no he's not!" He was, though. Devastatingly so. It was the kind of beauty you thought could only be dreamed up or only existed in lands with magic. Immortal creatures looked that way, not regular people. He knew it too, which just made him all the more insufferable. Eira turned to her, "And he's no one, just..."

She couldn't even lie and tell her he was an old friend. They had never really been friends. "An old acquaintance," Eira finally added.

"Okay, well, table three needs refills."

The click of the lock in the pub door echoed through the still night air. Eira hugged Nell goodbye and headed home in the opposite direction of her. It was a cool evening, cooler than usual. She could see her apartment across the street, the doorway dimly lit by the street lamps. She stopped for a moment to smell the fresh night air. There was something different about it tonight, it wasn't the usual wafting of warm salty ocean mist and eucalyptus she had come to know all too well, it was fresher somehow, almost frosty as if she was suddenly back home inhaling the crispness of an early winter morning. It was a familiar smell. The lovely, enticing scent of oncoming snow. *That can't be right?* Eira shook her head to try to ward off the insanity. It must have been her encounter earlier. He got into her head and was now causing hallucinations of the olfactory variety. The very moment she stepped off the curb, ready to cross the street to the sanctuary of her apartment, it began to snow, halting her in her tracks. It was that fine diamond dust that sparkled as it fell. She had always loved the snow and believed that the first snowfall of the year was a moment when time could stand still. It's amazing the power a mere bit of precipitation can have. The fresh white coat covering all the dirt and sorrows of the world creates a clean, fresh start for everyone and everything in it. Perhaps that is why it had always resonated with Eira, as she had longed to do the same for so many years; a fresh start. That's what Adelaide was supposed to be—but now?

She had no idea what was going on. *What the hell?* She stared at the sky and watched as those soft flakes cascaded downward and brushed her face. No, she must be hallucinating. Did she faint? Perhaps she was just dizzy and the snow was those little flecks of light you see before your eyes when your blood pressure is off. This can't be right. Eira looked ahead of her and tried to see if someone, anyone, was around and noticing this strange phenomenon too.

The snow began to fall harder—faster, creating a curtain of cold white flakes glistening in the moonlight. She stepped forward in an attempt to escape this daydream and found herself falling right off the edge of the street, which she had never known to end, and tumbling down the sides of a cliff finally rolling to a stop on the dirt-laden ground. *Well, that's new.* She lay there for a moment, eyes blinking, waiting for her brain to come to terms with what her eyes were seeing.

She was certainly no longer on the street outside her apartment, and she was very sure she was no longer in Adelaide. She had this sinking feeling deep within her core that she knew where she was, and it was the last place she wanted to be. She placed a hand on her brow, as one does after they have just tumbled down a cliff unexpectedly, and carefully moved her various body parts to check for signs of damage. Sitting up on her elbows, she noticed that the sun was past its highest point in the sky, but still very prominently hanging overhead, and wondered if she had been passed out for so long that it was already midday. Immediately, she went to her pocket to retrieve her phone hoping it was not completely smashed. It appeared that only Eira took the brunt of the fall, however the familiar words that read: *No Service*, were as clear as day on the screen. She didn't know why she did it, perhaps out of instinct from living where she had her whole life, but she knew there would be no service here. They don't even have phones if she recalls. Unless this world had suddenly become way more technologically advanced in the last decade or so, the phone in her hand was going to be utterly useless to her from now on—if only for playing *Candy Crush* perhaps. Who knows how long she'd be stranded out here, maybe it would help her pass the time. *Shit!* Eira frowned at the realization that she was now stranded without any way of contacting someone for help. She glanced around but did not recognize anything. There was no pile of snow around her which wasn't strange as there hadn't been snow in this land for the last hundred years, or so she had been told. Eira did think it a bit strange though, as it had been snowing when she fell into this damned place.

She looked toward the sky and noticed something small circling overhead. She watched its hypnotic circling for a moment or two but as it made its way closer to Eira, the object grew larger and larger until it was clear that it was headed straight for her. There was no time to get up and run so she quickly rolled over onto her stomach and raised her hands above and behind her head in an attempt to shield her from the massive beast now headed her way. Suddenly she was lifted off the ground by the talons of a massive snowy owl; nothing compared to the size they had back home. The owl carried her far from where she had landed and soared high above the trees of the forest. Eira wriggled in its talons, trying to free herself, but then realized that was probably a bad idea as she certainly did not want to face her death falling into the forest below.

"Put me down!" she shouted toward the bird. "Put me down! Put me down!" She was still squirming feverishly in the owl's talons until it finally lowered out of the sky and landed Eira safely on the forest floor. She stumbled backward once free as her heart was doing a great imitation of a freight train, beating out of her chest, when the ordeal was all over. She tucked the hair that was pulled loose from her braid by the wind during the flight behind an ear and turned around, only to see that she was no closer to figuring out where she was. *How is this any better?* She looked around in every direction only to find tree cover; dense forest, so much so that the sunlight was only barely peeking through the massive fir canopy. She looked at the sky and watched as the owl got smaller and smaller. Suddenly, it let out a loud cry and soared in the opposite direction. It circled once and cried again, as if to tell her something, then headed off. Was it trying to tell her which direction to head in? It's not like she had any better options, so she turned in the direction it screeched. *If you know where I'm supposed to be, why didn't you just drop me off there?* Eira was growing increasingly furious at the situation. She wandered for a bit hoping, praying she was headed in the right direction. By the position of the sun, there was not going to be much longer before her world would be shrouded in darkness, and who knows what kind of creatures wandered these woods at night. She stopped at a point in the path and turned to the large embankment at her side. It seemed tall enough. If she could just make it to the top, perhaps she could see more clearly where she was going. Eira scrambled up the side of the hill—more like a miniature mountain. *Damn, I need to work more on my cardio.* Once at the top, breathing heavily making herself the only sound she could hear radiating through her ears, she could see some sort of town and what looked like a castle poking out of the tree line in the distance. She knew that castle. Had seen many pictures of it growing up. *Thank you! Finally.* While she didn't exactly want to go there, she did know it was her best bet, so she begrudgingly headed in the direction of the town—toward a fate she had been running from for as long as she could remember.

Eira was beyond over whatever was happening right now and all she wanted was a warm bath and a comfortable bed, both of which she knew lay within those castle walls. She would figure out how to get out of here later, but at this point, her hunger and exhaustion were getting the better of her. She decided to take a quick break. From her best guess, she was still hours away from the town and while she did want to make it there before nightfall, her legs could not bear her weight for much longer. She was sitting on a boulder, playing *Candy Crush*, when she heard something rustling in the trees behind her.

*Please be a bunny. Please be a bunny.* Nope, of course not, because clearly, this wasn't her lucky day. A couple of wolves began making their way toward their newly found prey; undoubtedly her. Eira started to back up slowly, not having any weapon or any idea what to do when facing wolves. A crack came from the woods beside her. Oh great, more wolves probably. She did know that sometimes they trick their prey into looking one way when the rest of their pack is stalking from behind. Before she could summon her body to do something other than act statue, a white stallion and its rider charged in between her and the wolves. *Oh, come on! Nell would love this.*

The stallion reared a couple of times and pounded his front hooves on the earth, which seemed to give the wolves a good enough reason to flee. A glimmer above the horse's head caught Eira's eye and she looked closer at the white stallion, now calmly padding the ground. As he turned his head slightly, as if to look back and check to see that she was alright, Eira noticed that the glimmer was a white horn shimmering in the sunlight peeking through his forelock. At that moment, she just wanted to get the hell out of where she was. While she was immeasurably thankful to whoever had just saved her life, she also desperately wanted to go home and have nothing more to do with this land. In an effort to sneak away unnoticed, she backed up slowly to avoid the gaze of the man and then turned quickly, picking up a decent run and charging into the forest not knowing which direction was the right one.

"Wait!" Eira could hear him calling after her as she darted deep into the forest.

*Damn it.* She knew that voice.

In a moment he was able to catch up and cut her off, "Now where do you think you're going?"

"Can you please move?" she barked furiously back at him. "I just want to go home." She spun around on the spot as if searching for some glimpse of the correct direction. "Damn it, I think I ran the wrong way."

He dismounted the unicorn in an attempt to be on the same level as her, even though he towered over Eira. He probably figured he'd be more successful in this manner. Boy was he wrong. "This *is* your home whether you like it or not," he barked back.

She turned and faced her saviour, although to be honest, she probably would have preferred the wolves. She looked him up and down as he ran a hand through his deep chestnut hair, taking a deep breath to calm the fire that was undoubtedly brewing inside. He was the worst person and the last person she wanted to see, and now it had been twice in one day. Or at least she thought this was still the same day. She wasn't actually sure. He was wearing a deep navy jacket and black riding boots. Eira studied him over from head to toe and back again. She could see on the arm of his jacket a gold and silver crest with two polar bears facing each other with a silver snowflake between them and various decorative embellishments surrounding it. She knew that crest—knew it too well. She took a breath,

"While I am grateful to you for saving my life just now, I really don't want anything to do with you, so if you could please just leave."

"Eira," he said so calmly it was unnerving.

"Don't!" Eira cut sharply. "You know I don't want to be here. You all know I don't want this, so why are you trying so hard to turn me into something I'm not?"

"No one is trying to turn you into anything, but we do need your help and you know it, so stop acting so selfish," there it was again, calling her selfish for the second time, "and just come with me to Trillium Nivale and we can figure everything out!"

"I don't want to!"

"Well, suck it up, *Princess*. Sometimes you don't get to do what you want in life."

"Don't call me that," she gritted through her teeth, the anger welling up inside. If she wasn't already angry, that comment sure did it.

"That's what you are, isn't it?"

"No, I'm not. I'm *not* a princess. I'm *not* going to be queen. I don't want any of it."

"There's no one else, you know that."

"You can do it. You can be king and deal with all this."

"I'm not next in line to the throne."

"Sure you are, your dad is king right now. You can have it after him."

He rolled his eyes, "No, my dad is regent after your parents died, it doesn't work that way."

"Fine, then I hereby appoint you my successor to the throne." She motioned her arms with some fanatical finger wiggles toward him as if to transfer some great power she had within over to him, "There, now you can have it."

"I don't want to be king—not like this anyway."

*What was that supposed to mean? Was he planning on killing me? No, don't be stupid.* "Well, I don't know what to tell you." Eira stormed off back in the direction she had come from, hoping it was the right one but she only made it a few steps when she felt that same tug at her elbow being pulled back toward him, spinning her to face him.

"You really refuse to help us, to help your people? Everyone is suffering. This land is dying, Princess, and you're the only one that can stop it." He let go of Eira's arm and took a step back, eyeing her up, "You really are the Queen of Winter; is your heart just pure ice or is there—" Her hand stung as it made contact with his lightly tanned cheekbone. "*Ow,*" he said touching a hand to where she had slapped him. "You know what, *fine.* Maybe I should have just let the wolves deal with you. Or that bus, for that matter. It seems like we're better off without you anyway." He turned and started walking back and she watched as he mounted the stallion and gripped the reins in his hands. Maybe she shouldn't have slapped him.

"Okay, *fine.*" She hated herself for the words coming from her mouth, but she was smart enough to realize he was her only way out of this forest before nightfall. "I'll go with you back to Trillium Nivale and *maybe*," she emphasized, "we can figure something out."

He paused a moment, considering her proposition, then dismounted and held out a hand to her. He was smart enough not to say anything more. Eira walked toward him and mounted the stallion *without* his help.

"You're going to be the death of me, you know that right?"

She raised her brows as if to say, *hopefully.*

"This is Harwin," he continued, stroking the stallion's pure white forelock. Then he pulled himself onto the horse behind her, his strong arms reaching around and grabbing the reins. "Hold tight, Princess," his lips a whisper close to her ear, "not sure you're used to something so strong and powerful beneath you."

*Prick!*

## 3

With a kick of Harwin's side, they were off. The stallion with his two riders was soon out of the forest and emerging into a field. Eira could see the town she had spotted atop that hill in the distance and at the end of it, a castle towered above as if protecting the town below. There it was, Trillium Nivale, the home she had never really known, but was expected to protect. The sun was moving closer to the mountain tops, creating a lustrous glow in the sky. Harwin slowed to a walk as he made his way through the town. Eira couldn't help but notice that the town they were in seemed very modern. She knew this land was somewhat medieval, but she didn't know how deep that mentality ran. The town looked very similar to the European towns she had seen pictures of back home. It had paved streets, beautiful storefronts, and streetlights lining their way.

A voice interrupted her train of thought, "We're almost there."

She looked ahead and sighed. While she was looking forward to some comfort, she was not looking forward to what might await her inside those white stone walls. Eira didn't remember it well. She was a toddler, practically still a baby, when she left this place and was taken to another world for her *protection*, or so they tried to make her believe. It was a horrible childhood, filled with training and lessons all of which were to prepare her for a future she never wanted. To become the saviour of this land, to fulfill a prophecy she had nothing to do with. It wasn't all bad, though. She had her aunt, or at least the nanny they sent with her to raise her. Eira knew she wasn't her aunt, but called her that anyway, and she was the only mother Eira had ever truly known. She had vague memories of her own mother, but they were so distant she didn't truly think they were actual memories. Just the feeling that someone once looked after her with all the unconditional love of a mother. Eira's aunt did her best to make her childhood normal. When Eira was being indoctrinated, from as early as she could remember, about the history of this land, her duties to protect it along with swordsmanship and fight training, and who she was always meant to be, she was also baking, playing dolls, and having adventures with her aunt. She was wonderful and the only one Eira truly missed from this world. And then there was the prophecy, that stupid prophecy that started it all. She could still hear her aunt's voice echoing through her mind. Sometimes reciting it. Sometimes singing it to a little tune,

*A daughter born*

*With the first light of winter*

*To the king and queen of the land,*

*Will break the heat's powerful clutches*

*And take down the mighty beast's hand.*

*When a queen with the name of snow*

*Takes the throne at Trillium Nivale,*

*The world shall be restored*

*As it once was,*

*And snow will again grace the land.*

Eira had it memorized. She had heard it enough times growing up. She had heard all of it enough times growing up. That she was the one this land had been waiting for. That on the night of her birth, a hush grew over the castle. Many in the land had long forgotten the prophecy, but within the walls of the castle, it still rang true. It was on everyone's mind any time a queen was pregnant. Always waiting, and hoping that this time it would be a girl, a girl born on the first day of winter. But it never was. For one hundred years, it never was—until Eira. She was told her parents died not long after that. Her mother got sick and the pain of losing her tore her father apart until there was nothing left. She guessed she wasn't even enough for him to fight for. Eira spent almost three years in that castle, but honestly, she didn't remember much. Then one day, she was told she needed to leave for her *safety*. She needed to be sent away to a land where she wouldn't be found, to train in secret until the day she would come back to claim the throne and bring back the snow; a lot of pressure for a child. So Eira pushed. She pushed back hard. She didn't mind the training and her life at first, but as she got older she grew more and more resentful of her parentage. She wanted a normal life. She wanted to be whoever *she* chose to be, not who she was *told* to be. She wanted more.

Eira could remember the stories well about this place. She was told all about the day the dragon came. Her aunt had told her the stories as if they were made from her imagination to entertain a child before bed. As if a bedtime story was all it was.

It always began with the great battle that occurred nearly a century before Eira's birth. It was that day that a dragon descended on the land of Talvia in search of a new home. The country of Talvia remains snow-laden all year. The people and creatures of the country lived in harmony with the snow and everything that it brought. Dragons, however, cannot live in the snow. They simply will not survive in the cold, harsh climate. When the great dragon set his sights on the Hoarfrost Mountains high above the countryside, he decided this would be his new home. The dragon made his way through the countryside of Talvia— and once a dragon has picked its new home, there is no stopping it. His sights were set on the desolation of the snowy vista. A battle was brought forth and warriors from all over the lands came to the aid of the Talvians. Wintren-elves emerged from their village hidden within the forest and rode to their aid on the backs of the great polar bears from the North. The white stags, snow leopards, and wolves with their piercing blue eyes and a stare that could turn enemies to ice all fought for their homeland. All the Talvians rode in and fought bravely in the battle. The dragon was too fierce for the great king's armies though, even with the help of their allies, for it is known that a dragon cannot be slain out of anger or vengeance. You must beat the beast at his own game. With one final shot of fire the dragon let piercing into the heavens, the snow gods' magic was destroyed. Fiery embers and smog engulfed the skies and fell to the ground taking with it all the snow that had once laid there. The elves and animals sought out immediate shelter in the forests of Evervell, however, it was unknown to them and to others how long they would survive without snow and the colder climate. The temperature rose and the countryside became a hot desolate valley suitable for a dragon to live. With that, the great reptile flew to his new home high in the Hoarfrost Mountains. That was the end of the Winter Country as it had been known since the beginning.

Eira's child eyes, filled with wonder and intrigue, always widened at this part.

But there was still hope. With the last embers that burned to the ground, fell a prophecy. None of the Talvians knew who this daughter of winter could be or when she would arrive. For nearly a century, Talvia remained a desolate wasteland and the dragon terrorized its people. Until one night, on the winter solstice when the season of Talvia truly begins, a baby girl was born to the king and queen. The princess grew for three years, her existence hidden within the walls of the castle. Word of her being eventually fell into the wrong hands. The dragon emerged from his cavern and made his way across the land to the kingdom. The Wintren-elves emerged from the safety of Evervell forest for the first time in nearly a hundred years. No one had seen or heard from them until that night. The girl was given to them and they stole away with her. They sent her to another land with a guardian of their kin to protect and train her. When the dragon made his way to the kingdom, no sense of the girl could be detected. When the girl could not be found, the dragon fled back to his home in the mountains, remaining there for eighteen more years.

At first, it was just a fairytale, told to her by her aunt. But as Eira got older, they were no longer just the fantasies of a little girl wanting to run away to a faraway land and be a princess. She learned of her aunt's true lineage—her pointed ears, hidden for years by some magic, being revealed to Eira. *Those stories I told you as a child before bed, they're real.* She could still hear the words, her aunt's elegant voice trilling them to her. Then it began. The stories were becoming Eira's reality—quickly. Quicker than she had ever imagined and now they no longer seemed fun. It was all just an elaborate ruse; to trick her into thinking it was her destiny and she belonged in another world entirely. Eira saw through the plans as she got older and realized this wasn't the life she chose for herself.

Harwin was approaching the castle now. There was a long stone bridge hanging high above a tree-laden ravine connecting the castle with the world around it. It was covered in arched boughs all the way across. The guards opened the tall wrought-iron gates and they rode through. The courtyard was barren and grey except for a cluster of three tall skinny evergreen trees in the centre, wrapped with tiny luminescent orbs hanging from the branches that cast a soft glow on the courtyard. Two grand staircases soared upward on either side of the front doors, meeting at a large balcony. The castle climbed into the sky with white stone walls. Its turrets were tall and the pinnacle was as green as the forest below. Beyond its northern walls was a great lake nestled in the mountains encompassing the castle and stretching far into the north and east. Harwin halted and they dismounted. Eira was led through the front doors of the castle and gazed upon the details of a home she could not remember, yet it all felt strangely familiar. She figured she had been there before and perhaps somewhere deep, deep down in her mind, the memory of this place remained.

"Come with me. Gideon's been awaiting your arrival." He took Eira's hand which she swiftly ripped from his, and he led her farther into the castle and down a corridor.

Walking through the corridors, she got a glimpse of some of the rooms and the utter opulence of this place. For a land that had been plagued for a century, the castle sure held up. They passed a large open-air seating area with long sheer curtains dancing gently in the small breeze and a fire pit at the centre. Every room she caught a glimpse of seemed to have towering windows carved right from the white stone, and expansive views of the mountains beyond. The first room Eira was officially taken to was the library. It was not as impressive as she thought a castle library would be, however her expectations might have been slightly out of scope being raised on *Beauty and the Beast*—another one of her aunt's attempts to present herself as a normal human and to give Eira as much of a childhood as possible; now that was a library.

No, this one was quite small for the number of books it contained, but served its purpose well. Again, it was carved right from that white stone, and as she drew her attention to the ceiling the pristine smoothness of the stone got rougher, more jagged, as if to mimic the mountains. It was very dimly lit with only the light from the sun coming through the stained glass windows displayed with images of snowflakes dancing across them. It was quite beautiful the way the sun cascaded through the panes of coloured glass, tinting their surroundings. The library held books from every decade containing all sorts of scholarly topics along with various fictional topics simply for pleasure. By now, the sun had dipped farther in the sky and the room held a deep orange glow. Suddenly, the room got much brighter and Eira turned to where a switch had been flipped illuminating the large chandelier hanging from above.

"You have electricity here?" Eira blurted without thinking of the oddity of the question before it had slipped from her lips. She had noticed the sconces hanging on the walls as they walked through the corridors, but had assumed they were lit by candles. She didn't know why. Castles where she had grown up had electricity now, but she had always gotten the impression that this world wouldn't. Eira couldn't say why.

His eyebrows rose at her remark as if to say, *yes stupid, did they teach you nothing about this place?*

"Sorry, I just assumed you wouldn't with this being a different world and all. This whole place seems kind of...old-fashioned."

"So, you think we have magic but can't figure out electricity?" Eira smirked at his sarcasm. "But, you are right. We do tend to do things kind of, *'old-fashioned'* here."

The low voice of a man came from above them, "Who's there?" he asked.

"It's just me. Why was it so dark in here?"

"I like the dark. I find that sometimes the best things in life can only be seen when someone turns out the lights." Eira looked up to the shelves that soared into the ceiling and found the man to whom the voice belonged. A man was sorting books high above in the balconies. He could not have been much older than middle-aged. He wore long robes the colour of deep evergreen and his brown hair was somewhat unkempt. His eyes were wise and his manner of speaking was comforting as if he knew more than you suspected.

"Ah, Leon my dear boy. When did you return? Did you find what you were looking for?" the man asked as he climbed down the spiral staircase. When he got closer he paused, staring at Eira with deep soulful eyes, "Oh, I see you have." He held out a hand to her, "I am Gideon, master of all knowledge of Talvia—of all things past told, and about to be told. It is an honour to finally meet you, Your Majesty."

"I wouldn't call her that if I were you," smirked Leon. Eira shot him a glare.

Gideon continued as if he didn't even hear Leon's comment, "Although, I suppose we have met before, long ago, I'm sure you don't remember. So maybe I should say it's nice to *re*-make your acquaintance." Eira gave him a fake smile, so he wouldn't know how desperately she didn't want to be here. However, there was a part of her that suspected he knew. "So," he continued, "how much of this place have you learned about, how much of the prophecy do you know?"

"Enough," she stated hoping he wouldn't pry. This wasn't a test. She didn't wish to be quizzed on her knowledge of this place.

"Well then, I suppose there is not much for you and me to discuss then." Eira and Gideon exchanged glances for a moment, "Unless there is?"

Eira wasn't going to, but she found herself asking, "Well, what if I didn't want it—any of it? What if I didn't want to be queen, to defeat the dragon, to bring back the snow? None of it. Is there a way?"

Leon rolled his eyes. Gideon continued to look at Eira for a long agonizing moment until he finally spoke, "I'm afraid I don't think there is. Unless everyone is fine with the land staying as it has been for a hundred years. Unless the people of this land are comfortable with their lands dying and being forced out to find new homes and new ways of life to care for their families. Unless everyone is comfortable with the monarchy falling and the status quo of this world beginning to fail. I'm not sure what the repercussions would be if that happens."

*Great. Thanks for the guilt trip.* "And, there's really no one else who can defeat the dragon?" Eira asked, knowing full well she wouldn't like the answer, but hoped nonetheless.

"Some have tried, but easier said than done. Well, sort of. I mean, it is still a dragon," said Leon.

"Those fools," Gideon began in a dismissive tone. "Everyone knows you cannot simply kill a dragon with brute force."

"Everyone?" Eira questioned. They seemed to pick up on the fact that *she* did not know. That little tidbit had been left out of her training.

Leon spoke again, "A dragon's scales are stronger than anything known to this world and they possess an ancient magic. Every dragon has a secret about them and to slay a dragon, you must win at their game. A dragon possesses only one weakness that will cause their armour to wane and a sword may penetrate their diamond-scale exterior. When they know they have been defeated by you, their protective magic disappears. Only then can a dragon be slain."

"Well, that's not at all intimidating," Eira groaned.

"What? But defeating a dragon wasn't?"

"Well, I figured I wouldn't be alone. But yeah now that you mention it, it *is* intimidating. *Especially* for a little girl to be told her whole life that she has to be queen, and defeat a dragon while I'm at it!"

He ran a hand through his dark hair and those glimmering hazel eyes gave away his utter annoyance with the situation. "Look," began Leon turning to Eira, "I have some things I need to do quickly and then I'll meet you back here. But please try to listen to him. Don't be such a—"

She pierced right through his core with a scowl that made him dare not finish that sentence. "Okay then," she turned to Gideon as Leon left, intending to humour him, "I was told my whole life this is what had to be done, but I still don't understand. Why is it that the snow needs to be returned? What is the harm of having summer all the time?" Maybe no one had thought of that, and everyone just figured it would be better for things to go back to the way they were. Sometimes change can be good, right?

Pulling out a very old map and unrolling it on the mammoth ash wood desk carved with various animals and foliage, Gideon gave greater insight into the land of Talvia. Eira had seen this map before—not as old, however. As a child, she had spent hours memorizing every inch of it: all the hills and mountains, the various rivers that ebbed and flowed through them, the different lands. She imagined and looked forward to the day she would finally get to visit these places, much like people do where she grew up. But then it all changed—she changed. She grew up and didn't want to live in a fairytale anymore.

Eira could see Talvia and at the top of the map it read, *The Winter Country*, in beautiful scrollwork, and she could see everything that made up the land. There was Trillium Nivale in the northwest corner of the map. The surrounding lake to the north that also stretched far into the east was Lake Isas, expanding far beyond the bottom edge of the map. Past the lake, there was a forest that bordered the Hoarfrost Mountains. There were small towns in the south and on the edge of Lake Isas. There was another forest in the southwest corner of the map, which she figured out was the forest she must have landed in. There were more mountains in the western part of the map as well behind the castle. Then Gideon began to tell a solemn tale of the Winter Country,

"You see my dear, as you may know, in this world there are four countries: Kevatia: the Spring Country, Kesa: the Summer Country, Syysia: the Autumn Country, and Talvia, of course, the Winter Country. It is meant to be winter all the time here. This does not mean anything bad. Living here is quite nice for us as we were born here and know the snow. A dragon comes from the Dragon Country far beyond any borders ever travelled. They rarely choose to leave, but if they do they are in constant search of a new home and you pray they do not come across yours to claim as their own. When this happened, it disrupted the equilibrium of this land. The balance of nature shifted when the dragon rose from its homeland. The four countries work in harmony with one another creating a great balance. The plants and animals that thrive here began to die off and are still dying off. Most are endangered or have become extinct. The snow was also a major source of fresh water for this land, and now without it, the land is struggling to survive." Maybe if someone had told Eira this long ago, she wouldn't have been so set on not coming back. Gideon continued, "The Wintren-elves and the fairies have become legends of old. We do not know where they sought refuge from the fires of the dragon. The ice on the lake surrounding this castle began to melt, which brought new hardships for the people living near its icy edge."

"What types of hardships?" Eira asked.

"Pirates, my dear. And others, but with no ice, the pirate ships are free to venture inward to our land and plunder the villages."

"There are pirates in this land?" she winced.

"There are now. The people of Talvia made do with what they could, but as the years went on, times became harder and harder. Many people lost their homes and journeyed farther than they had ever known to seek salvation. Once a year, the dragon leaves his cave in the Hoarfrost Mountains. The villagers in the city around the mountains call it the Day of the Dragon, and he comes down and collects the baskets of gold, silver, and jewels left out in the hillsides for him." Gravely, Gideon finished the last few words of his tale.

"I—I don't think I can do this," she admitted for the first time without stubbornness toward the fact she was being *told* to do it, but for the fact that there was now an immense weight hanging over it.

At that moment, Leon came back into the library to collect her. Changing the subject, "So, where did you run off to?" Eira asked.

"You'll find out soon enough."

They left Gideon in the library and made their way through the castle. Walking toward the great hall, Eira noticed many murals on the castle walls. Many of them looked like Trillium Nivale and the country that surrounded it however, there were no paintings of what it looked like now—the only Talvia she had ever seen. All works were depicted covered with snow. After her time with Gideon, she now knew that the Talvia she had experienced briefly was nothing but a shell of its former glory. Now she knew all that Talvia was supposed to be. Eira had not realized it when first landing here, she assumed it was simply summer. It wasn't until now that she realized her mind had played a trick on her and what she saw was no summer, but a land suffering—stuck in the moment in her world before the beauties of spring would awaken the land—a time of depressive brown. The world she saw had all the attributes of winter: the barren trees, and hard earth, but without the snow to make everything belong, and a heat that seemed suitable for well, a dragon.

Eira came to one grand painting in particular that halted her. It was what looked like a family portrait: a mother, a father, and two children. One was a girl about the age of two or three and the other was a baby wrapped in its mother's arms. The woman looked like an older version of Eira, with the same long dark honey-blond hair and fair complexion. The man shared the same eyes she had looked upon every day of her life—a deep, icy blue. They were both very important and statuesque in appearance. Even the children looked as though they had significant destinies in play for their futures.

"That is King Ronan and Queen Adela, your parents." Eira knew before the words left Leon's mouth. She had been told many times throughout her childhood that she looked like her mother. It was the only way she could create some sort of semblance of what she might have looked like. He paused a moment and uncharacteristically breathed, "I'm sorry you'll never have the chance to meet them. They were both wonderful rulers, the likes of which Talvia has not known for many years. Or, so I'm told."

"Who is the baby?"

Shock came across his face, "That's your brother, Oren. You—you didn't know about him?"

Eira shook her head, "I guess they felt it wasn't important to know." She didn't know why. Perhaps if she knew she *had* family in this place, she would have been more inclined to fight for it.

"He left Trillium Nivale when he was eighteen and never looked back. Seems to run in the family," Leon gave a wry smile. "No one's seen or heard from him since. He had no desire to be a king and when your mother died giving birth to him, he always felt as though it was somehow his fault—that you'd never get to know them. No one knows—"

"Wait, go back," Eira stopped him. "My mother died in childbirth? I was told she got sick and died."

"That's weird. I suppose maybe they meant she contracted an infection after giving birth which led to her death, but it's weird they entirely left out the fact about your brother."

"Yeah." She was going to have to get to the bottom of this. And where was her brother now?

"As I was saying though, no one knows where he is now or if he is even alive. It is a shame, he and I were great comrades as children—playing games throughout the castle and making mischief. He was like the little brother I never had." He glanced at Eira, "Sorry."

"Don't be. You didn't keep it from me."

"I honestly assumed you knew."

Without warning, Eira's eyes began to well up and there was nothing she could do to keep the tears from making their way out. It was all suddenly too overwhelming. She had never seen her parents before, only what she had imagined they looked like in her dreams.

"I need to get out of here." She turned and began to run down the hall, not knowing where she was going.

Eira could hear Leon calling after her but didn't stop. She could hear the click of his boots on the stone floor as he started to run after her, almost catching up when he was stopped in the hall by an older woman. Eira pushed past her and kept going, finally finding a room that looked good enough to be alone in. She made her way through it and out onto the balcony, racing over to the stone railing pressing herself against it, breathing in the fresh air, and looking out at the kingdom beyond. The sky was now an array of pink, purple, and orange hues. She could barely see the sun peeking through the mountains. She drew a few deep breaths from within and she wiped her tear-stained cheeks. Suddenly, there was a hand on her shoulder.

"Leon, I don't—" Eira turned to see a new face. "Oh, I thought—"

The woman smiled, "I'm Brenna, Leon's mother."

"Oh," Eira said wiping more tears from her cheeks, then mustering up a smile, "It's nice to meet you."

"The pleasure is all *mine,* my darling. I've been waiting to see you again for a long time."

"It seems a lot of people have."

"I know how difficult this all must be for you to understand, especially not having your mother around to reassure you. All a mother wants to do is comfort her child and make all their problems go away for them." Brenna spoke with such a comforting tone, the way a mother should speak to their child when they need a helping hand. The way Eira's aunt would speak to her when she needed it.

"I wish I could have known them."

Brenna smiled, "Trust me when I tell you that everyone here is your family. They want what is best for you and for you to be the woman you were born to be." There it was, that extra little bit. Be the woman she was born to be. They meant, be their saviour.

Brenna hugged her. That strong motherly hug Eira had missed over the last few years. They made their way off the balcony and back into the corridor where Leon was waiting, leaning against the wall next to the open door.

"Well darling, I will leave you in my son's capable hands." She shot Leon a look that said, *be nice to her*. "I wish I could stay a bit longer, but I'm leaving to visit my daughters who are staying with my sister in Syysia right now. Please trust me when I tell you we thought it was in your best interest to send Leon to train with you once a month when you were younger." That was it—twenty-four times from age sixteen to eighteen for two hours each was all the time she had ever spent with that man. Forty-eight hours total.

Eira didn't respond, just gave a suggestive crinkle of her lips as if to say, *really?*

Brenna sighed, "We had our reasons. Maybe one day you'll understand." She touched a hand to Eira's tear-stained cheek as if to say, *sorry*, then dismissed herself down the hall.

She wanted to change the subject quickly, "You have sisters?" Eira turned to Leon who was still leaning against the wall, his arms folded against his chest.

"Yes, one's your age, and the other is a few years older than me."

"Middle child, huh? Explains a lot." Leon frowned. "Do I have any other family?" Eira asked trying not to sound too hopeful. "Aunts, uncles, cousins?"

"Sorry, I'm afraid your parents were both only children."

Of course they were. Eira let out a heavy sigh.

Leon led the way back down the hall, not saying much. Walking through the archway that led into the great hall was like walking into another time entirely. It was covered in gold leaf and grand windows that climbed three stories, arching at the top and curving into the ceiling creating a clear barrier between the outside world and the safety of the castle. Eira could almost picture the feasts and balls that would take place there. The girls dressed in gowns made of exotic silks or velvets and the men dressed in fanciful jackets in various jewel tones. Her eyes did not know what to gaze upon first. They were drawn to the large three-story chandelier hanging at the heart of the arched ceiling and then to the ornate scrollwork bordering the crown moulding. At the end of the hall, there sat two large thrones for the king and queen. Eira could always imagine the two thrones sitting in a castle, like in all the fairy tales and history books—but there was still something about acknowledging it in person. Behind the thrones, on either side, there hung two large banners stretching from just above the back of the thrones high into the ceiling. They were a beautiful twilight blue sapphire with the same silver and gold crest upon them that was so delicately embroidered on Leon's jacket. Leon led her to where his father along with a few others were waiting eagerly for her arrival—the arrival of their queen.

When Eira took her gaze off the surroundings long enough to notice the other people in the room, she stepped in front of them looking somewhat apologetic. As annoying as it was, she was beginning to feel apologetic about everything she had done. Maybe it was just a spell they had cast over her when she came here, but it seemed she was going to be thrown into this war whether she liked it or not. Eira just hadn't decided yet if she was going to fully let them.

Most of them seemed to look at her with a mutual feeling of sobriety. The staring contest they all seemed to be partaking in was beginning to make her feel a bit uneasy. Some looked utterly shocked at the sight of their soon-to-be queen—a twenty-one-year-old girl in her limited edition Disney Princess sneakers, which she paid far too much for but it was worth it, and her short-sleeved polo shirt and jeans—the pub's uniform; hardly a noble appearance. Regardless, Leon's father was the first to come up to her. Or, she assumed it was his father. They clearly shared familial traits. He was a tall man, not unlike Leon himself. He had the same dark chestnut brown hair, almost looking black in some lighting, although his eyes were not the same golden hazel as Leon's. He must have gotten those from his mother.

"Eira, it is a pleasure to finally meet you," he held out a strong hand, engulfing hers as she took it. "I am Charles, Leon's father, and was an advisor to your father. I am now regent of this kingdom until the rightful heir should take the throne. We hope you can bring peace to the land and return the Winter Country to its former glory." Such formal confident words. So *rehearsed* sounding. Perhaps he was nervous.

Eira simply smiled with the face of someone who would certainly do their best—if she chose to, that is. She turned and looked at the figures lined up beside Charles. "Eira," said Leon turning his attention toward the men, "I would like you to meet some of Talvia's most valiant warriors. This is Theo," he said pointing to a man about the same age as Leon, or perhaps a couple of years younger, standing beside his father. He was also tall, but slightly darker in complexion than Leon or his father. Perhaps it was by the sun's doing, or perhaps not. Theo smiled at Eira, giving a quick bow, and then upon rising bearing his exceptionally white teeth that played opposite to his dark eyes, and brushed his hair from his face in a boyish way. "This is Killian," continued Leon turning to the next in line. Killian certainly was a specimen of a man—that's for sure. A real stalwart gentleman. He towered over Eira with his broad shoulders. He had a neat beard trimmed to the curve of his chin, the same russet colour as the long curly hair that brushed past his shoulders, neatly pulled back into a half ponytail. Eira couldn't help but stare a bit too long. That was until...Leon stood in front of another tall gentleman about the same height as Killian. "And this is Boreas," he announced. Boreas was tall and muscular. Someone you would want fighting on your side. His shoulder-length icy-blonde hair brushed the sides of his face as he nodded to Eira while standing with his arms crossed—emphasizing his muscles only more.

"Boreas? Like, the god of winter?" Eira realized.

"The same," he smiled standing up a little straighter. She was stunned; she had never met a god before. Sure, some men who thought they were, but not a *real* one.

"Wait, you're the actual god of winter—bringer of the cold winter air? Then what do you need me for?" Eira glanced back at Leon.

"I cannot bring winter back without your help." His strong deep voice echoed through the great hall, "Your presence here has only just begun to help restore my powers. Until the dragon is slain, I can only help you fight your way to him." Eira released a heavy breath and looked at the three companions she had just been introduced to. They all looked about the same age as Leon, give or take a couple of years, except for Boreas who only looked about ten years older than Leon, Theo, and Killian however, those ten years could easily be tens of hundreds for all she knew.

"Eira, we don't expect you to be happy to defeat a dragon. There are few that will willingly face one, seeing as there are certain *risks* associated with it." If she was being honest, she was slightly distracted by Boreas. Eira nodded along, not fully listening to what Leon was saying.

"Wait—what?"

"Like incineration," chimed in Killian. Wide-eyed, Eira looked toward him.

"Gee, thanks. That hadn't occurred to me until right now." The blank stares filled the silence. "Don't tell me you expect me to actually fight that thing! I was never told *anything* about that! I was just told there was a dragon that took over and it's my destiny to become queen and bring the snow back by defeating it—and now that I am saying this out loud it does sound like I actually need to *fight* a dragon—yeah, okay." *Why did I never clue into that before?* She guessed she was a little preoccupied with not wanting to be a queen in a magical land.

"Seriously? What have you been thinking defeating a dragon meant for the last decade?" asked Leon.

"I just figured when I came back the dragon would be able to be slain—that was how I would defeat it. I didn't know I would have to come face to face with it."

"Well, only for a little bit," reassured Leon. "We'll take care of the actual slaying. You just need to weaken it." Weaken it—sure. She rolled her eyes in response. "Well, how about some dinner now, or would you rather get some rest? It's been a long day for you and a good night's sleep will do you some good."

"I think I just want to go to bed."

As the group left, Leon turned to Eira, "How do you feel?" he asked.

"Well other than learning *defeating* meant *fighting* a dragon—and feeling a little stupid about not cluing into that—pretty good." She paused a moment and then continued, "And I mean, come on, you have an actual *god* here. That's so cool. I mean have you seen his arms?"

"What?" responded Leon. Eira raised her eyebrows in unison with nodding her head—more to torment him—before heading out of the great hall. "Yes I have actually," Leon called after her; the aggravation radiating in his voice. "I have arms too. Everybody has arms."

Eira found her bedroom in the castle quite inviting—and far more lavish than expected. The bedroom itself was as large as her entire apartment with a fireplace and sitting area added on. The arched windows cast a shimmer of moonlight onto the floor and the light from the crackling fire created an inviting glow. She walked over to look more closely at the welcoming flames when she felt something small brush up against her ankles. Eira knew that feeling. She glanced down to see a familiar face staring up at her, "Pix?" she said picking up the small cat and holding her out in front of her. "How did you get here?"

"Meow," was all the little cat had to say, so Eira placed her back on the floor and watched as she scurried off toward the bed, leaping onto it and making herself comfortable. She then made her way into the bathroom and was taken aback by the large white stone soaker tub in the centre of the room, sitting nicely under a crystal sky made to mimic the stars, reflecting the moonlight coming in from the towering windows that opened completely so it was like bathing in the sky and mountains. The bathroom was ornately tiled, floor to ceiling, in white marble with sapphire-coloured tile accents embedded into the stone of the castle. As she scanned the room, her eyes stopped on the pristine white toilet in the corner. *Oh, thank God.* It had never crossed her mind until right this minute that this world might have more of a chamber pot or outhouse-type situation and there was no way she was doing *that.* Eira noticed that the bath was already done up with various oils and bubbles swirling together in a beautiful harmony, inviting her to indulge in its warmth—which was extremely well received after the day she had.

"Wow, now this is top drawer." Eira quickly threw off her shoes and clothing and slipped into the bath, revelling in the scents and silky oils taking her away from everything, just for a moment. Once she was sufficiently leathery and done letting the warm water wash the troubles of the day away, she dried quickly, stepped out into her room, and opened the closet to find it filled with gowns, the likes of which she had only dreamt of wearing. Eira couldn't help herself—let's face it. While she was resisting being there, she may as well take in some of the perks while she can. Eira had to try a few on.

A knock came at the door when she was on the third dress, "Just a minute," she called picking up the skirt and hurrying over to the door. Eira flung it open to reveal Gideon standing on the other side. Her appearance didn't seem the slight bit odd to him, as she would have expected—unless people sleep in ball gowns here—but he seemed utterly unfazed by it. He merely smiled and said,

"I see you are embracing your new role quite nicely."

"Oh, yeah, well." Eira looked down and tugged at the garment, "I was just having a little fun."

"Well, perhaps this can add to it," he smiled and then moved his one hand out from behind his back. He had a small box tied with a little gold bow in his hand. "I almost forgot," he began again, "happy birthday. Twenty-one, right? That is a magical age." He handed the small box over.

Eira hesitated a moment, taking in the simplicity of it, "Thank you."

"Go ahead, open it."

Eira did just that, gently pulling on one of the bow's ends and releasing the neatly tied ribbon. She lifted the lid of the box and pulled back the tissue paper covering what was inside. "Wow," was all she could manage to say as she carefully pulled out a jewelled crown carved from crystal lying so comfortably inside. Gideon took the box from her as she examined the crown more. The crystal made it look as if the crown was made from ice, and the delicate intricacies of it touched with pale blue diamonds sparkled in the light.

"It was your mother's," he said after a moment. "I figured she would have wanted you to have it. And, if you're willing, it will be yours one day." Eira just looked at him, not knowing how to respond. The crown symbolized so much, and she was not sure how she felt about any of it. "Look," began Gideon again. "I know this is all a lot for you, even though we trained you your whole life for this exact moment, it can still be quite overwhelming and take some getting used to. I don't want you to think that by me giving you this, we are forcing you to take the crown right away and rule a land you don't consider your home. Your mother wore that for many years and ruled the land alongside your father with grace and dignity. If it does only one thing for you, maybe it will bring you closer to your family, and help you understand where you came from."

"Thank you," Eira said willing the tears not to burst free. "It's beautiful." He then left her for the night.

Eira sat on the sofa looking at the crown resting in the box. She couldn't think any longer. Finally, she decided to walk over to the mirror and put it on. It felt so strange— nothing like the tiaras she wore as a little girl playing dress-up; those were easy to wear. No, this one felt heavy atop her head and full of a burden she was not sure she was ready for. Physical and scholarly training over the years tried to prepare her, but Gideon was right. The weight of it right in front of you hits differently. It was best that it remain in the safety of the box for now.

Eira fell into a blissful slumber almost immediately after climbing into the grand four-post ash wood bed. Modern yet perfectly fitting into the simple elegance of the room; the mattress lovingly topped with cream-coloured duvets and pillows—the luxury of which she had never known. For the first time in her life, she dreamt of her mother and father. She had never known them or even what they looked like until now. Eira was walking the halls of Trillium Nivale, dressed in a beautiful lilac-coloured gown. Everything around her seemed foggy and unclear until she came to the throne room. Her mother and father were sitting there waiting for her. Just before she could reach them, flames broke out around her and they were consumed by the fire. She tried to call out to them, but no sound came.

She looked to the sky and saw the mighty dragon circling, looking for her. It descended and—she awoke, her heart pounding and sweat on her brow.

There were times in Eira's youth when she would have dreams of a woman and a man caring for her and watching over her as she grew however, they were always faceless figures brought on by her longing for a family— more of a family than just her aunt.

Eira drifted back to sleep and awoke the next morning to the golden sunlight pouring across the sheets, warming her face. It was not until morning, with the enlightening daylight, that Eira got the true sense of the all-encompassing surroundings of her room. She could see the mountains and evergreens outside as if her room was built right amongst them. She could only imagine what they would look like snow-covered as they were supposed to be. She would be warm and cozy inside her plush room with a magical snowy scene unfolding just outside her windows. A lady's maid entered the room with breakfast, headed to the closet, and pulled out a gown for Eira to wear that day.

"Good morning, Your Majesty," said the girl. She could not have been much older than Eira. Her golden hair was done neatly in a braid, starting from one side of her head and flowing across the back and down her opposite shoulder. She wore a modest lavender-coloured gown with a cream-coloured apron around her waist.

"Good morning," Eira replied. "And you don't have to call me that, Eira is fine." The girl just smiled and went back to placing Eira's breakfast on the table. "What's your name?" Eira asked as she got out of bed.

"Ceilidh, Your Majesty." She frowned slightly at the girl's formal response and looked down at the breakfast now beautifully plated before her. Eira didn't even realize how hungry she was until there was a plate in front of her. "Would you like me to help you get ready?" Ceilidh asked. Eira looked up from a mouthful, surprised at the question. No one had ever asked her such a thing before. Ceilidh motioned to the dress she had hung on the bathroom door. She hadn't even noticed it was there until now. "Your dress, Your Majesty."

Her mouth opened at the sheer elegance of the periwinkle and gold gown that hung across the room—not at all her idea of everyday wear. It had a beaded bust with cap sleeves and a flowing a-line skirt. "Nice," Eira smiled. "But, where are my other clothes?"

"They were taken to be washed, Your Majesty. Would you prefer them? I can see if they are ready."

"No, it's alright," Eira shook her head. She had never had the chance to wear such nice garments in the past.

Eira certainly was not used to being fussed over but enjoyed having someone else do her hair and take the stress out of coordinating an outfit for once. When she was transformed into something that looked as if it belonged in a castle, she headed through the door and down the corridors to explore, all the while thinking about going on a journey to slay a dragon. She wandered down the halls looking at the various castle displays such as knights' armour and tapestries. There were many paintings too, of the past kings and queens of Talvia; her ancestors. She came to one knight displaying the same coat of arms she was becoming more familiar with—that gold and silver crest. Looking both ways down the corridor to make sure no one was coming, she carefully took the sword out of the knight's hand and began to swing it around pretending she was in battle. It had been a long time since she held a sword. She had almost forgotten the weight of one. With one swift move, she took the knight's helmet clean off and sent it crashing to the stone floor producing a rather loud clang reverberating down the hall. Three years, but she shouldn't have been *that* uncoordinated. Standing up straight as if nothing had happened, she grabbed the helmet and tried to place it back on the knight's shoulders and then carefully placed the sword back with him as well, scurrying off to where she could not be found and blamed for the incident. Eira found Boreas, Theo, and Killian in, what she assumed was, the maps room pouring over various accounts of the landscape and trying to decide the best route to the Hoarfrost Mountains.

"Are you sure that's the best way? What if we hit it from the western front, it's an easier trail upward," Theo was saying as Eira crept inside the room, but still lingered in the doorway.

"Ah, you don't know what you're talking about," Killian nudged Theo out of the way. "This route is a sure thing, the most direct." He pressed a firm finger against the table.

"That is preposterous! That will send us in the opposite direction and take at least a day longer!"

"Not if we cut through Evervell here," another finger against the map. Evervell, Eira knew that name. She had seen it many times while pouring over the maps of this land.

"You can't cut through Evervell there." A shove from Theo sent Killian bumping back to where he stood before, "It's too dense, and gods knows what lurks in that brush."

Eira couldn't help but smile a bit at their squabbling. While they did seem to be getting on each other's nerves, it was the type of bickering only done by close friends—family. Eira felt as though she was stepping in on a casual Sunday dinner, with them getting into the latest debate about something.

"Better get used to it." Eira nearly jumped at the voice coming from behind her. "They never stop and it's a long journey." Leon caressed himself around where she stood in the doorway and into the room, glancing back at her appearance. His eyes burned on her from head to toe until he finally smiled and said, "You look nice."

She suddenly felt completely overdressed, seeing as he was simply wearing a t-shirt and joggers. "Yeah, well, it's not like I got to pack first."

"You would have if you came willingly." The others had noticed Eira's presence by now so she followed Leon into the room. "We're taking this route," said Leon placing a finger against the map, "it's the most efficient. We don't need to spend more time out there than needed." Theo and Killian glanced at the route,

"Yes...well, that's what I was going to suggest next," Killian puffed.

"Oh, yeah, clearly the way to go," added Theo. Boreas simply rolled his eyes from where he had been leaning against the wall, arms folded across his chest, smart enough not to step between Theo and Killian—or simply just didn't care enough. He was there for the journey, no matter the route taken.

Leon rolled the maps as if to say, *enough cartography for one morning,* then turned his attention back toward Eira. "Good morning, Princess, how did you sleep?"

She thought back to her dream, "Alright."

"What was that crashing a moment ago?" Leon turned to the men as if he thought it might have come from this room, and given the tension between Killian and Theo Eira had walked in on, he had fair reason to suspect that much.

"What crashing, did you hear something? I didn't— it was probably ghosts," Eira's face remained composed. "So...when are we leaving?" The group stared at her. "I will admit I am a little scared about slaying a dragon but it seems to be for a good cause."

"A little scared?" asked Killian. "Darling, it's a dragon. I'm terrified and I am considered one of the bravest warriors in the land."

*Well, that makes me feel better,* Eira stared blankly.

"I wouldn't go telling people that," Theo smirked at Killian.

Boreas rose from his position on the wall and strode over to Eira. His gaze never left hers as he gently took hold of her hand and pressed a gentle kiss to the top of it, "It is my great pleasure to journey alongside you, Your Majesty, and fight for you when needed." He then released her hand and made his way out of the room, leaving the rest of them dumbfounded in his wake, and Eira more flushed than she'd like to be in front of the guys.

"Anyway," Leon spoke first, "we'll leave at dawn."

*Why is it always dawn? Can't adventures start later in the day?*

Theo and Killian left the room, leaving Eira and Leon together. He perched himself atop the edge of the table, one leg still outstretched, and folded his arms across his chest, then glared at Eira with those deep mysterious eyes.

"What?" He stared longer, narrowing his gaze. "What?" Eira asked again—sharper this time.

He pursed his lips, "Just trying to figure you out. Suddenly you seem all for this little adventure. What happened?"

"Nothing happened. I had a change of heart—what, people aren't allowed to change their minds?"

"Oh no, they can. You were just hell-bent on *not* helping, so I'm wondering what happened is all?"

She shrugged, "Nothing." Maybe it was the vision of her in her mother's crown last night, or her dream, or the true story of Talvia she was told, but something did change in her during the night and she awoke with a sense of home here—a sense that she belonged. Eira had never really felt that before, so she figured she should try to fight for that feeling.

He hopped onto the floor, "Well, Princess, it's your first official day here, what would you like to do?"

"I don't know," Eira responded, "I haven't really thought about it."

"Well, how about I leave you to explore—unless you'd like the company?" He was unnervingly close to her now.

She turned her head upward, "From *you*—I don't think so." He didn't move, just towered over her, his scent wafting into her like a cool breeze; sandalwood and citrus.

"But now that you mention it, company might be nice—maybe I'll go find Boreas."

He smirked, "Trust me, Princess, you're far too mortal for him." He breathed in deeply as if taking in all the perfume Ceilidh had spritzed onto her hair that morning and took a step back, "Well, I have things to get ready before we leave tomorrow anyway." He strode off toward the door, "Come find me if you get lonely."

*Pig.*

Eira explored the castle on her own for a few hours until finally deciding to root herself on a beautifully plush chaise, waiting so invitingly on the balcony of her bedroom. She stared blankly out to the courtyard beneath her room and watched as the various members of the castle staff moved about. She looked beyond the castle walls themselves, to the great big world beyond. Eira could see all the way to Lake Isas, its waters glimmering in the mid-afternoon sun.

She heard a knock at her door and turned to the open doorway to see Leon standing there. She rolled her eyes but got up from her perch and met him halfway in the middle of the sitting area. "Good afternoon," he started. "Just came to see if you're hungry."

Eira hadn't thought of eating—not after the mountain of food she had consumed for breakfast. But now that he was planting the idea into her head, she was a little hungry. "Sure." He looked past her for a moment and walked out onto the balcony. Eira trailed behind, "What are you looking at?" she finally asked him.

"Just—the beyond." He leaned a little closer into her—he seemed to keep doing that, and while all her instincts kept telling her to elbow him in the gut, she annoyingly also liked it for some reason. He held out his arm pointing into the distance. "You see that? That's where we'll be heading tomorrow, around the lake and to the forest. That tiny little bit of mountain just barely peeking up over the treetops, that's where we're headed." Eira glanced in that direction as well. It seemed so far away—and yet, not far enough. "Getting used to it yet?" he asked moving his hands into his pockets and turning to face Eira. "That all of this is yours." He gave a slight nod to the courtyard below and the forest, lake, and mountains, just tiny figures littered in the background landscape.

The corner of her mouth curved slightly upward. It was the way he had said it and the sunlight touching every exposed piece it could find, "You mean, everything the light touches is all *my* kingdom?"

"Um, yeah, I guess if you want to put it that way. But," he pointed outward, "that shadowy place over there is yours too." Eira couldn't help but chuckle under her breath.

"Anyway, you said something about food."

The afternoon was filled with more trying to occupy herself, while others were busy preparing for the journey. Eira walked around the gardens for a bit. They were not your usual gardens as most things don't grow in the snow. While the castle did have a greenhouse, the outdoor space had evergreens and other plants that can survive in a Talvian climate. There was a small pond that Eira was informed used to be a skating rink. She met the two large dogs that roamed the castle: Olaf and Polar—big, fluffy, and white. Perfect for a land of eternal winter, but they looked utterly uncomfortable in the current climate. Gideon had said they were once bred as reindeer herders, but these guys were simply the palace pets; loveable and not good for much else. They kept Eira company for the rest of the day following her around the castle and making sure she didn't get too lost—or into any trouble. Eventually, she ventured out, past the palace gardens. She was walking around for what seemed like hours when she came to a large hill behind the castle and decided to climb it to get a better view of the kingdom—*her* kingdom. When Eira was getting closer to the top, she could see two large stone figures becoming more and more visible. The dogs were circling them and sniffing the ground. The closer she got the more familiar they looked. It was a man and a woman gazing stoically over the land. She walked up to the statue and read the inscription: *For our beloved king and queen. We will be reunited with the snow one day, just as we will be reunited with you in another world. May the next world serve you well while we remember you in ours.*

Eira realized the figures were her parents. The pure white, as if carved from snow, stone figures towered above her as she stared deeply into their faces. She knelt on the ground below them and whispered,

"I wish I could have had more time with you. I wish you could have tried harder to hold on for me—for *both* your children." She realized she was not the only one who had lost their parents. She had no right to be angry with her father—she didn't even know him, know the situation. But Eira couldn't help that little bit of anger bubbling inside. He could have tried harder; at least she could have had a father. Eira took a breath. There was no point in being angry, what was in the past was in the past—what's done is done. She cannot bring them back, they cannot come back. She needed to move on. "Everyone here seems really nice and they seem to have so much faith in me. I never signed up for this destiny." But that's the thing about destiny—no one ever knows what theirs is until they've lived it and looked back. Eira wished she could look back on this, and know that it all turns out alright. A few solemn tears rolled down her cheeks. At that moment she heard a voice behind her and quickly wiped them and turned around.

"Are you alright, Your Majesty?" Ceilidh asked. Again—*Your Majesty*. Eira smiled, trying not to give the impression that she was upset. "I was looking for you, what are you doing?"

"I was...walking the dogs." Eira looked at Olaf and Polar who were nosing Ceilidh for attention—more likely treats held within her apron pockets.

"This is just a memorial to them," Ceilidh nodded to the statues, "if you were wondering? They're not buried here. It is Talvian tradition for royalty to be cremated and then their ashes are scattered across the mountains at sunset." Eira looked in the direction of the mountains. "Anyway, I came to get you because Leon and the others would like to go over the plan for tomorrow."

Eira nodded and strode alongside her as they headed back toward the castle. They walked mostly in silence the whole time. Eira wasn't really in the mood for small talk and Ceilidh seemed to pick up on that so she let her be. She led Eira to a sitting room where the others were already going over the plan and listing various supplies needed. They informed Eira about everything—all the ins and outs of a journey of this calibre. It would take about two weeks—one there and one back. Eira knew what she was getting herself into, but the reality of it hadn't truly hit her until this moment; weeks trekking through the wilderness with three men—and a god.

"How are you feeling about all of this?" Leon asked once he was done and the two of them were once again left alone in the room together—that also seemed to keep happening. The others had gone to get started on dinner, which was ready in the dining room.

"Okay," Eira replied. The thing was, she *was* up for an adventure. She thought she would regret it if she didn't go along, but the risks were becoming more and more evident the longer she spent in Talvia—for herself and for Talvia. But along with the risks, the benefits were also beginning to take over.

Eira sat there at the dinner table watching Leon, Killian, and Theo tear into each other in a brotherly way and she got a sense of what she was fighting for—and she liked it. Maybe was even beginning to love it. This family that one day she could be a part of too.

Eira was tossing and turning, trying to find that blissful slumber she so desperately wanted—especially since she had to be up at *dawn*. It was late. So late that it was early. The whole castle was asleep and she wished so desperately she could be too. No matter what she had tried, sleep just couldn't find her. Anytime she thought she had drifted off, that recurring dream woke her again with visions of the dragon. Neither the relaxing bath with the massive floor-to-ceiling windows open so the cool night air could breeze through, nor the hot mug of tea and the roaring fire with Pix snuggled up next to her did the trick. She finally decided to head out into the castle in the hopes that a change of scenery might help. The halls were not as dark as she had thought they would be in the dead of night.

The moonlight trickled through the massive arched windows illuminating the shimmering hall. The sconces glowed a dim yellow, giving the hall that bit of extra light needed to see. Eira didn't know where she was going: the Library, or perhaps the pool for a late-night swim? No, she didn't have a bathing suit and wasn't going to risk skinny dipping. Maybe the kitchen for a late-night snack? That is, if she could find it. She remembered passing it once, but all the halls in this castle looked the same to her.

"Oh, hello," Eira said as she was finally led down the correct corridor by the smell of freshly baked goods wafting down the hall. She had assumed it was the castle bakers, readying some last-minute provisions for their journey tomorrow. The kitchen was massive—as it should be for supplying food to a castle this large. Like every other aspect of the castle, it was crafted with the finest attention to detail. It wasn't like typical castle kitchens that were made to be hidden, usually in the lower levels so the aristocracy could not catch a glimpse of the servants and staff. No, this kitchen was made to be seen; a focal piece of the castle. Like kitchens in the homes where she grew up. It gave off the essence of the heart of the home, where people gathered for more intimate meals and celebrations. Where friends and family laughed and enjoyed together. Eira's gaze was guided upward to a massive skylight above the large stone island and like everything else in this castle, it had a slight ethereal quality to it. She couldn't explain it— but she felt it. It was not a cold stone castle, but a warm inviting one.

"Hi," Leon answered, hands wrist deep in kneading some sort of dough. Great, as if he couldn't get sexier; he bakes too. "Can I help you with anything?"

"What are you doing?" Eira asked wandering farther into the kitchen, surveying his surroundings. He was the only one in there, save some cookies cooling on a baking tray. As he delved back into kneading, Eira noticed something black peeking out of his rolled-up shirt sleeve on his forearm. A tattoo? It looked like triangles with rough edges, but she felt weird asking him about it so she diverted her gaze so as to not draw his attention.

"I couldn't sleep, so I figured I'd make something for our journey tomorrow."

"I didn't know you could bake?"

"Why would you?" he shrugged then placed the dough into a bowl and covered it with a damp cloth to rise. He then clapped the flour off his hands and Eira watched as the plumes of white circled and landed gracefully atop the counter. He headed to the sink to wash. When he was done, he turned back to Eira, "What are *you* doing up this late?" She didn't like the suggestive tone and glimmer in his eye. "Missing me?"

"I can't sleep," she said sharply. "And when I'm home and can't sleep, I usually watch T.V., but that doesn't seem like an option here. So, I figured maybe a snack would help."

His lip turned up slightly in one corner as he reached for a cookie and handed it over. She took a gingerly bite, then her face relaxed. They were good—oh they were good. The chocolate was still melted and they were soft and warm. He didn't say anything, just smiled at her reaction, and then continued to clean the flour off the counter. Eira finished the cookie—and a second and third in silence while he cleaned. It was a bit awkward, but she didn't know what to say and he seemed content just cleaning while she ate. At some point, he poured her a glass of milk and handed it over still without a word. What was he doing? What was his game? She didn't know. When they were both done she stood from the stool at the counter and glanced toward him. They still didn't speak.

Eira finally broke the silence, "Well...goodnight."

He was leaning against the opposite counter, his arms crossed as he was finished cleaning, "Goodnight, Princess," he smiled back.

After a bit of hall wandering, Eira finally found her room again and quietly opened the door. She quickly hopped into bed and snuggled down, thoughts of Leon racing through her mind. *No—stop it.* She shook them from her mind and finally began to feel the weight of her eyelids. Before she had realized it, she had drifted off into a sound slumber until she was awoken by something, or rather someone.

Eira screamed, scrambling out of the bed and turned on the bedside lamp.

"You know, Princess," Leon said casually turning onto his side and propping himself up on his elbow. "I usually like to get to know a girl before I let her in my bed."

"What are you talking about?" she snarled back all too aware of the fact that Leon was naked from the waist up—at least she hoped it was just the waist up.

"You're in my room."

She glanced around, and while it looked very similar to her room, she now realized it wasn't quite the same. "Well, all these damn rooms look the same."

"No they don't, but you can tell yourself that."

"Prick!"

She still stood there. "Well, are you going to leave?" He turned onto his back and settled in as if trying to go to sleep. "I mean, I don't really care. I'm going to sleep either way."

Eira let out a low groan and headed toward the door just as a small cat trotted into the room, bounced onto the bed, circled, and then finally laid down. *Traitor*, she glared at Pix.

She paused when she hit the doorway. "It's three doors down, to the left," called Leon from the bed. Eira's eyes rolled upwards and she stormed off down the hall—to the left.

The morning sun rose all too quickly. The next day was upon Eira and her companions and she had not benefitted from as much sleep as she would have hoped to. She was given a more suitable outfit for the journey for the gown she was draped in yesterday might not be the best attire for defeating a dragon—unless she had planned on seducing it into submission. Some pants, a nice pair of riding boots, and a warm shirt and jacket. She didn't know how cold the weather might get, but she could already feel it changing. It was slight, but it was colder than it was when she had arrived.

Eira threw open her door only to find Leon leaning in the doorway about to knock. He looked down at her, his one arm pressed against the doorframe above her head. He quickly righted himself and took a step back. "Ready?" She nodded in response. Eira was then led to the castle stables where Killian, Theo, and Boreas were readying their horses for the long journey across the field to the water's edge. Leon had said it would take about a day's ride to reach the town of Huurre on the edge of Lake Isas where they would stay for the night.

"Sleep well?" asked Leon breaking the silence as he tacked her horse for her. Eira smirked in response. "This will be your horse," he said as he handed her the reins. A rather beautiful strawberry-roan coloured mare with a white mark on her forehead padded the ground as she walked closer. "Her name is Maeve—and *Harwin* is quite fond of her."

Eira knew how to ride—knew how to shoot an arrow while doing it too; all part of her training. They lived on a small plot of land, large enough for a couple of horses and secluded enough to train a would-be queen. Her aunt taught her to ride—amongst other things. She was dangerously good at them all. She was an elf warrior after all. Eira rubbed a hand against Maeve's velvet nose, then felt a hand place itself atop her shoulder. She turned to see Gideon standing behind her.

"Eira, my darling," he began. "This journey is going to be difficult but I want you to remember something." Gideon took her shoulders in his hands and leaned in, "You may have been born into this life, but it is *you* who makes it your own." He held the stirrup out for her and she placed the toe of her left boot into it hoisting herself up and over the horse. "I'm glad our queen has come home."

Eira's heart was pounding but there was no time to succumb to it. The others had all mounted their horses as well and before she knew it, Killian and Theo were off having just made a wager on who would reach the gates first—loser bought first round at dinner. She watched as their horses were pushed harder and soon they were nothing but the faint sound of hooves on the stonework in the distance. She looked at Leon who seemed to be waiting for her to start moving first. She nudged Maeve with her heels and the mare jolted forward.

5

The journey outward was quite pleasant, apart from
the cursing Killian was doing at Theo for beating him.
Apparently, it wasn't a fair race, but Leon diffused the
situation—as it seemed he usually had to, and the rest of
the time they spent laughing and telling stories. The ones
from Killian were particularly Eira's favourite. He had a
knack for storytelling that was very satisfying and
humorous. They travelled up and across the varying
gradients of the landscape, seeking shade from the noonday
sun under small patches of trees where they could be found.
While she slightly missed the comfort and convenience of a
car, there was something beautifully simplistic about a
journey on horseback—at least as long as the weather
holds. Eira didn't know what they were going to do if it
rained, or got immensely colder.

"So where exactly are we headed again?" she
finally asked.

"We're headed to the town of Huurre, to Iceman's Wharf. From there, we will travel around Lake Isas. We will have to stay in the town overnight though," said Theo.

"Good," added Killian. "I can already taste the roast and pint." His mouth was practically salivating at the mention of it.

"Do you ever think of anything other than eating and drinking?" said Theo.

Eira pushed Maeve to move slightly faster into a trot and rode up beside Leon. His head had seemed to be somewhere else for the majority of the journey so far, "Hey, you okay?" she asked slowing back to a walk.

"Yeah, I'm fine. Why wouldn't I be?" he smiled.

"I don't know. You just seemed kind of...distracted."

"It's nothing, Princess."

"Fine—whatever. Here I am, trying to be a little nicer to you even though you're the last person I want to be on this adventure with."

"Well, you don't have to keep reminding me." They were most likely about to erupt into a full-blown argument when a voice sounded behind them.

"What are you two chatting about up here?" Killian rode up alongside Eira and Leon, "Leaving the rest of us to fend for ourselves. I don't know about you, but I've had just about enough of that god's stories. He's not very funny." The two chuckled at his boldness. "Now, I've got a story for you." Mischievousness gleamed in his eyes as he looked at Eira, "Involves a goat and a rather large amount of whiskey—as all good stories do. And a poorly thought out plan involving a razor and a bonnet."

"Don't tell her that one," pleaded Leon.

"Hush, you. Now, I know you're hooked already, but if that hasn't got you, this certainly will…"

By nightfall, they reached the town of Huurre. Huurre was quaint. There were markets and shops along the main streets with wooden signs swaying beside the doors indicating what types of services were provided inside, and little cottages and townhouses housing its people along the outer borders. It had once been, long ago, an ice fishing community and still was minus the ice. Most of the shops and dwellings were well maintained—the people doing their best to keep the town alive even in the hard times. Street lamps lit the cobblestone underfoot as they rode into the centre of town. Eira would have loved to see all this town used to be, but things seemed to have degraded more and more since the dragon came. Killian led the group over to the local pub for a well-deserved meal. They didn't bring any attention to themselves by simply walking into the pub, it was later that evening that the people began to wonder who this strange girl was. Even though she now looked the part of a true Talvian—wearing more appropriate clothing. It was as if the people could sense she was not from around here—or rather, didn't grow up here.

The five sat around a small table by the hearth of the fireplace, strategizing and planning the next days of the journey to the Hoarfrost Mountains' foot. As Leon had mentioned before, most had long forgotten about the prophecy. There were a few elders in the pub who would have sprung from their seats if they had known who Eira was. The elders made a mission of telling and retelling the stories of old along with the prophecy to any who would spare them an ear. Many of the people still believed in a free Talvia and that an heir to the throne would one day return, but as the years went on, many gave up hope. It seemed as though the elders were the only people brave enough to hold on to the past, or perhaps because of their senility they were the only ones able to get away with it. The younger generation would tell them to let it go and that things were not going to change, but the elders had grown up in an age where they had things to believe in, which was lost on the younger generation.

Looking around the pub, Eira could see that she stood out among the regular crowd. There were a few women, including a waitress—not unlike herself back in Adelaide. Leon had just returned to the table from talking to a gentleman he seemed to know.

"Good news," he started. "I have just appropriated us a ship and a captain to sail across the lake so we don't have to go around. It should take about a day off the journey." He sat down close beside Eira, reaching behind her chair and resting an arm on it—a little too close for her liking.

"Why are they staring at me?" Eira queried as she glanced toward a group of men sitting in the far corner of the pub. Another hooded man caught her eye sitting next to the group of men, trying not to draw any attention to himself.

"They're not staring at you," answered Leon, "they are staring at me—because of my father. There are still those whose allegiance lies with the nobility of this kingdom, not with my father. They believe he has no right to rule them."

"But, he's done a good job hasn't he?"

"He has done adequately enough for what he was left with after your parent's death. When there was no heir to take the throne, many Talvians revolted. Some fled to other lands forming a new authority and others remained in waiting for the day the heir would return. It is hard to say who is left and who still believes. Many think they have waited long enough and it is time to move on. There's another family vying for the throne. They believe they're the true heirs to it. They even sent their own men into the mountain to try to defeat the dragon and win the people's favour, but none were successful." A sudden uproar behind them stole all of their attention. An old man stood up from his table and made his way over to the group shouting.

"She's here. I know who you are. I have seen that face many times over the years. You look just like the old queen, may she rest in peace. You are here to save us from the dragon." Most people in the pub thought he had too much to drink for the night and was a foolish old man talking nonsense. Eira wasn't sure if that was lucky or not. He *was* right, but did she want everyone in this pub to know it?

"We're just passing through," replied Theo, "I'm afraid she just has one of those faces," he smiled at Eira. It seemed to satisfy the man, or perhaps he was so intoxicated that he wasn't even sure of what he just said. He went back to his seat and ignored them for the rest of the night.

"Do you want another drink?" Leon glanced at the almost empty glass clutched between Eira's hands.

"Probably not," she replied, "I'm kind of a lightweight." He smiled taking a sip of his.

"I do!" said Killian downing the last of his beer and bumbling over to the bar. Eira had learned over the last couple of days that Killian did, in fact, think mostly of eating and drinking. Fighting was in there too. She watched briefly while he trained with Leon and Theo in the castle's sparring ring yesterday. Leon tried to get her to join, but she wasn't in the mood for training and Killian's rippling pectorals on display had her breathing more heavily than she would have liked. Better not risk it. Eira had done enough training for eight years anyway. And the last time Leon and Eira met in the sparring ring—it didn't go well. She could still kick his ass, she was sure of it, but she wasn't in the mood to go there, so she politely declined to his chagrin. Two days, she had already spent two days in Talvia, getting to know these people and—

"What?" Leon asked, noticing the change in her facial expression.

She tilted her head sideways to look at him, "It's Christmas." He didn't respond, just smiled back.

"What's Christmas?" asked Theo.

Eira's eyes widened and her head bounced back as the words made their way to her, "You don't have Christmas here?" She was shocked, but then pausing a moment she realized, of course they wouldn't have Christmas here. Some other winter celebration maybe, but not specifically Christmas.

"No," responded Leon.

"Well, it's just a winter celebration where you give each other gifts and spend time with your loved ones. If you really want to get down to it, it's actually just a massive birthday celebration for one guy who lived over two thousand years ago."

"Wow, he must be important," slurred Killian, sitting back down with a new overflowing pint.

"He is to some people," Eira nodded.

"We do have something like that here, though. It's not in celebration of anyone in particular, just to celebrate the winter solstice. Same idea, though, with gifts and spending time with loved ones." Theo was solemn for a moment, "Honestly, it hasn't been celebrated here in a while. I don't remember my last Solstice."

"Well, maybe I'll bring that back too—being queen and all."

"I guess it will be like a massive birthday party then too, given your birthday is also on Solstice," added Leon.

"So, what did you do back in your world?" inquired Theo. He seemed very fascinated about where she came from and how she lived. While Talvia did have similarities to her world, it wasn't quite up to speed with the twenty-first-century goings-on.

"Well, I was a university student back home."

"What's that?" asked Boreas.

"It's the school you go to as an adult to learn how to do the job you hope to have one day and to prepare you for life in the *real* world. Or at least, they like to think it is. It really just teaches you how to memorize trivial facts you'll never use in your day-to-day life or your future career, and how to manage being insanely broke and in debt, and how to function with only a few hours of sleep."

"And, you have to go to these schools?" he asked. "It's mandatory?"

"Well...no," she replied.

"Then why on earth would anyone willingly go through that?"

"You know what? I keep asking myself that same question. Unfortunately, though, it's kind of how it works there. You can't really get anywhere without it."

"Well, that sounds dumb," chimed in Killian.

"What else did you do there, other than be sleep-deprived and broke?" asked Boreas.

Eira took a breath, "Well, when I wasn't in school or studying, I was working at the bar a few blocks away from where I live."

"You were a barmaid!" gasped Theo. Leon nearly choked on his drink at the accusation.

"I guess—if you want to call it that. It's just called a waitress there, and many people my age have that job. I wasn't exactly a princess back there."

"What was your favourite part of that job?" asked Leon.

Eira thought a moment, "Probably watching the people when I'm not at their table talking to them. You catch little snippets of their conversations or you can't hear them at all and then you just make up what they're talking about. First dates are the most fun to witness. You can tell the couples who have just met their lifelong partner and the ones who will probably never see each other after that night."

"Wait a minute," said Theo holding up his hand, "people go to places like *this* on a date?"

"Well," she scanned her less-than-appealing surroundings, "yeah—maybe not exactly like this place, but close enough."

"There's nothing better to do than go to a smelly bar?"

"Well—no, there are lots of fun things to do on a date, but people do like bars. Maybe they're a bit different there, although they do have ones that have the same atmosphere as this."

"Well, I wouldn't take a girl to a bar is all I'm saying."

"You haven't taken a girl anywhere," joked Leon.

"You couldn't resist, could you?" Theo sneered.

"Well I'm sure *you* have," Eira snidely remarked to Leon. "Blonds I'm assuming, too."

"Nah, he seems to like brunettes," added Killian, but was met with daggers from Leon.

"Okay Kil, where would you take a woman?" Leon asked fully expecting Killian to waver.

"The fjords at sunset." He seemed a little too prepared with that answer. They all turned to look at him, "The sun hits the waters just right and you can watch as the world turns from orange to pink to purple. As the sun lowers more and more behind the mountains you get that last radiant beam of soft light that cascades over the world and then it's gone. You sit by a roaring fire watching as the stars dance in the sky above you, and you just know nothing will ever be more perfect than that moment right there as you breathe in the night air and breathe out all your fears about what's going to happen next." The group stared silently as Killian sipped his drink when his tale was over. "What?" He looked back at their frozen faces, "real men are romantic and not afraid to show it!"

"Here, here!" Eira toasted, holding up her drink, not missing the chance to send a death glare to Leon.

He threw back a, *what?* expression, as if he didn't know what she was talking about. Their glasses clinked and then the topic was changed. When all were satiated, they left the pub and headed back to the Icicle Post Inn for the night. They had stopped there briefly before the pub to secure rooms for themselves. Killian stumbled out of the bar with Theo and Boreas close at hand should they need to catch him. Eira followed, grasping her arms as the cold night air swam through her. Just as she hit the last step onto the street, a voice behind her grabbed her attention. The woman was tall and had a light olive complexion. Her long dark hair was braided nicely over one shoulder, and she wore pants and tall boots with a corseted vest made of leather over her shirt and under her jacket. She looked as if she was ready for battle—not entirely inappropriate in a bar such as this one.

"Wait, wait," she called and then finally caught up. "The old man, he was right. I have heard many stories about this day, from my father and grandfather. They still believe and I do too. I knew it the moment I saw you." She held out a hand to Eira and she took it, "My name is Clea, and I am at your service, Your Majesty."

"Thank you. That is very kind, but we do not need any assistance," Leon reacted sternly.

"With all due respect, I think you will. You will need all the help you can get when it comes time to slay the dragon." Turning back toward Eira, Clea continued, "You may think you have this covered, but if I were going up against a dragon, I'd take all the help I could get."

"She has a point," Eira agreed. "I have never killed a dragon before." While she did have extensive weapons and fight training growing up, a dragon wasn't exactly something she could practice against.

"That's what we're here for," assured Killian, now being propped up by Theo and Boreas.

"That may be, but what happens when the dragon is more of a match for four men?" answered Clea.

"I'm a *god*," boasted Boreas, also quite intoxicated.

"And what would you like me to do about that?" Clea raised an eyebrow.

"Never mind," he sunk back into the group.

"She may have a point. What's the harm in being overly prepared for the dragon? Besides, I could use another girl on this trip," Eira said looking at the group and frowning slightly. Leon's displeasure was written all over his face so she simply looked back at him and claimed, "Queen," asserting her authority over him. He did not like that very much, and he let her know it with a rather peeved facial expression, but he also knew that this was a battle he probably was not going to win and a waste of his efforts to even try.

"Alright," he finally sighed, "she can come. Meet us at Iceman's Wharf at sunrise."

Clea nodded in thanks, "Thank you, Your Majesty. Goodnight boys—oh, and *god*." She turned and headed in the other direction to wherever it was she was going for the night.

They walked in silence the rest of the way to the inn. The Icicle Post Inn was quaint. Everyone was assigned rooms; the guys split between two and Eira in her own. It was the type of place you knew had been run by the same family for years, and the elderly couple at the front desk were more than happy to have guests. Especially because there had not been much tourism in Talvia since the land ran dry and desolate. The elderly woman who escorted Eira to her room was sharing the inn's tale as they walked up the old wooden staircase from the lobby. It was once the most popular inn in the town, everyone travelling through Talvia or just coming for a vacation would want to stay there. Its old-world charm coupled with the happy hosts made it the perfect place for rest and relaxation. It had that Scandinavian charm with wood carving details in the framework and the colours of red, green, white, and blue, now faded, but representing the vibrancy they used to hold. Eira's room had a brick fireplace with a fire already dancing inside. It was a small room, but not the bad type of small, the cozy type that makes you feel at home. The bathroom was just large enough for a claw-foot tub and a small sink. After a long day on horseback and then a long evening with the guys at the pub, a warm bath before bed was just what she needed. She also did not know the next time she would be able to indulge in such privileges, so she took the chance while she had it. Leon had said that the journey was mapped out with their stops in various villages or traveller's cabins littered along the way, but she knew nothing of how *rustic* those places might be.

Eira revelled in the warmth of the water, soothing her aching behind and thighs. Sure, she knew how to ride, but it had been so long her muscles had adapted to not being on a horse and the first time back took its toll. A set of red and white striped pyjamas were folded on the bed waiting for her. She slipped into them and then went over to the fireplace and closed the doors so the fire would die down. She then crawled into the bed and watched as the fire flickered slowly, drifting in and out of sleep. Finally, when all the embers ran cold, she fell into a deep sleep, that for the first time since being here, would take her all the way to morning.

Eira awoke to a loud knocking at her door. Opening one eye, she looked to the window and saw that it seemed the sun was just starting to rise over the horizon. Groggy and still with sleep in her eyes, and pretty pissed at whoever was at her door, she pulled herself from the warmth of the bed and sauntered over to the door, fumbling to get it open in her sleepy state.

"You're still asleep?" asked Leon when she finally figured out how to use the door handle, weirdly chipper and awake for the time of day.

"Yes—you're not?" she growled at him.

"Of course not, we have a boat to catch."

"Well, you didn't exactly tell me what time we would be leaving in the morning."

Leon frowned, "It's fine, you can get ready and we'll meet you downstairs."

"Okay," she smirked and shut the door in his face. Eira was not a morning person and would never be.

She finally dragged herself down the inn's stairs to see the group waiting for her at the bottom. None looked particularly annoyed with her tardiness, so she didn't see why she couldn't have gotten a few more minutes of extra sleep. Killian looked the worst, but not because of having to be up early. His state was purely due to the amount he had to drink last night.

The ship was ready when the group finally made it down to Iceman's Wharf. There was an unfamiliar, yet familiar chill in the air; a chill that had not been felt for a hundred years. It was cold for a summer morning and it was all due to Eira's presence in Talvia. There was new hope, and the magic of the snow was beginning to slowly return. When they reached the docks, the pungent smell of fish mixed with the early morning air hit them like a ton of bricks. It hit Killian the hardest though as he ran to the edge of the dock and proceeded to empty his stomach into the lake. Fishermen were gutting and cleaning their catches, readying them to be sold in the markets and the sight of it didn't help his situation.

"There are so few fishermen," Eira said. "I thought this was a fishing community?"

"With the increasing temperature of the water since the dragon arrived, the fishing industry is getting more and more difficult. With the decreasing oxygen levels in the water as it warms, the fish that normally swim in the lake had to migrate to find cooler living conditions or they would die. The sudden warming of the waters was too stressful on most of the fish populations. Now fishing trips take longer than usual, resulting in smaller catches," replied Theo. "That is why many people had to leave Talvia to find a more stable way of life."

"Please stop talking about fish this early in the morning," begged Killian, finally able to stand with them again.

The ship along with its captain, an old friend of Leon's, was ready to set sail. His name was Arlo—a fine captain who, since the ice had melted, spent most of his years sailing between lands. Leon had not known what had come of him since their last encounter. They were boys who had played together many times as knights and explorers. He was telling the group about his adventures with Arlo when Clea met them at the docks as promised.

"Good morning," she chipped, again a little too enthusiastic for the time it was. Was everyone in this land a morning person—well, everyone except Killian.

Boreas piped up, "Oh good, the scary battle-maid made it."

The now six of them climbed aboard the ship. It was a rather large ship and crew. The ship took on the resemblance of an old Spanish galleon, made of beautifully carved wood; a prize to be owned by any captain. All were welcomed on board by the first mate. There was no sign of Arlo yet, but their welcoming was as if by an old friend to them all as the crew helped to load their belongings below deck. This was a far more lavish ship than she had expected. Eira wasn't sure if ships here were just bigger or if some sort of magic was at play, but there was a rather large living room below deck; comfortable and welcoming. Killian found a quite comfortable-looking settee and decided to take up root there for the rest of the day.

"Holler if you need me to kill something," was all he said as he pushed past Theo and slumped onto the cushions, crossing his arms and closing his eyes.

A sudden realization hit Eira, "What about the horses?"

"They'll head home. They know the route well and are better off there. They don't like ships much and there's not enough room, except for Harwin. He'll meet us on the other side of the lake. Unicorns can run incredibly fast, faster than any horse and they don't get tired. He'll probably beat us there, to be honest." Leon could already tell by Eira's expression that she felt like he was forgetting a crucial part of the rest of the journey—she was *not* walking the rest of the way. He smiled, "Plus, Arlo has a few horses on board already that he's willing to let us borrow for the rest of the journey."

"Oh—that's nice of him."


Most of the crew looked as though they were veterans of the sea. They set sail not long after boarding. Eira braced her arms against the railing, looking out to the mountains beyond the lake. They were headed east toward the Hoarfrost Mountains and it was still early so the sun hung in front of them providing a warm glow on the surface of the water. She looked over the edge of the ship and watched the waves crashing against the port side. Not long after the ship had set sail, they were taken back to the living area for tea. Killian was still slumbering peacefully, and rather loudly. The crew above was busily manning the ship deck while Arlo welcomed them with open arms.

"Leon!" He embraced his old friend with a hug. "You've gotten taller."

"Or perhaps you've shrunk," joked Leon.

"No, I was always taller than you. You just finally caught up." He moved to sit in an armchair and motioned for the group to join him, "So I see not much has changed since last I saw you. Still rescuing those damsels in distress?"

"Yeah...something like that."

Eira chimed in at that moment, "So, how do you two know each other?"

"We grew up together—in the castle," said Leon.

"Yes, my mother took a job as a maid in the palace. We packed up and moved, just the two of us, from Kesa to Talvia. She was one of your mother's favourites. She was even there the night you were born. She died about ten years after that but by then I was old enough to be on my own. I travelled back to Kesa and bought a ship. I've been on the water ever since."

Captain Arlo was a handsome man. His dark skin made his light brown eyes stand out against his solid face. He spent more time talking to Leon than the rest of them and asking questions—the kinds of conversations old friends catching up would have. One of his crewmen came in about halfway through their conversation and gave him a slight nod then excused himself again. Captain Arlo stood at that moment, walked slowly toward the porthole and peered out. Eira noticed the cascade of light that was trailing in through the window gradually disappear. It seemed as though there was a sudden wave that had washed over the captain. Something was troubling him and perhaps it had something to do with the fact that the ship was now straying from its designated course.

"Why are we turning?" Eira asked. She had never been on a ship but knew enough to know they were headed off course.

"Don't worry, Your Highness," replied Captain Arlo. "We are heading in the right direction. It is difficult to tell when you are below deck," he said with a strangely assuring voice. Clea walked over to a window across from Arlo and peered out. Eira could hear the footsteps of a crew working hastily above deck and little did they all know, the crew was working to alter the sails and a new flag made its way up the mast; a flag that every young child playing make-believe would know the colours of.

"Her Majesty is right," Clea interjected, "we are not heading for the eastern shores of Lake Isas. We are turning toward the inlet in the north that will take us out of Talvia."

"Arlo. What's going on?" Leon asked with every ounce of skepticism in his body.

Arlo sighed but did not take his gaze from the porthole, "I am sorry old friend, but I have to do this."

"I don't think this is a mere trading ship," said Theo.

"What ship *is* this?" Eira asked warily.

Arlo turned and looked at her with only a glimmer of remorse in his eyes, "A pirate ship, my dear."

"Well, fu—"

# 6

Killian had awoken right at that moment, and the verbalization of the particular sentiment they were all feeling had come from him. Never had it occurred to Eira that she would have to deal with pirates on this journey. The voyage across the lake was supposed to be smooth, a calm sea voyage where she could relax. Now she was staring a pirate in the face, wondering what to do next. The rest of the group seemed to share her feelings as she glanced around at the rest of their faces.

"Alright, what did you guys do?" Killian asked, rising to his feet from the settee.

"Arlo, what are you talking about? This is a joke, is it not?" Leon's voice was stern.

"Well my old friend, while you clung to the pathetic hope that your queen would someday return and bring back the glory of this land, I had to make a living for myself. Not everyone could remain in the palace—living a carefree, lavish life, getting served whatever they wanted day and night. I took to the seas to fish and trade but that was not enough to sustain a way of life. I was taken aboard a pirate ship one day and saw all the wonders that being a captain could bring. The captain of that particular ship was rich and I wanted it too. But more importantly—he was old. When he died, he bestowed his ship and crew onto me."

"But she's back now. The rightful Queen of Talvia has returned and all will be restored. Take us across the lake and you will see."

"I cannot do that, Leon. My greed has overtaken me—and I love it. There is a treasure in that cave with the dragon."

"That money belongs to the people!" Eira interrupted.

"Oh, but my dear, I am the people. I lived here once, that money is partly mine."

"You gave up that right when you chose the life of a pirate! What happens when the lake freezes over again and you can no longer pirate these waters?"

"That is why you are here, so I can make sure that never happens. Or, for me to get adequate compensation from the treasure. It won't matter anyway if you give in or not. Many people beyond the borders of your precious Talvia will pay immensely for the capture of the queen. I am not the only one who has benefited from the lake melting. Many other pirates and people use these waters for trade. They too would want to make sure this lake never freezes again."

"Arlo—what have you done? You've gone mad. This is not you!" argued Leon.

The captain looked at them, "It's the new me—the one who likes having it all. Take them to the brig," he ordered.

His crew marched in and took hold of them. They fought back hard, but it was no use and soon they were being wrestled into the hold below deck. Their weapons had been taken off them before boarding and placed securely in the hold below—that maybe should have been their first sign.

A few hours had passed when Captain Arlo sent for one of the crew members to release Eira, and only Eira, into his company. He tried to persuade her to see his side and give in, but she was not going to give in so easily. She may not be crowned queen yet, but for some reason, Talvia was starting to feel more like a home to her than her previous one.

"Dear little princess," Captain Arlo began, "you should just give in now. I'm not asking much, just a share of the treasure and then I will be on my way and leave you to rule in peace."

"Somehow I find that difficult to believe. I will not be swayed so easily, Captain."

"You will drive me out of this land when the snow returns! I deserve compensation for that!"

"You deserve nothing! You chose the life of a pirate and you can leave it. If you choose to change your ways then there will be a home for you in Talvia, otherwise, you can sail away knowing you will never be able to return."

"Bold words for someone who is not even queen yet. What happens if you don't succeed? What if there is no queen to fulfill all these promises you're so willing to make without any forethought?"

He looked at her, glaring with those daring eyes. He was not going to give in so easily either. He knew that when she defeated the dragon, he would be forced out. A pirate cannot sail on frozen waters.

"Take her back to the other prisoners," he ordered when her time with him and his patience had expired. They were getting nowhere. They were headed out of Talvia and Eira didn't know how to stop it. She was shuffled back to the cell but on her way out of the captain's quarters, she noticed a young boy scrubbing the deck. He glanced up at her with longing in his eyes. She could not help but think of the chance this boy might have had if the dragon had never come. He would have a life, more than that of a pirate.


"What happened?" asked Theo as she was pushed rather rudely back into the cell. She would have walked nicely on her own, no need for that.

"What do you think happened? He's not giving up and he wants to be paid off."

"I'm sorry," Leon began, "I got us into this. He was supposed to be my friend."

"Ah, it's not your fault," Killian reassured him. "How were you to know he was a traitor? But um, we're probably not going to listen to your judgement for a while—just saying."

Eira wandered over to the bench and sat beside Killian. Sighing, she moved her hands from her lap and ran them from her forehead back through her hair, trailing her fingers down the loose curls, pulling some over her shoulder. When she dropped them again, she looked to Leon and gave a half smile, reaffirming what Killian had just said—the not his fault part. They sat there in silence. Eira stared at her hands folded in her lap and felt the gentle swaying of the ship on the water. Every so often they could hear a wave crash against the side as it broke the forlorn silence.

"I can't take this anymore. I'm getting us out of here." Killian's frustration soon set in and he went running at the cell gates with his full strength trying to pull the door open, but no matter how many times he struck at it, he could not break the hinges that kept them from their freedom.

"What are you doing?" asked Leon.

Killian took another run at it, but it only resulted in him being knocked out for a second or two. He returned to his feet and shook off the blow.

Patronizingly, Eira suggested, "Why don't you just try to take out the pin in the hinges instead of just banging at the welded iron?" She had finally had enough of his use of brute force that was clearly getting them nowhere. Killian stood there, the look of obvious realization brewing on his face.

Boreas proceeded to try to loosen the iron pins from their holds, but they were stuck tight. He managed to loosen one a bit, but that didn't help much when there were three to get through. In time he managed to loosen and somewhat remove all three, but the door would still not budge. Exhausted, he sat back down with the rest of them.

There was clearly a party happening above deck. They could hear shouting and fighting—the kind that men do for fun. By this time, it was nightfall. They did not know what hour it was, but it was certainly late. When the commotion above them had died down for the night, they assumed most had gone to sleep or had passed out from the drink. Suddenly, they heard footsteps coming down the stairs toward them. Killian quickly manoeuvred himself in front of the hinges they were trying to pry open in an effort to hide what they had done. But as the click of boots drew nearer, it was becoming more obvious that the person who belonged to those boots was not one of the crew. It had to be someone lighter—not a fully grown man. There was no light down there, save the small oil lamps floating precariously in random spots. A shadow began to grow closer and closer to them until they were finally met with who the boots belonged to.

It was the boy Eira had seen scrubbing the deck earlier. He motioned for them to be quiet, grabbed the keys and unlocked the cell, causing the gate to fall from having its pins loosened. Killian and Theo tried to grab it, but their efforts came up short. It came down with a heavy crash. They all froze, hoping—praying no one above heard the noise. Some were staring at the gate on the floor and others toward the ceiling, listening above for more footsteps when the boy piped up.

"Hurry—hurry. Most of the crew have gone to sleep. There are a few standing guard above deck, but honestly, they're in no condition to fight anyone. If you hurry you can sneak to the longboats and escape." Eira looked at the boy and did not know whether to trust him or not.

"What is your name, boy?" Theo asked.

"Thomas. I was sold to the captain to work aboard the ship. When I saw you come aboard today I snuck off and listened to what you and the captain were talking about."

"Why are you helping us?" Eira inquired. "We certainly don't want you to get in trouble with Arlo. Who knows what type of temper he has?"

"Because I still believe in a free Talvia and remember the stories my father told me. Before I was aboard this ship, I heard tales of the queens and kings of old. How they were so good to the people and how one day a queen would return. I have never lost hope." Hope. A lot of people here seem to have it. Just another reason Eira was beginning to feel for this place.

Leon ordered Eira, Clea, and Boreas to follow Thomas upstairs to the boats, while he, Killian, and Theo headed to find their weapons and packs. They could see the guards standing watch and Thomas explained where the longboats were and how to get there. With the dark of night as their cover, they snuck up onto the deck and over to the boats. One would be enough to carry all of them. Clea and Boreas began to ready it: unhooking the covers and releasing the knots holding it in place. Killian and Theo returned with not only their weapons neatly stashed in their holders once again but with two large sacks filled with fruit, meat, and vegetables. If it were up to Killian, it would all be meat but thank goodness someone else was there to ensure a proper diet. They threw the sacks to Boreas who was standing in the boat and then piled in, not before cutting the ropes of all the other longboats hanging off the side of the ship. Thomas began to lower the boat and Eira looked back at him.

"Wait, aren't you coming with us?" Thomas looked shocked at the question and didn't answer. "Get in," she hurried. "A pirate ship is no place for a boy." Eira paused a moment, *but then again, neither was going after a dragon.* Either way, she motioned for him to come along. Thomas agreed and tried to climb into the boat. As he was stepping up over the edge he slipped and fell backward onto the deck. His sword clanged against the metal of the cannon beside him and the guards made their way over to see what was happening. When they noticed their captives had escaped they drew their swords at Thomas. Leon and Theo leapt out of the boat to his aid.

"Lower the boat," Leon called to Boreas, "we'll catch up." Boreas did as he was told and began to lower the boat into the water.

"No!" Eira called grabbing Boreas's arm to stop him. It was like grabbing a tree trunk and her small hands were accomplishing nothing against him. "We can't just leave them."

"We can and we must. Leon and Theo are brave warriors. They can certainly take on a few drunken pirates." While Boreas and Killian were distracted with lowering the boat, Clea seized the opportunity to sneak off the edge and climb up the side of the ship.

*Now where is she going?* She was not going to let the boys have all the fun with the pirates.

On deck, Leon, Theo, and Thomas were battling the pirates on guard. The clanging of the swords was all that could be heard as Eira was lowered in the boat. The noise awoke the other crew members who once seeing that the prisoners had escaped, joined the fight—to the best of their abilities. They were still quite intoxicated. Theo and Leon were skilled with a blade and, for a young boy, Thomas was able to defend himself quite well.

Captain Arlo stormed onto the deck, "What is going on aboard my ship?" he demanded as he swung open the door to the captain's quarters. Captain Arlo saw the battle and unsheathed his cutlass stomping his way onto the deck. As he walked toward Theo and Leon, his crewmembers parted and ceased all fighting.

"How did you escape?" Captain Arlo demanded from Theo and Leon. The two did not answer. "Well, maybe a walk down the plank will jog your memory." Theo was seized first and his hands were bound. He was forced down the plank at the tip of a sword.

"Arlo, you must stop this," pleaded Leon with a deep anger brewing inside. "This is not you, what happened?"

Theo was being forced farther and farther down the plank. When he reached the end he turned around and looked toward Leon. Leon knew what he had to do, even though the thought of it hurt him. Arlo had once been his friend, although it seemed to Leon that his friend was long gone and he was never returning. Leon then twisted free from the clutches of the men holding him. He grabbed his sword and clashed the end of it against Arlo's. The battle had begun again. From the side of the ship, Clea leapt up onto the plank and cut Theo free from his bonds then moved quickly to defeat the pirates emerging onto the plank. She fought ruthlessly with her sword and knocked most of them off into the cold waters below. Theo sprang from the plank toward the deck of the pirate ship and grabbing his sword he joined the fight, taking out many of the crewmembers. It was four against many, hardly an even fight, and Leon, Theo, Clea, and Thomas could not hold off the pirates much longer.

From the longboat far in the distance Killian, Boreas, and Eira watched the fighting aboard the ship. They could not see much of what was happening, just shouts and lights flickering in the distance.

"I think it's going well," Killian smiled, to fill the silence between them. His comment was met with identical frowns from Boreas and Eira.

When they had the chance, Leon jumped off the side of the ship with Thomas under his arm and swam to the boat waiting in the distance. Theo and Clea, seeing Leon and Thomas leap overboard, soon followed, diving into the deep indigo waters.

Captain Arlo ran to the side of his ship and scanned the waters for any sign of them. All around him was darkness and he could not make out where they had escaped to. Leon, Theo, Thomas, and Clea were swimming as fast as they could to the longboat. From the deck of the pirate ship, a long cry of rage from Captain Arlo sailed through the night air. Arlo turned to his crew.

"Should we go after them?" one of the crewmembers asked.

"No," replied the Captain, "they're as good as dead out there anyway. There is no way that girl will defeat the dragon." His crew stayed silent in the aftermath of the battle. "Well, what are you all standing there for? Continue on our course to the neighbouring lands. There are many other villages beyond these borders to plunder. I do not want to see these waters again."

It was dark and it was difficult to tell what direction to head in. They were now a day, or possibly more, behind with only a small rowboat to carry them to the water's edge. The air was getting colder and colder. Theo and Leon quickly ripped their clothes from them and changed into dry ones from their bags and Eira admittedly struggled to avert her gaze as much as she probably should have. Thomas was shivering but Eira found a blanket in the supply bin to help stop the cold from seeping into his bones.

"Sorry it's so cold. I guess that's kind of my fault," Eira said. Killian had given him one of his shirts to wear for warmth, but he was so skinny, it didn't seem to help.

Leon grinned at her attempt to make light of the situation. "We should all just try to make do for the time being. We will be in this boat until morning," he added.

"You should try to get some sleep," Eira said to Thomas who had stopped shivering; a warm contentment now glossing over him.

"I would say we are about a day in the opposite direction," added Killian. "If we try to head back it will take too long. We should just head for shore and backtrack in the shelter of Evervell instead."

"Evervell?" Eira asked. She knew it was the forest beneath the mountains, but they all seemed wary of going there.

"Yes. It will be about a three-day journey through it to reach the foothills and we have no more horses, so I guess we will walk," he replied.

*Oh yeah, I forgot about the horses,* Eira scowled but no one saw.

She sat down beside Thomas who was curled up trying to rest. He sat upright when she came over, clearly having no luck finding sleep. She didn't blame him. After the night they had, it was going to be hard for any of them to sleep.

Killian was already passed out.

"So—how old are you?" Eira asked. She pegged him for an early teenager.

"Fourteen," he replied. Fourteen. Way too young to be bound to a pirate ship for the rest of your life.

"How did you end up on Arlo's ship? You said you were...*sold*?" She cringed at the word. The fact that someone could still be sold as property made her sick.

He nodded, "I was taken from my family about three years ago. They couldn't pay their taxes and so I was taken as collateral. My parents begged and pleaded, trying everything to get me back. My father pleaded with them to take him in my place, but he was too old. They wanted someone young, someone like me they could get a better price for. Someone would pay well for a strong young boy willing to do any work." Eira was struggling to hold back tears. She felt for him. She too was taken from all she knew and while her upbringing was a loving one, it was still nothing compared to what it should have been. "I was sold to the old captain of Arlo's ship and when he took over, he kept me on board."

"We'll get you back home." She wrapped her arms around him, "I promise." And she truly hoped it was not an empty promise. She would make it her personal mission to deliver him to his parent's front steps.

The night was cool and dark. The men all took turns sleeping and rowing. By the time the clouds parted, the sky was scattered in tiny lights making it difficult to get any sleep. The boat was hardly as comfortable as the bed back at the castle, or the inn for that matter, but the gentle rocking back and forth of the waves eventually lulled Eira to sleep. She didn't sleep for long though. Turning over in her sleep resulted in her falling off of the bench and landing hard on the boat's bottom. When she awoke with the stars still dancing overhead, it was only Boreas who was awake, rowing slowly in the direction of land.

"Hi," Eira greeted in a whisper sitting across from him and wrapping a blanket around her shivering shoulders. He didn't say anything, just kept looking past her at the dark horizon and rowing. "How long have you been rowing for?"

"Not long. I just switched with Killian." Killian was back to sleep already, curled up off to the side, snoring like no animal Eira had ever heard before. It seemed as if he could sleep anywhere and for the first time in her life, she wished she could too.

"Oh," Eira answered. She didn't know what to say to him but felt awkward being awake and not acknowledging his presence. "So, we haven't really talked much," she finally said.

"Yes." A simple answer.

Eira cranked her head to the sky and then circled it back around again thinking of what to say next, "So…what's it like being a god?"

His eyes moved from looking past her head to focussing on hers, "What's it like being mortal?" he replied.

"Pretty. Freaking. Awesome." He didn't seem to get her humour. Her head bobbed up and down while she thought of how to keep the conversation going. This was definitely one of the more awkward conversations she had ever had but for some reason, she persisted. "Although I've got to say, I'm not sure I would like being immortal. That's a long lonely life if you have no one to share it with."

"Everyone I know is immortal. You're the first people I've known who aren't."

"Ah, touché." Eira let out a small laugh. "Well, you know, you're the first god I've met." She paused for a moment and then realized he may be the one person on this boat that she could actually be honest with. He didn't care about who she was meant to be and he wasn't putting any pressure on her to be something she's not. "So, how did you get here? I thought all the snow gods were destroyed? At least that's what the stories say."

"It takes a bit more than some dragon fire to kill me," he smirked. "Destroy our powers—sure, but not us. Anyway, I am actually here as punishment."

"Gee—thanks. But...what do you mean?"

"I bargained myself out of exile by agreeing to come down here and aid the princess in her fight."

"Exile?" Her tone changed serious and intriguing, "What did you *do*?"

"It is not important. What is, is that I am here to serve you and restore mine and all the other gods' powers."

"So...where do gods get banished too?"

"The Kingdom of Nightmares and Storm."

He was far too casual saying that. Eira's eyes widened, "Oh—that sounds like a fun place." She's not sure he understood her sarcasm. "Why would you have a place like that?"

"For banishing people." Well, duh. "It's not as bad as it sounds though, but this was still the better alternative."

Eira nodded, "Good to know." The silence grew around them again and after that, she didn't want to pry more into the life of the gods. "Okay—good talk." She turned around to look back at the sky. Something stirred from the other end of the boat and a figure stood up. Leon sat down next to her a moment later and stared in the same direction as she was.

"What are you looking at?" he yawned.

"Nothing really, just trying to avoid more awkward small talk with Boreas." She raised an eyebrow and glanced back at Boreas. Leon turned his head around and smiled at Boreas who had moved back to looking past them.

"Yeah, he's not much of a talker, is he?"

"Not really. But have you heard about where the gods get exiled to?"

"Do I want to know?"

Eira shook her head. "How long do you think it'll be before we reach the shore?"

"We should by morning."

A loud snort came from the dark shadows of the boat where Killian was sleeping and Eira was reminded that she should probably be sleeping too. She looked at Leon in the darkness and paused for a moment taking in the way the shadows played across his face, and the moonlight highlighting every curve and line. Then inhaling the cool night air, Eira said, "Goodnight," and stood up.

"Goodnight," he replied.

She paused a moment looking for a place to claim as her own for the rest of the night, this time opting for a spot on the bottom of the boat rather than risking falling off the bench again. The only available spot was next to Killian, and while she didn't really want to be snuggled up next to him, and his snoring, at least his body heat might keep her a bit warm. Her blanket made a nice cozy layer of plush on the hard planks of the boat and, surprisingly, it did not take long for her to be rocked once again to sleep.

In dawn's light, the makings of Evervell forest could be seen on the horizon and a small grey mound was rising up beyond it.

"Morning, darling." Eira was awoken by the shock of a kiss being placed on her forehead and Killian stretching away from her. She had not realized that during the night she had rolled over into him and cuddled his firm muscular body for the rest of the night. "Well, I slept well... how about you?" he gave a suggestive teasing wink, then smiled and got to his feet holding out a hand to help Eira to hers. Eira simply rolled her eyes in response and took his hand.

The sun beat down on them, adding a ray of warmth against the ever-cooling air around and the ones who had the pleasure of a midnight swim were able to dry their wet clothes draped over the side of the boat in its beams. It seemed as though since they started this journey, the air was getting colder and colder. Eira knew it was—they all did. She supposed that was a good sign to some, but while she may be a queen of winter—damn she needed a sweater. The warmth of the sun would not be enough though, to keep them warm during the rest of the journey.

"Row. Row. Row," shouted Killian from the bow of the boat as Theo, Leon, and Boreas held the oars and dipped them simultaneously in and out of the water pulling the boat closer and closer to shore.

"You know, you could help us," said Theo.

"Nah, you guys need the exercise. I, however, am a top specimen of muscle and strength. Would be useless for me." Clea, who was sitting behind Killian, reached an arm up and pushed him straight into the water.

"Thanks," nodded Theo.

They reached the rocky shore just as the sun was beginning to colour the sky in warm yellow light, breaking free from the pink and orange of it rising from behind the mountains.

The now seven of them pulled the boat ashore onto the banks of Lake Isas. Theo and Thomas went to find some logs and soon a roaring fire was crackling. They sat around warming themselves—especially a sopping-wet Killian. Soon, some breakfast was prepared from the food Theo and Killian had swiped from the pirates. Eira had never tasted anything so good: the bacon, the eggs—which she wasn't sure how they made it without being broken, and the various fruits. Perhaps it was because she was now sufficiently starving. None of them had eaten since tea with Arlo the day before. Soon enough, they were all satiated and planning their next course of action. They were indeed far from the course originally planned, but an alternate route was found quickly and it shouldn't put them too far behind. Eira was sitting with Clea while the boys were off doing their manly outdoor things—not sure what that entailed, but it was only Clea and Eira left by the fire.

"So," Eira began, "how is it that you can just leave everything and come on this adventure? Doesn't your family miss you?"

"No. My family doesn't really care. They know this about me—that I like adventure." Eira's expression soured at the fact that her family just didn't seem to care that she ran off to fight a dragon. "My parents haven't spoken to me since I ran out on my wedding last year. I've been on my own ever since. I have a sister who I talk to once in a while, mostly just for proof of life, but I'm not sure she tells anything to my parents. I'm pretty sure I'm dead to them, and the feeling is pretty mutual."

"Why did you run out on your marriage, if you don't mind getting into it? It's okay if you'd rather not."

"It's fine. He was terrible, just some nobleman from another town my parents were hoping to make some money off of. He didn't exactly take well to the whole women being warriors thing. I guess I was too much for him. He wanted me to play happy little wife while he spent his days fucking any woman who looked his way—sorry for the brashness. I guess that's another thing he didn't like about me."

Eira's eyes widened, "Well, I'm glad to have you along. This journey would be exhausting without another woman."

"Well, no time like the present," greeted Theo. "We should get going."

Their belongings and the rest of the food were tucked inside their packs. They no longer had any horses so everything they needed from then on, they would have to carry. Eira was amazed at Killian's and Boreas's packing abilities. She was convinced there was no way they would be able to carry as much as they were attempting to, but sure enough, it all fit into their packs—with only a few seams busting. They left what they didn't need in the boat at the water's edge and put out the fire. It was a long journey ahead now, but one they had to make. *Eira* had to make.

# 7

The days were long and tiring, but the forest was beautiful and a shelter from the cooling outside world. Eira dragged her feet along after they had already been walking for hours.

"You alright?" asked Leon, looking back at her forlorn expression.

"Yeah—fine," Eira huffed. "It's just been a while since I did this much walking." She would like to say she had kept up with her training more, but after she left at eighteen, she hasn't worked out since. Perhaps just another way to break free from the life she was being pushed into—a way to stick it to them, to disobey.

"We can take a break if you need it?"

"Nah, it's fine, just getting my hiking legs back," Eira said, remembering how much she hated hiking.

"Okay then, we'll keep going."

They made it farther than their first day when they stopped earlier than expected at a traveller's cabin. The next one wouldn't be for hours, and none of the group could make it that far. Traveller's cabins were not at all what Eira had expected. She had pictured a small derelict place in the middle of nowhere, just an empty shelter from the cold. She was wrong. It was as if little homes were built into the forest at various points on different paths.

They were coming up to their next stop for the night. Leon had said the cabins were built by the Wintren-elves long ago and were enchanted to always have what you needed in them. And right now, Eira needed a hot shower and a cozy bed. They all took turns showering and found their beds quite comfortable for the night.

Eira was asleep in no time—until she was awoken by her dream again. Someone was already awake, though. She wandered over to where Leon sat in the dim glow of the fireplace with a drink in his hand.

"Sorry, did I wake you?" he asked as Eira sat in the chair opposite him.

She shook her head, "No, just a bad dream is all." She didn't know why she told him that. She felt weird saying it. Children have bad dreams, not adults. But he seemed to understand where she was coming from.

"You want to talk about it?"

*Weird.* "Not with you," she replied casually.

"You know, sooner or later you're going to have to stop hating me." He took a sip of his drink.

"No thanks. But I will agree to tolerate you for the rest of this journey."

"Tolerate, huh? We'll see how long that lasts." He took another sip.

"What's that supposed to mean?"

"Whatever you want it to, Princess."

Eira rolled her eyes, "Well, as soon as this journey is over, I never have to see you again, so..."

"Is that so?"

"Why wouldn't it be? I'll be queen, so you don't have to live in the castle anymore."

"If you think you can just do it all on your own? My father was advisor to your father. It'll probably benefit you having him around."

"Yes, but you're of no benefit to me."

"I might be, you never know." He poured another ounce of amber liquid from the decanter into his glass. "Want one?"

"No."

"It might help with the sleep. Or you *tolerating* me more."

"The last thing I need is to be drunk at midnight around you."

"Why? You won't be able to control yourself?"

"From punching you in the face—probably not." He chuckled and put the stopper back on the glass container. "So, why are you up so late?"

He stared at the fire as if trying to find a suitable response, "Just thinking about things. But you're right. I should probably go to bed." He downed the last sip of his drink and placed the glass on the table next to his chair. He stood and walked over to her, resting his hands on the arms of her chair, and leaned down to her ear, "Unless you want to keep telling me how much you hate me?" He didn't let her reply, just stood and walked past her to bed leaving her heart racing. Why? Why did his extremely close proximity keep doing that to her? She shook it off and waited the appropriate amount of time before going to bed herself. She didn't want to risk running into him again.

When morning came, they quickly had breakfast and then were on the road again. They didn't want to waste any more time seeing as they were now on foot.

"It's so quiet here. I haven't seen any wildlife or heard anything since we started walking." Eira broke the silence in the group. They had just spent the last hour listening to Killian and Theo have a heated debate on whether that girl from last week really did like Killian or not and if he did, in fact, screw it up by opening his mouth. Clea and Eira were on the same page—he probably said something stupid, but for the life of him, he just couldn't seem to remember what he would have said to make her turn her nose up at him.

"There are still some in the forest," replied Leon. "They just tend to keep to themselves. The only ones you really have to worry about are the wolves, which you've already met," he grinned. "This forest used to be full of life, or so the tales go. The Wintren-elves and fairies had their home here too. They took care of the plants and animals that thrived in the harsh winter climate. When the snow left, so did the creatures. Slowly. One by one. No one has seen or heard of them since. Some were able to remain, the ones that could survive in the warm climate, but so many of the animals that called Talvia home depended on the cold and snow to survive. The elves and fairies cannot live in the warm weather either, not for long anyway. There were stories of the old days and how vibrant and full of life this forest was. As time went on, the animals disappeared and the fae folk haven't been seen or heard of since the night you were stolen away from this land."

"Were there ever giant snowy owls in Talvia?" Eira queried.

He shrugged his shoulders, "Probably, sounds like something we'd have."

"Damn, I wouldn't want to see where those things live. Birds are already disgusting. And *giant* birds—no thank you," added Killian.

"Just wondering," she answered staring absently into the forest ahead of them. She turned back to Leon once more, "Do you still believe they're out there, or that they will come back when the dragon is defeated?"

"I hope so," he answered. She never mentioned the owl she had encountered on her first day in Talvia.

They walked for another few hours, stopping only briefly to rest their legs then right back to hiking. Killian and Theo were back at it with their banter, Leon adding a quip here and there, *not* to their amusement. Eira was letting her mind wander having had enough of conversations about who could win against...insert various animals or mythical creatures here, when she noticed through the trees a large white bear staring at her. He stood still, just watching for a moment.

"Do you guys see that?" Eira turned to the group.

"See what?" asked Boreas.

"A bear, just—" Eira turned to point where it had been but it was gone.

"I didn't see anything, and I'm eagle-eyed. Nothing gets past me," huffed Killian. Clea smacked the back of his head—except that.

"Never mind then," Eira sighed.

The camp they had set up for lunch was in a small clearing in the dense forest. They were staying off the forest road for a more direct route though. Thomas and Eira had just finished prepping the food for lunch when she caught a glimpse of the bear again wandering through the forest in the distance. It looked so out of place, not at all able to camouflage with the surrounding greenery. Every time it seemed as though she was the only one who could see it and that it was following her. Perhaps she was beginning to hallucinate. Some overwhelming presence washed over her and she found herself not being able to hold back from following it into the forest. Eira walked to the edge of the clearing, deciding which way would be best to enter the forest. She could still distantly hear the others going about their lunch preparations, utterly oblivious to what she was seeing or doing.

"Well then, who's cooking?" started Killian. "I'll go get some firewood." He grabbed an axe and threw it over his shoulder.

"Are you sure you can handle that?" teased Boreas.

"Are you sure you can handle this?" argued Killian shoving the axe in his face. Eira made her way into the forest a bit more, their voices getting quieter behind her.

"Guys—enough," started Leon. "Killian, go get the wood. Boreas can stay here and watch the camp. Eira and—where's Eira?"

"I don't know," answered Clea. The rest of them shrugged their shoulders in response.

"She probably finally had enough of you lot and left," chuckled Killian now trampling into the forest.

Crack! Eira turned her head toward the distant sound. She had followed the bear as far as she could but it disappeared when she tripped over a log and lost sight of it. Unfortunately, she had disoriented herself and lost track of where she was and was now wandering through the forest alone. She made her way to the forest road when the air was disturbed by another loud sound. She paused a moment, listening to the silence around her and then she heard it again. Crack! The vibrancy of it breaking through the silence. This time it was accompanied by the sound of hooves, racing over the gravel road. From where the path curved out of sight, came a stampede of hooves and wheels. The carriage raced toward her down the road. The driver was forcing the horses on and shouting for them to go faster. He looked up and saw Eira standing on the side of the road ahead of him. She backed into the forest behind her when she noticed his hands pulling back on the reins. Just a little at first, but then when they made eye contact, harder. The horses slowed to a trot.

"Eira, there you are," said Clea coming up behind her. "What were you doing?"

"I—"

"Oh good, you found her," added Theo. "What are you doing?"

"Well—"

"Eira, what are you doing?" joined Leon. She rolled her eyes at their identical questioning and let her shoulders fall in response. She would have happily answered all of them if they didn't keep interrupting her attempts to.

"And what are you lovely folks doing on the side of the road?" came a voice from up high. They all turned to see the carriage driver sitting atop his carriage, holding the horses still at the reins. "Are you lost? In need of some assistance?"

"No, we are just fine thank you," said Leon taking Eira by the shoulder and turning her away from the carriage driver, trying to head back toward the woods.

"Well, perhaps you can help me then? I am lost."

"You were going pretty fast for someone who's lost," Eira sneered. The man just glared down at her with a devilish twinkle in his eye. An uncomfortable stare from someone Eira was getting the feeling she didn't want to know.

"Look," began Leon, "if you just keep following the road, you'll eventually get to a small town, but we do really need to be going."

The man continued to glare down at them, pursing his lips. He stood up and straightened himself toward the sky before stepping off the carriage and making his way to Eira and Clea. He glanced back and forth between the two women. An unsettling glare. Then stepped back. Leon and Theo had their hands on their swords, ready to pull them out if needed. The man turned quietly to board his carriage again and lifted a foot onto the step when he reached into his pocket for something. He pulled out a handful of what looked like sand. With rapid precision, he spun around and threw the dust directly into their faces. There was no time to react. The man was too fast. The dust spread around them in a flash and they were out. Darkness.

Another man from inside the carriage stepped out to see what was happening.

"Good catch," he said to the carriage driver, "they'll fetch a pretty price." The two worked quickly at carrying the group from where they fell to inside the carriage. The carriage driver sat atop his driver's seat again and with a crack of his whip, they sped off into the distance.


Boreas ran back through the forest after catching the tail end of what had happened to the others. He had grown impatient of waiting for the others to come back and decided to go search for them. When he heard their voices in the distance, talking to the carriage driver, he made for that direction and caught a glimpse of the group just as the last of them was being pulled inside the carriage.

"Alright," began Killian as he was making his way back to the camp, "too big of a job for me? Well...take a look at this pile you self-righteous—" He dropped the bundle of wood and scanned the campsite. Only Thomas was left, sitting on a stump. A crashing of footsteps came through the forest from the other side of the campsite and Boreas appeared in front of him, "Running away, were ya? Too afraid to face me when I showed you. I thought so."

"There's no time for your games, Killian. The others have been captured and dragged off down the road in a carriage. If we hurry, we can follow them before they get too far ahead." Boreas then ran back in the direction where he came.

"So… no time to eat then?" Killian called after him. He then hopped to, running after Boreas, "You see what happens when you leave them alone. I'm gone for two minutes and they get themselves kidnapped," he muttered.

Eira awoke to the distant sound of men talking. When her eyes were strong enough to let her in on her surroundings, her head was tilted to one side and her hair had fallen out, disrupting her vision. She raised her head and moved the hair from her face. She could now see she was in a cell and the only person who was accompanying her was Clea.

"What happened?" Eira asked making her way to her feet. She was a bit shaky and had to use the wall to stabilize herself.

"I'm not sure," replied Clea. "The last thing I remember was Leon talking to that carriage driver and—wait," she looked around, "where are they?"

Eira looked around the small cell. It would be hard not to notice if two men were also in there with them. "I don't know."

All she could see was a faint flicker of light coming from the hallway beyond the cell door. A shadow started moving down the hallway, growing larger as it made its way closer. A guard came around the corner right up to their cell. He didn't say anything though, he was simply passing by, but following him were Leon and Theo and then another guard behind them. The guard opened the cell beside Eira and Clea and motioned for the guys to go inside. The door was then slammed behind them and locked; the guard putting the key into his pocket.

"Eira! Clea! Thank gods you're okay," said Theo walking toward the bars that divided them. There was only a small strip of bars stretching from the ceiling to about Eira's eye level. The rest was constructed of solid stone.

"What's going on?" Eira asked hoping that wasn't a rhetorical question and one of them did have an answer for her.

"Well, we are in what is called a prison cell," quipped Theo. Eira rolled her eyes.

"That's what we were trying to get to the bottom of," said Leon.

"And?"

"And… it seems we are meant to be sold."

"*Sold?* Sold for what?"

"Does it really matter?" added Theo. Probably not. Being sold is hardly ever a good thing. "The point is, we need to find a way out of here, and negotiating with the guy in charge of all of this, didn't seem to work."

Clea asked, "So now what?"

"I'm not sure. The only thing I know is hopefully Killian and Boreas are looking for us."

"Well, maybe I can negotiate with him. I am the future queen after all," Eira suggested.

"I tried that already. He doesn't believe us, and why would he? Most people don't think the heir will ever come back. Many of the people who live here now aren't even Talvians. They moved here when the weather got warmer and took advantage of our depleting prosperity. He just wants to make money," sighed Leon.

"We can give him money. Surely the castle has some kind of wealth attached to it."

"Yeah, but we didn't exactly take it all along for the journey," smirked Theo. "I don't think he'll accept it in good faith."

Just then there was a commotion outside of the cells. One of the guards was on his feet, yelling at another,

"Hey, you cheated!"

"Did not! I won fair and square. I'm not the one who plays with cards up my sleeve."

"Fine! Best two out of three." The guards continued playing their game. Theo walked over to the cell door and watched the guards as they picked up and put down cards in various orders.

"I think I know what they're playing," said Theo.

"Are you any good at it? Maybe you can win our freedom?" Clea said sarcastically. Yeah, he could. They looked at her with an idea growing in their minds. "I was joking guys, come on. Do you really think they're going to let us go if he wins a little card game?"

"It's worth a try," started Leon. "What do you think, buddy?" he said clapping Theo on the shoulder. "You feel like playing a little *game?*" The way he said, *game* had Eira thinking something else was brewing between those two.

"Got nothing better to do," he smirked in response.

"Hey!" called Leon to the guards. "Hey—you two." They looked up from their hands and saw that Theo was motioning them over to the cell. They placed their cards down and walked over.

"What do you want?" the guard ordered.

"We saw you like to play cards, and thought you might want to play against a real opponent," Leon answered.

"You want to play?" laughed the guard to the other.

"No, but he does," Leon smiled and pulled Theo forward. The guards looked at each other. "Here's the deal, if he wins we all go free. If you win, your boss can sell us as planned," Leon smiled.

"What on earth makes you think we have the power to let you go if you win a little game? The boss won't allow it."

"Go ask him then."

The guard talking to Leon thought for a moment and then motioned to the other guard to go ask the boss. A few moments later the same carriage driver they had met on the side of the road came down the winding steps into the dungeon and over to Leon and Theo's cell.

"So, I hear you want to try to win your way out?"

"Sure—why not?" replied Leon. The carriage driver thought for a moment. Leon was banking on the fact that he was a gambling man and could not resist the chance to give in to his vice.

"Alright. Why not?" That was strangely easy. He motioned for the guards to open the cell and let Theo out. "Cuff him though, we don't want any funny business."

Before the cell door was open, Leon turned to him, "You got this right?" he winked.

"Oh, yeah."

The guard led Theo over to the table and then proceeded to put cuffs around his ankles and wrists.

"How am I supposed to play like this?" asked Theo holding up his hands.

"Fine," said the carriage driver. "His ankles will suffice." The guard leaned over Theo, exposing the pocket where he had the cell key, and unlocked the cuffs around his wrists, then sat across from him. "No, no," the carriage driver motioned for the guard to move, "I'll be playing against this one," and he took his seat across from Theo.

The cards were dealt and the game went on for about an hour. Eira, Leon, and Clea watched as best as they could from their cells, but it was hard to make out if Theo was winning or not. The guards stood on either side of Theo, making sure he played fairly. Finally, the game was over and the carriage driver stood up and looked at Theo. He didn't say anything, just smiled and shook his head placing his cards back onto the table. He then turned to walk back up the stairs and the guards led Theo back to his cell.

"What? Is that it? Who won?" asked Eira. Theo was now by the door of the cell waiting for the guard to open it. "How did it go?"

"Um—not well, I don't want to talk about it," replied Theo walking into the cell.

"Great," Clea rolled her eyes.

"You said you knew what game they were playing?" asked Eira.

"No, I said I *thought* I knew what they were playing. Turns out—I did *not*."

"Great! Now we just wasted all that time while we could have been trying to figure out a way out of here," said Eira.

"It wasn't all wasted time," winked Theo pulling a small key from his pocket.

"How did you do that?" asked Eira.

"Fastest hands in all of Talvia," he boasted. Leon was smiling.

"Did you guys plan this?" asked Eira.

"Of course, Theo can't play cards," replied Leon.

"Hey, I gave it a good try."

"Okay, so now that we have that, how do we get out of here without those two noticing?" asked Clea.

"Hey!" Theo called to the guards, "Yeah, you two. Go get your boss and tell him I want a rematch!" The guards looked at each other and then proceeded to the staircase. "Wow...I didn't think that would work."

They quickly unlocked the cells and soon they were all making their way up the staircase trying to find their way out. When they stepped out of the dungeon they walked up the steps and out onto the dirt ground. They were being held in the basement of some building. Eira looked at the sky and the sun blinded her for a moment. Then she turned to look behind her to see what the building looked like. It looked like just another large stone building, the kind that was built about a hundred years before she was born. Suddenly, out walked the carriage driver with the two guards behind him.

"Get them!" he demanded. The guards started advancing on the four of them. They had no weapons to aid them in their fight and nowhere to run. While they probably could all hold their own in a fistfight, they were at a serious disadvantage given their opponents had weapons and would likely use them.

Atop the roof of the building surrounding the courtyard, Killian and Boreas were making their way to them. Eira glanced toward the sky when a figure caught her eye, making his way across and down the roofs with surprising ease. When the moment was right, Killian and Boreas made their way into the fight. They quickly disarmed two of the guards and tossed Theo and Leon the fallen swords.

"Buddies," Killian said to Theo and Leon, embracing them both with one arm around each. "You know, if you wanted to make it up to me for not letting me have it out with the pirates with you guys, you could have thought of something better than getting yourselves kidnapped." He kicked a guard out of the way and slashed another with his sword.

The carriage driver called for more of his guards, who seemed to appear from out of nowhere and started to fight. The carriage driver made his way over to Eira, who was unfortunately still unarmed.

"You were going to make me rich!" he called. "I could have got fifty for you easy."

"Ah, come on. I've got to be worth more than that." She was backing away from him slowly.

"She certainly is." Leon jumped in between them and tossed Eira a sword he snagged from the guard he had just disarmed. "You still know how to use one of these things, right? Remember, pointy end into the thing you want to die," he smirked.

She swiftly and without mercy took out the guard that was creeping up behind her, "Like that?"

"I'd suggest we get out of here, Princess," Leon took her hand and pulled her toward the gate where Clea was waiting. They left no guards still standing.


In no time, they were all running down the road, through the forest, back to where they had left their camp. When they arrived, it was as if they had never left. The pile of wood Killian had dropped was still lying on the ground by the fire pit.

"Who was that?" asked Boreas.

"Just a man trying to make a living in this world. It's a horrible thought, selling people off like slaves, but times have been tough," Leon turned to Eira, "since the fall of your father and mother," he said. "Are you okay?"

"Yeah, I'm fine," replied Eira. But was she? She had trained all her life for moments such as these, but the sight of it right before her eyes had taken her aback. The blood and fallen guards were like nothing she had seen before. She had never *killed* anyone before. She dropped her sword and fell to her knees. That was a real battle, with *real* people and *real* dying. Albeit, a small one—but still. She breathed heavily through her thoughts of what had just happened—what she had done. Leon put a hand on her shoulder and knelt down to face her.

"Hey," his voice calming and kind, "you're going to be okay. I get it. You can practice in the ring as much as you want, but nothing prepares you for that first real taste of battle. But they were bad guys, okay. Selling people. They deserved it."

"Well," began Killian. "You lot should consider yourselves lucky that you all left me when you did otherwise you'd be doing who knows what for the highest bidder right now."

"Um, I think Boreas was the one who saved us actually," said Clea.

"No. Who do you think gave him that idea? Do you think pretty-boy could have come up with that plan himself? Plus, I was all the muscle in that fight back there."

"What plan?" questioned Clea. "Sneaking in on the rooftops? Yeah, *real* original."

"It doesn't matter." Eira stood, "Both of you—thank you."

"You guys are back," another voice called from behind them. Eira hadn't even noticed that Thomas wasn't with them until now.

Eira turned to Killian and Boreas, "You guys left him here all alone?"

"Um...well," started Killian. "He's fine—we left him all the food."

"Yeah, and we were coming right back," added Boreas.

"He's fourteen and in the middle of the forest, *alone*," Eira argued.

"You don't want to know what I was doing at fourteen. He's fine," Killian brushed off her disapproval of them.

"And what would have happened if we didn't come back?" argued Eira.

"Well, in that *extremely* unlikely scenario, he would have figured it out. What? Did you want me to bring the kid into battle instead?"

"He could have waited outside, or somewhere you knew he was safe."

"Oh yeah, that's fun," Killian rolled his eyes. "I knew he was safe right here."

Eira was about to open her mouth again when she got cut off by Theo, "Okay, enough. We're all fine, let's just cool off for a minute and figure out what's next."

Eira took a deep breath and walked toward the fire. She sat down, resting her tired legs. Leon sat down beside her and rested his forearms on his lap. He tilted his head to the side and looked up toward her, "You sure you're okay?"

"Of course," she sighed.

Killian joined them a moment later with some food in his hands ready to grill. None of them actually got to eat the last time they were here. He sat next to Eira and put an arm around her in an effort to say, *sorry*. Then he placed a kiss on the top of her head. Killian was like a golden retriever: loyal to a fault and always comes back.

"Shouldn't we get going?" asked Theo.

"We should eat first," answered Leon, "it's still a bit until the next cabin and we all know what will happen if Killian doesn't get to eat."

"Fine."

Killian looked up from the fire and through a mouthful of food came a muffled, "What?" He then swallowed, "Anyone want some?"


Eira noticed the white bear once more the next day. The rest of the group seemed not to notice as usual. Despite what had happened the day before, she walked away from them for only a few moments, creating new tracks through the brush. The bear remained ahead of her, walking slowly along. It paused for a moment and turned to gaze upon Eira. At the same moment, she paused as well. He did not look like a bear to fear, he simply turned his head back and continued walking, indifferent to Eira's presence. She slowly took a few more steps forward, moving the boughs of the trees aside to walk through. The bear suddenly disappeared from sight and as she pushed the next few branches out of her way, they revealed a snowy forest ahead. The branches snapped back into place behind her and Eira was now standing in a magnificently snow-covered paradise.

"Where's Eira?" asked Clea looking around.

"What?" asked Leon. He scanned the distance, "Not again."

"Oh great, you lost her again? Well, if she's kidnapped, I'm not going after her this time," said Boreas.

"What is it with you guys and not being able to keep track of the Queen of Talvia?" asked Killian. "She's just a girl. She's not even that small."

Theo rolled his eyes.

As far as she could see, the forest was a winter wonderland with large feathery snowflakes drifting softly around her. The air was as still as stone and the sound of her breathing was all that could be heard. Irving Berlin himself couldn't write a song that described the beauty of this white world. Eira made no movement and remained standing there in awe of what she had just found. She noticed a tree branch bending low to just above the top of her head. A cardinal flew by and perched on it. It was beautiful, adding a sharp red contrast to the white world around. She turned to go back and find the others, moving the branches again she looked out at the green forest. It was as if this snowy scene was invisible to the rest of the forest. As if a giant invisibility cloak was draped over part of the woods. Eira did not want to lose sight of this magical place. She called loudly for the others, who were looking for her at that very moment.

"Do you hear that?" Clea asked as she tilted her head in the direction of the sound, "this way."

The group went running to where they had thought the source of the sound was coming from. They arrived in a small clearing with trees surrounding them.

"Eira!" called Leon into the empty forest around him. As if out of nowhere, Eira's hand reached out and pulled him into the wintery world. The others were stunned. Leon had just vanished before their very eyes.

"It's all right," Leon's phantom voice called from the spot where he had disappeared. "Follow my voice and see for yourself." The group followed his voice into the trees and they too were pulled into winter. They all looked around shocked by the sight before their eyes.

"Where are we?" asked Killian.

"I don't know," Eira replied. The group walked deeper into the forest, wandering for about an hour.

"So this is snow," started Killian. "You know, I'm having a hard time figuring out what the fuss is about. My feet are getting cold." He shook the piles of snow from his hair and brushed his shoulders clear. He was then hit in the back of his head with a snowball.

"Well, it does have that benefit," smirked Theo.

The game was on. Killian leaned down and scooped up a handful of snow and formed it into a ball, throwing it right back at Theo.

"Guys—come on. We don't have time for this," added Leon, but he was only met with a snowball from each of them hitting him on either side.


The same cardinal began to chirp and flew to another branch. As they continued Eira noticed something most peculiar, "The trees—the branches are turning to...gold," she said in awe. As they continued walking, they came to a path lined with gilded trees. At their bases were various flowers made of solid ice, giving off the impression they were made from glass. They bared no leaves and it was as if someone had painted them to shine like a golden sunrise. The cardinal again landed on a golden branch in front of Eira as if he were leading her to something.

Without warning, out of the forest came an army of men and women. They drew their bows and swords and surrounded Eira and her partners. They looked very similar to humans. Their hair was long, some as white as the newly found snow they were standing on. Their ears came to a curved point at the end. Not noticeable until you took a closer look. They were dressed in white, blue, or silver. They looked as though they belonged in the snow and Eira recognized their appearances instantly. A voice called from behind the group and the group suddenly lowered their weapons and parted letting someone walk through toward Eira.

She almost cried at the sight of her.

## 9

Leon smiled too when the face of the woman coming through the line of elves was visible. Eira rushed to embrace her in a long-awaited hug, "Feya."

"I've missed you too," the elf smiled, "but I always knew we'd meet again here one day. Even if you were dead set on never making it back here."

Eira released her hug and took a step back smiling at her aunt. Then she turned to the rest of the group, "This is my aunt Feya. Or rather, the woman who raised and trained me, she's not really my aunt, but as good as one."

Leon gave her a nod as if to say, *nice to see you again,* while the others still seemed in awe of the fact that they were surrounded by Wintren-elves.

"You're Wintren-elves!" gasped Theo. "Sorry, I just—"

Feya smiled at him, "Yes, and we are all very thankful to you for bringing our queen home."

The elves all bowed as if on cue in a welcoming gesture.

*Well, that's new,* thought Eira. No one, let alone an entire group of people, has ever bowed to her in a synchronized manner before. Back at the bar where she worked, she was lucky if people even got out of her way when she was carrying drinks or food. Another elf walked through the crowd—a male this time. He was tall, his long wavy silver hair brushing past his shoulders and his deep blue eyes radiated beauty. He walked up to Eira and ever so gently took Eira's hand and kissed it with the weight of a feather landing upon it.

He rose to meet her eyes and said, "I would recognize you in a heartbeat, my dear one. Our borders have remained secure for a hundred years. Only a true queen of Talvia could find us. My name is Evian, High Lord of the elves. Long ago we created an allegiance with the kings and queens of Talvia." He raised his hands, "Welcome friends of this realm, to the Valley of the Ethereal."

When they reached the kingdom of the Wintren-elves, it was a beautiful town hidden amidst the forest. The gates were made of woven tree roots sprinkled with frost, and amongst them, various snow flowers were placed. Glory-of-the-snow and snowdrops were woven in and it shone with embellishments of silver. At the base, snow crocus flourished along with other bushes that thrive in the snow. Lord Evian's palace stood beyond the gates and he led the group into the great hall.

"Welcome to our home. I am sure you will find it quite comfortable. Please feel free to take advantage of the natural hot springs that run through these parts. Even though our magic comes from the cold, we do not always favour it," Lord Evian smiled.

"Hot springs?" repeated Killian perking up at that moment. "Where? Right—if anyone needs me that's where I'll be. Oh, yeah!" he exclaimed as he began removing his jacket and boots in anticipation of the warm water as he headed in the direction that Lord Evian had pointed out. Theo sauntered along behind him. Evian ordered some of the elves to lead the rest of them to their rooms where they would stay the night.

The rooms in the elven palace were exquisite. Eira had never seen anything like it. The beds were made from carved silver wood, and a shimmering canopy that looked like fresh sparkling snow fell from the ceiling and cascaded around the bed. She had a balcony that overlooked the Wintren-elves' kingdom. Even standing on the balcony, there was some sort of magic at play that didn't allow the cold in. Eira retired into a warm shower and as the water poured over her, she thought about how convenient it was that this journey had so many luxurious stops. New clothes woven with elven magic to always keep you warm even in the harshest of winters were given to all. Eira was dressing when a knock sounded at her door. She glided over to the exquisitely carved wooden door and pulled it open.

"How are you settling in?" Feya asked. She stood there, the picture of beauty and grace. While she was one of the Wintren-elves top warriors, she always had this elegance about her. As if even amidst the roughest battle, she was always poised to perfection. Her long ash brown hair was woven into a crown around her head and she was dressed like Eira had never seen her before, in a long ethereal gown that made it look like she floated along the floor. She glided into the room and the both of them sat on the settee opposite the roaring fireplace.

"I missed you," Eira began. "You're the only thing I really missed from my old life, from growing up."

"I know, sweetheart. I missed you too, but I knew as much as you tried to push this away, you'd end up here. We never meant for you to feel forced into something. We were simply trying our best to prepare you for your future." Her voice was as calm and understanding as ever. She had always been that way while Eira was growing up. Merciless on the battlefield and teaching Eira to be the same, but tender and kind in every other aspect of life.

"Why was I never told about my brother?" Eira had to know. It was straight to the point, but there was no other way around it, and Feya would appreciate that.

She took a breath, "My brother," right—she was Lord Evian's sister, "believed that it was the best course of action. We could not risk you wanting to come back here and see him, or him going there. He was told it would not be safe for him to meet you until you were returned here safely. Anyone of the royal bloodline could potentially be tracked by the wrong kind of people—or creatures." Eira thought of the dragon hunting her down.

"What if I never get to meet him?"

"You will. I know you will. Maybe not anytime soon, but one day in the future your brother will come home, they always do eventually." She always had a way of saying things like she knew more than she let on. Eira hoped Feya was right, and that one day she would get to meet her brother.

Later that evening there was a grand feast in Eira's honour. She felt quite uncomfortable about it but wasn't going to argue with Lord Evian. The group was sitting down to dinner when Killian finally made his way in.

"What happened to you?" asked Theo, looking at a particularly red of face and hands Killian.

"I fell asleep, alright."

"In a pot of boiling water? You look like a steamed tomato," stated Clea. Killian threw them a peeved expression and took his seat at the table grabbing a pitcher of water as he sat, gulping down its entire contents. They were all dressed in the finest of elvish formal wear. The plates started to come out from the kitchen and the delicious smells wafted through the doors toward their table. The servers were not all elves however, they were small creatures resembling trolls but their hair and beards were made of icicles. Eira turned to Leon and asked him what they were.

"I think they're barbegazi," responded Leon. "They are part of mythology. Creatures with icicles covering their hair and they only live in the cold snowy climates."

"So Talvia would be a perfect home for them," replied Eira. She was not sure how they managed to serve all the food and pour the wine, seeing as they were not much taller than the table. The question was answered when one came up beside her and clicked a button on the table right next to her knee. Out popped a set of stairs and quickly the barbegazi climbed up and laid the plate in front of her with perfect precision. Then backed down the stairs and returned them under the table.

"I had no idea there were any still in existence, or that they did exist for that matter," added Leon.

"There are many things that are rumoured to be no longer in existence. You should not believe everything you hear," piped in Lord Evian. He then turned to Eira, "So," he continued, "you have quite a journey ahead of you." He moved his gaze from Eira to the rest of the group.

"Yes," replied Eira.

"Well, you have the help of the Wintren-elves on your side. You have always. We will be there when you need us."

"Thank you," she smiled. Eira wanted desperately to know more about the Wintren-elves and Talvia, but it seemed that Lord Evian was not going to answer any more questions that night. It was time for celebration. They laughed and drank all night long. When the festivities were dying down, they made their way to their rooms for the night. As they were leaving the dining room, Eira could see that there were elves and barbegazi hastily rushing around carrying chairs, plates, platters, and many other things. It looked as if they were redecorating.

"What's going on?" asked Eira to one of the elves walking past carrying what looked like a bundle of silver sheets.

"It is Myrrvintrel, my lady," the elf bowed. "It is our New Year. The festival starts tomorrow."

*New Year?* wondered Eira. She wasn't exactly keeping track of time, but she was sure that the new year must have come and gone already. Perhaps the elves and Talvia follow a different calendar. No—of course they would.

"I hope you will be staying for the festival," said Lord Evian coming up behind the group. "It lasts four days, and on the fifth is Myrrvintrel: the New Year."

"That's very kind of you, but I don't know if we have five days to spare," Eira replied with a smile.

"Sometimes, it is important to embrace the unexpected. It is the unexpected that makes the journey worthwhile," smiled Lord Evian.

"I for one would not want to miss an elven festival. Especially one that lasts five days," added a slightly intoxicated Killian. The rest of the group didn't seem to oppose.

"Well...as long as you're sure it's okay?" said Eira.

"Five days sounds like a lot, but in the grand scheme of things, it won't hold us up that much. Besides, I think we need a rest and some fun," smiled Leon. It was strangely accommodating of him. This whole time, he seemed to want to be getting to the mountains as quickly as possible. Why waste time now?

"Well, it is settled then. You will be my guests for the Myrrvintrel festival," smiled Lord Evian.


When Eira arrived at her room, she wrapped a blanket around herself and wandered out onto the balcony where she could see the Wintren-elves preparing for the festival tomorrow: setting up tables and stringing lights from the trees. She watched them for a bit and then watched as the stars twinkled down on her. Every once in a while, she could spot a shooting star. She closed her eyes and wished for everything to turn out alright in the end. There wasn't much else she had to wish for. She took a deep inhale and let the fresh winter air seep into her lungs. Her head turned at the faint sound of knocking on her door. "Come in," she called and was soon met on the balcony. Leon rested his hands against the railing next to her and peered out into the sparkling night. The moon reflecting off the pure white snow illuminated the world around them and even though it was the dead of night, it was far from dark.

"I just wanted to see how you were doing?" he asked quietly. "We haven't really talked much since we got here—since you saw Feya again."

"I'm good," was all she replied. They stared out in silence for a few heartbeats. "So," she started, "I never asked you how you know Killian and Theo. It seems like you have for a while."

"Yeah, since we were boys. I spent months out of the year in Syysia, seeing as my mom is from there and her entire family still lives there. My father was from Talvia and working for your father, which is why when they got married they moved here. My sisters and I would always go back though, and that's where I met Killian and Theo. Theo's mother was a maid at my uncle's estate, so he lived there with her, and Killian we met one day in town. He was about to do something dangerous and stupid that probably would have got himself killed," his expression at those words said, *I know, shocking right?* "So we stepped in. Been friends ever since."

"So, Killian and Theo are Syysian?" Leon nodded. "Then why are they fighting for Talvia?"

"Why not? They're my friends and fighting for Talvia is fighting for our whole world. If the snow doesn't come back, it *will* start affecting the balance of our world entirely—it already has to a small extent. They know that."

Eira was sombre for a moment then said, "I asked Feya about my brother."

He glanced at her, his expression asking, *oh?*

"She said Lord Evian thought it would be best if I didn't know of anyone tying me to this land. They didn't want me to have a reason to want to come back here and risk anyone, or anything finding out I was here. It was safer that way. They told him he couldn't visit me for my safety also."

"Makes sense, but I can tell you it tore him up inside." She lowered her brows. "He's always loved you, even though he's never known you. He hated that they kept you from him and that you had this destiny surrounding you that took you away from him. He lost his whole family the moment he came into this world. I think that's one of the reasons why he left. He couldn't stand the feeling of waiting around for you to come back anymore. He couldn't stand Talvia anymore."

"I understand the feeling." Eira looked back out over the balcony.

"He'll come back one day, I know he will. He's not going to give up the chance to know you. I don't get it, I mean you're a pain in the ass, but he doesn't know that yet." Eira laughed and smiled up at him—a true smile. A bright, honest smile across her face—his eyes sparkling in the moonlight as she felt something shift in her.

He stared for a moment, just taking it in. As if time had frozen around them. Then he finally said, "You know," he smiled back, "I think this is the first time you've ever smiled at me."

"What?" she was taken aback.

"I think you've smiled around me, to other people, but never directly at me."

"That is the stupidest thing I've ever heard. Of course I've smiled at you." And then she thought back to the few encounters they had together and realized she probably hadn't. Especially given the fact that most of her thoughts revolving around him were those of detestation. She sighed.

"No—no, I don't think you have."

"Oh, please. How could you possibly remember something so trivial?"

His eyes never left hers the entire time, "Believe me, I would." She scoffed at him—a challenge in his eyes. Then he added, slowly and confidently, "You think you wouldn't remember the first moment time stood still, because you just saw the most beautiful thing you've ever seen?" Her heart raced against her chest, battling against her to be released. He turned as if he hadn't just said that and leaned against the railing again, "Why do you hate me so much?" he quietly asked.

Her pulse calmed, "I don't know." He was hoping she'd say she doesn't hate him. "I just—"

"I've never done anything to you—as far as I know."

"I know...I just—" She didn't have the words. Had no idea what to say to get herself out of this situation.

He turned to face her again, "Is it because I represent everything you've never wanted in your life? All of this?" He motioned around, "The crown, the kingdom, everything?"

"Maybe," was all she could think to say.

He sighed and looked back out over the balcony. "Well, I think I'm going to go to bed. Goodnight, Princess. Maybe one day you'll hate me a little less." He brushed past her and for a moment she wanted to reach out for him and...

She smiled at him again—apparently for only the second time in her life, but he wouldn't know that seeing as his back was turned to her. "Goodnight," she whispered in his direction. A rare pleasant exchange between the two of them and she could feel her walls beginning to slightly crumble around her.

Eira couldn't sleep that night. Not for lack of comfort in the elves' sumptuous beds, but for the fact that she could not settle her mind. She was plagued with thoughts of what Leon had said and thoughts of what faced her once they left the safety of the Wintren-elves' kingdom. Alas, sleep didn't seem to be coming to her anytime soon, so she got up and wandered out of her bedroom. All around her was silence. She wandered the halls for a bit until she came to a room with its door cracked open. She peeked inside and it looked to be a study. There were bookshelves and various knickknacks. One thing, in particular, caught her gaze though. As she scanned the room, she stopped on a massive wood-carved door just standing by itself in its frame. She pushed the study door open just enough for her to slip in and walked over to admire the beautiful woodwork. The wood was a grey colour as if it had come from the bark of a grey ash tree, and the door itself came to a rounded arch at the top. Roses and various other floral details were carved into the face creating a frame around the edge and they were coloured to match their reflection in nature. A beautiful cherry blossom tree developed in the centre of the door and stretched its branches to the corners of the frame. Around the door frame itself were carved animals. There were unicorns and the great polar bears, lynx, and foxes. There was a single doorknob on the right side midway up in the shape of a snowflake. She reached out to touch one of the carvings and the door swung open.

She was taken aback by the scene she saw on the other side of the door. It was her apartment back in Adelaide. It looked just as it did when she had left for work the day she was taken to Talvia. Nothing had changed. She took one step in, but that was all. She stood in the doorway. In front of her, her home, behind her was another world entirely. Then without thinking, she stepped back through the doorway and shut the door. She wasn't sure if what she had just seen was real or just some Wintren-elf magic trick. Was she really that close to going back? Could she just walk through that doorway and pretend this never happened? She turned and walked out of the study and back to her bedroom with an uneasy feeling in the pit of her stomach.

After that, she did not seem to have any trouble falling asleep and the sun was shining high in the sky when she awoke next.

# 10

It was a time for celebration; a new beginning in the history of Talvia and a new year for the kingdom of the Wintren-elves. The festival of Myrrvintrel had started that morning when Eira awoke in the Wintren-elves kingdom. Even the barbegazi were enjoying the festival after their workday was done. Their disproportionate feet made it easy for them to get around in the snow, like built-in snowshoes. The elves certainly knew how to throw a party—it did last five days, after all. Yet, while they seemed to know how to party with a passion, they also knew how to keep the civility of it all. The main activities were drinking and enjoying frivolity with friends. The whole point was to end the year toasting to the new one and what better way to go out than with five days of indulging in everything that makes one happy. Eira however, was not much for this kind of fun. She could enjoy the party and the time with the people who were now becoming more friends rather than travel companions, but she wasn't about to hit it hard for the next five days. A sentiment some in the group seemed not to share—Killian. The food was outstanding, full of elvish delights the likes of which Eira had never seen nor tasted. Some looked familiar to things she would find back home at festivals, such as mini powdered doughnuts, but these were elvish doughnuts, so they tasted way better and left you feeling without regret after eating a dozen or so. That part, Eira really liked about the festival. Her favourite drink, she found out, was a Wintren-elf specialty called a snowdrop, and Eira liked the sound of that. It didn't have anything in it that would leave you making questionable decisions or give you a headache the next morning. However, it seemed that even with those types of drinks such as the extremely popular elvish wine, the elves seemed to find a way to combat that side effect of indulgence. She really didn't know what was in a snowdrop, but it tasted of lavender and freshly fallen snow. It was served to her in a champagne flute carved from ice and was rimmed with sparkling sugar snowflakes. It was that drink exactly that she was sipping when she was joined by a familiar face.

"I trust you are enjoying the celebration?" asked Lord Evian, taking a seat beside Eira as she was curled up under a blanket the colour of snow around a crackling fire.

"Yes, I am," she replied with a smile. "This really is something. I've never seen a festival like this."

"We try to make the last few days in the old year something to remember. To forget about the hardships in the previous year and celebrate what is yet to come, and all the good the last year gave us." Eira smiled in response. "Well, I will leave you to keep enjoying the party. I have more things to attend to." With that, he left Eira sitting by herself again.

"Good afternoon," came a voice behind her. She turned to see Leon and then followed him with her eyes as he sat down next to her. "So, what are your plans for this afternoon?" he asked with a smile.

"Well," she said tipping her glass far back to get the last sip, "I was planning on getting some food and then starting on something a little stronger than this," she placed the glass down in front of him.

"While that does sound fun, and while I'm always up for something a little stronger, I had something else in mind."

"Like what?"

"Well, I thought it might be time for you to head back into the ring and begin training again."

"No thank you," she looked at him with a sideways smile.

"Why not? It's been three years since you've done any training."

"I'm fine. I dealt with the kidnappers, didn't I?"

"Yes, and while your skill remains, your stamina could certainly use some work. I remember you being pretty spent after."

She glowered at him, "I'll train with Feya if I feel up to it."

"Feya thinks you should train with me."

"Who asked her?" The annoyance in Eira's voice grew.

"I did, and you don't need me coming to your rescue every time you're a little out of breath."

Eira snidely remarked, "What, you're getting sick of coming to the rescue?"

"For you—never," he winked. "But it's good for you."

"Don't tell me what's good for me. A couple of times with you isn't going to improve my stamina."

"Well, it depends on what we do exactly," he winked. "I can think of a few things..." She walked right into that one. Eira rolled her eyes and groaned. By this time, Killian and Theo were standing beside them and listening in. "Look, I'll make you a deal. You meet me in the ring right now and if you beat me, I won't bother you about training again. But if I win, you train with me every morning here until we leave."

"Do it, do it, do it," Killian urged from behind Eira.

"Fine," Eira agreed.


When they had finally made it to the elves' training room, Eira could see all the weaponry they had hanging on the walls and the various training ones made of wood, most of which she was highly trained in. Thinking back, Feya did have an unusually large trove of weaponry at their cottage.

"Really? Training swords? Come on guys, I thought this was going to be a fight." Eira and Leon shot Killian a glare from the centre of the room and Theo leaned over to Killian and whispered a joke about Leon, Eira, and a different type of wooden sword. Killian spat out a laugh and tried to hold his composure when Eira and Leon shot him the same look again.

Five minutes into the fight, it was clear who was going to win. "You know man, I really wanted to be on your side but I think she might beat you," shouted Killian to the centre of the ring while Eira and Leon's training swords were clashing together and Eira had nearly beat him twice already.

"Yeah, I mean she was trained by Feya. She is general of the elven army, after all," added Theo.

"You guys really aren't helping," struggled Leon from the ring while pushing against Eira to free his sword. He finally managed to break free, but Eira was right there again, kicking him onto the ground with a blow to the chest. She clearly wasn't holding back.

"She really doesn't hold back, does she?" said Killian to Theo, both still standing on the sideline with their arms folded across their chests.

"No. She seems to be getting out some pent-up anger toward him though. It's probably healthy," replied Theo.

"Remind me to never get on her bad side."

The fight went on for another ten minutes. Both Leon and Eira were getting exhausted, but neither would admit defeat. They lunged at each other again, Eira just dodging Leon's blow, but it sent her tumbling to the ground. She managed to get herself back onto her feet before Leon could make his way over to her and she tripped him before he could make it any farther. He stumbled slightly but managed to regain his footing just as another blow from the training sword hit him in the back causing him to lurch forward. He spun but there wasn't enough time, Eira had knocked him to the ground and was now straddling him with her sword to his throat. She released after a second and smiled, "See, I can still kick your ass."

"Not likely," he said throwing his weight into her and spinning on top of her in one quick movement. He stared down at her, her arms pinned above her head by his strong forearms. They stared at each other, time seeming to stand still.

"You think they're still fighting?" Killian leaned into Theo, not taking his eyes off the centre of the ring.

"All right, I'm calling it a draw," declared Theo. As if his words snapped them out of some sort of trance, Leon released Eira and stood over her. He reached his hand down to her so she could help herself up. She did, panting excessively. Eira dropped her sword on the ground and placed both hands atop her knees, panting toward the ground.

"You might be right about the stamina thing," she admitted to Leon.

"Well, I can help you with that later," he winked. She was too tired to smack him for the inappropriate joke, so she simply glared up at him, expression blank but eyes flaring.

"So...hot springs?" asked Killian.


Eira headed to her room and changed into the bathing suit the elves had left for their guests. She wasn't even sure if elves wore bathing suits up until this point, although to be honest, it was never really a thought that had ever crossed her mind. Why would that ever have formed itself into a thought up until this point in time? Of all the things running through her mind at any given moment, *do elves wear bathing suits,* would hardly be one. She supposed the elves would of course though, given the fact that they have hot springs. She was also thankful, a feeling that she never thought she would have after the fact, that she had let Nell convince her to get a leg and bikini wax with her a week before her birthday. After the bathing suit, she wrapped herself in the long flowing robe left with it, something that seemed far more like elvish attire and headed down to the hot pools.

She was the first one there, so she climbed into the perfectly heated water and sat on one of the rocks submerged in the pool. Around her, the snow was falling lightly, just enough to add the perfect atmosphere to the springs, and a cooling sensation on the parts of your body not submerged in water. It was as if everything in the Wintren-elves' kingdom was planned to perfection, and it most likely was. She watched as little snow butterflies fluttered around the edges of the pool and then dissolved into the piles of snow around her. The serenity in this place was utterly unmatched. She relaxed in the warm waters for a while, sitting back and closing her eyes. The hot pools were all natural and had healing mud that was meant to be put anywhere you felt like you needed some refining. She put some of the mud on her face and sank into the water again as if she were enjoying an afternoon of pampering at a fancy overpriced spa. She figured this was the closest she might ever get to one of those, and while five stars can be amazing, she was sure they had nothing on Talvia and the Wintren-elves' kingdom. No amount of marketing or fancy products could make something from the other world feel this enchanting.

A few minutes later, she washed the mud off and sat up in the pool. She was still the only one around even though there was more than one pool. All around her, down through different forest paths were other hot pools, but it seemed the Myrrvintrel celebrations were diverting everyone's attention away from this natural wonder. She liked the time to herself though; she hadn't gotten much of it lately. As she soaked in the waters, it almost felt as if time stood still and she forgot just exactly why she found herself in that very spot at that very moment. Her mind wandered back home for a moment. She would be working and not doing much of anything else. She might venture out with Nell for some after-Christmas sale shopping—that's right, Nell! Where did she think Eira had gone off to? She didn't exactly leave a note as to where she would be and she didn't entirely know if she could go back after all of this. Was her face now plastered all over the other world notifying the public of a missing woman? Well, there was nothing she could do about it now. Hopefully, no one was too frantic about it. Her panic subdued itself soon enough with the addition of the rest of her friends.

"Dude, I'm telling you, just wear the damn elven one," Leon was saying to Killian as they walked in.

"They don't fit right. Elves aren't built like me."

Eira turned to them to see what they were talking about, "Oh my!" gasped Eira quickly turning her head.

"What?" asked Killian looking down to his bathing attire that covered far less than Leon, or Eira would have liked—at least that's what Eira let on. "Ah, you're just jealous of this body. Not all can be as confident as I am. I get it," he said submerging into the spring, signalling it was alright for them to look again.

"Didn't the elves give you a bathing suit?" Eira asked.

"Nah, I brought my own. You should always pack a bathing suit with you when going on a journey. You never know what'll happen."

Sound advice.

When Killian found the right spot to root himself for the next few hours in the pool, he grabbed some mud and slapped it all over his face, then placed two cucumber slices on his eyes. Eira and Leon just looked at him.

"I can feel you two staring," started Killian. "There's nothing wrong with a little pampering—takes a real man to do this." They looked at each other with puzzled expressions on their faces then smiled. Eira glanced down at Leon's forearm, once again getting a glimpse of his tattoo—this time the full image. It stood out immeasurably against his skin tone. It was a mountain scene from wrist to elbow wrapping all the way around his forearm with snowflakes scattered around. The detail of it was exquisite, with each snowflake being unique, just like the real thing. It was definitely new. She didn't remember him having it when they used to train together. Eira was about to ask him about it but was interrupted by Theo joining them. She felt like it was maybe too intimate of a thing to be asking about while his friends were there, or perhaps she just told herself that to avoid looking stupid if she did decide to ask him.

"So," began Eira, turning back toward Leon who was now settling into the pool and resting his head against the edge. "I certainly didn't think I'd be relaxing in hot springs when I signed up for this little adventure."

"Oh yeah," said Leon, still not moving from his current position, "and what did you expect?"

"Well," she pondered for a moment, "I don't really know what I expected. Just not this, I guess. I don't really know what I'm saying." She looked down at the waters and dragged her fingers across the surface.

"Well, if it makes you feel any better," he still didn't move, "this isn't what I thought I'd be doing right now either when I signed up for this, 'little adventure', as you call it. Although, I'm not complaining."

"So, why did you sign up for this?" asked Eira still staring at the warm waters. This finally prompted Leon to raise his head from its position and he opened his eyes and glanced at her with a crooked smile.

"I figured you'd ask me this eventually."

"Well, all I really know about you is that your dad rules *my* kingdom," she smirked, "but, you're not a prince although you seem to have an affinity for being a stereotypical prince charming—saving the day and all." A grunt of agreement came from Killian.

Leon smirked, "You really need to know my whole story?"

"I don't know if I *need* to, but I would like to. We never actually talked when I was younger. You showed up, we fought, usually I won—"

"Hey," he cut in.

"Man, come on," added Theo, "I called that fight for your benefit, not hers."

Leon's face went rigid, "Anyway...when I was about eight years old, my family officially moved into Trillium Nivale so my father could take place as regent over the kingdom. Your father had just died, only a few months after your mother had. You had been gone for a couple of months at this point so my father, mother, sisters, and I all came to live at Trillium Nivale. We lived in an estate house on the other side of town before then. I didn't mind though, seeing as I had spent a lot of time there in the past. We even met a couple of times when you were little."

"I guess we would have," interrupted Eira.

He smiled. "So, my father did his best to keep the peace with neighbouring countries and the people of Talvia. As I got older, I learned of the day the dragon came and the prophecy. At first, I thought it was just an old tale, but Gideon and my father insisted it was real. He told me about you and why you had to leave. Eventually, as you know, they sent me to train with you once a month. I learned over the years that while on the outside the people and this country may have looked okay, it was suffering more than anyone could tell. There I was, a boy who had grown up never knowing what snow even looked like and all I wanted to do was fight to get it back. So, I started gathering people I knew I could trust to come along. Then we just had to get you to show up."

Eira didn't know what to say after Leon had finished his story, but luckily, she wouldn't have to fill the silence now growing between the group.

"Anyway..." began Leon, but was quickly interrupted by Clea joining them.

"What is that?" she asked looking at Killian.

"Best to just ignore it," replied Eira.

Leon took a deep breath and stood up in the pool, "Well, I think I've had enough hot springs for one day," he said striding through the waters. "I will see you ladies later," he added hopping out of the pool. "That includes you, Kil."

Killian simply flipped Leon a vulgar hand gesture without even disturbing the cucumbers.


After three days of Myrrvintrel, Eira was honestly beginning to hit her limit on festivities. She decided to take a walk through the Wintren-elves' kingdom, rejoining in the festivities later. Walking through the snow-covered forest, she imagined it was what Talvia normally looked like. The sun's rays radiated through the trees hitting every snowflake on its way down, making them fall to the ground like tiny crystals. She followed one of the walking paths the elves had made and wandered along for a while, just enjoying her own company. She loved the stillness of her surroundings. It was a place where time lost all sense of meaning. A few birds fluttered from branch to branch, high in the trees, but other than that, there was no other wildlife to be seen. She thought back to the day when they had found the Wintren-elves' kingdom, and the great polar bear she kept seeing. She reminded herself to ask Lord Evian about it when she had the chance.

She was coming up on a large valley and she could see a frozen waterfall in the distance. She made her way down into the valley and up to the waterfall. It towered above her; solid sheets of ice hanging off the side of the rocks. She saw a couple of otters playing in the snow and sliding down the bottom of the waterfall where it had made some ice slides. The sun had made its way over the waterfall and cascaded a giant rainbow over the entirety of it. She kept walking through the valley and eventually came back to the Wintren-elves' path. The only problem was, she was not sure which way to take it. One went back and the other led deeper into the forest.

A pair of piercing blue eyes watched as she was trying to make her decision. A twig cracked in the distance and out leapt a pure white wolf—so white it was almost blue. She had never seen anything like it. She froze in place. The creature was the same size as her, staring her down on the path, baring his teeth. Just as it was about to lunge, another massive white figure jumped in front of her and stared the wolf down. It was the great white polar bear. A staring contest was all that went down between the two animals. The wolf submitted and darted back into the woods. The bear turned around to face Eira. They were at eye level with each other.

"Thank you," she said. The bear did not respond, just kept looking at her with his great soulful eyes, scanning her for what, Eira didn't know. She held a hand up and the bear hesitated a moment, but then walked into it, pushing his large snout against her palm and moving his head downward for her to rest her hand on his forehead. The bear walked with Eira for a couple of minutes, and then when she was headed back in the right direction, he disappeared again into the forest.

"Eira, there you are," said Clea as she wandered back into the festival. "You're missing out on everything—come on," she urged her. Eira caught up with her and the two walked back into the festival.

They wandered through the various stalls with vendors selling different refreshments and treats. Eira was particularly fond of an elvish cake that tasted of honey and lime, with crystallized sugar coating it. She couldn't pronounce the name, but it satisfied her to her very core. She probably had about three a day. She was sitting with

Clea when Leon came over to her with one of the cakes in hand and handed it over.

"Thanks," Eira smiled. She wasn't going to turn down another one, even though she probably should have. Leon sat next to them and was about to say something when Killian appeared, also with a cake in his hand, followed by Theo doing the same. Eira stared at the two of them.

"What—she likes them," stated Killian, sitting down on the other side of Clea. "Fine, I'll eat it. But it's basically all I've seen her eat," he smirked. Theo handed his to Clea, who also didn't object to more cake.

"You really have these boys wrapped around your finger," she leaned into Eira and whispered.

"Apparently."

"I heard that," smiled Killian. "And it's just good sense to stay on the future queen's good side. She controls executions after all."

"What?" gasped Eira.

"He's kidding," assured Leon.


Later that night, massive bonfires were being lit and there was still lots to eat and drink. Everyone, especially Killian and Boreas who were now in a drinking contest with each other, was enjoying the unique elvish refreshments. It seemed as if every day they came out with a new concoction.

"You're not going to win," said Boreas finishing his drink. "I am a god."

"You seem to like bringing that up all the time. Is that because you have nothing else going for you?" hiccupped Killian.

Eira was sitting with Clea, Theo, and Thomas, enjoying their food and watching the elvish dancing happening around them. Thomas left soon after dinner with some of the Wintren-elf children and teenagers.

"Where have you been?" asked Theo as Leon sat beside them.

"Just enjoying the festival," he replied.

The evening turned to night and they continued in the festivities playing some sort of elvish game none of them understood the rules to. When it got later, they were all sitting around the fire enjoying the warmth. Thomas had fallen asleep in a chair and Killian and Boreas were still in their contest—now arm wrestling. It was obvious Boreas was humouring him though, as Killian was expressing a lot more force and Boreas looked as though he was not even paying attention.

"You know, I'm not sure this is the best for him," said Leon standing behind the chair Thomas was sleeping in. "Those two aren't exactly the best role models," he said looking at Killian and Boreas.

"Yeah, but better than pirates," said Clea.

"True." He headed over to Killian and Boreas to see if he could finally get them to quit their competition and enjoy the night with the rest of them.

"He's not like the rest of them is he?" smiled Clea.

"What?" said Eira turning away from watching Leon. She just smiled and raised her eyebrows to Eira. "What?" she asked again.

"Oh, come on. Anyone can see it," said Clea.

"See what?" asked Eira.

"Seriously? You're going to pretend like you have no idea what I'm talking about. Since the day I met you, it was pretty obvious how the two of you felt."

"Oh, it is not," Eira stated furrowing her brow.

"Yes it is," chimed in Theo sipping his drink.

Clea motioned to him as if to say, *see, even Theo knows it.*

"Okay, well you guys are all crazy. I despise him— always have."

"Really? Believe me, I've been around enough shitty guys in my life to recognize them a mile away. He's one of the good ones," smiled Clea.

"What?"

"Well he certainly doesn't despise you," added Theo.

"What's that supposed to mean?" Eira asked.

Theo stumbled over his words, the realization of what he had just said sinking in. "Oh...um. Well, he just doesn't despise you—none of us do. I don't know why you'd read anything into that." He cleared his throat and took a sip of his drink, averting his gaze from Eira. Then he redirected his attention to where Killian and Leon were now arguing about whether he would have won against Boreas if Leon hadn't stepped in.

"Look," continued Eira, "I'm not exactly here to get a boyfriend out of all of this. Leon is a nice guy, but I'm not interested." That was a lie and she knew it. Clea most likely knew it too.

"Well, maybe you should take Lord Evian's advice and embrace the unexpected," added Clea.

"I already am." Eira was getting a little short with her at this point.

"I don't mean this."

"Look, I've known Leon for a few years now, granted not very well, but still. In the time we've spent together, he's never done anything to show me that he cares at all about me. All he cares about is getting Talvia back to the way it was and just like everyone else in this damn world, using me to do it." Eira stood and stormed off. She wasn't exactly sure what tipped her over the edge and she knew the things she said about Leon weren't entirely true, especially after their first night in the Wintren-elves' kingdom. But even after that night, she still felt as though everyone only had one thing on their mind, and that was to get the snow back—whatever the cost.

She was halfway to her room when someone pulled at her arm and she whirled around to see Theo standing there. He had run after her when she stormed off. "Eira, wait."

"What?"

He ran a hand through his dark hair and sighed, "Look, Leon's probably going to kill me if he finds out I told you this, so don't mention it was me, but it's not true. What you said back there. He doesn't want you going up against that dragon. In fact, he's spent the last three years trying to prevent it."

"What are you talking about?"

"Something changed in him when he came back from the last time he trained with you. He spent that whole month buried in the library, looking for something. Do you remember the next month he was supposed to go train with you, but he never showed up? The time before you left and no one knew where you were for three years?"

Eira's eyes narrowed as if to say, *yes.*

"Well, he was gone looking for some sort of way out of this mess that didn't involve you having to go after the dragon. He's known from the beginning that it's dangerous and something most people don't walk away from. It ate him up inside for years knowing that you had to do this, and he was hell-bent on trying to find a way to free you from it—like he was desperate to rid you of this burden. I think he prayed that you wouldn't be found after we all heard that you left, not telling Feya where you had gone. But once you were, his hands were tied, he couldn't do anything. He's been asking Lord Evian if there's some other way, some solution only the elves know about."

Eira couldn't respond. There were no words that would be an appropriate response. Theo simply looked at her with remorse in his eyes and turned and headed back to the festival.

Eira continued to her room, willing the tears not to begin until she was in the safety of her bed when she was stopped by Feya. She knew instantly the anger and hurt hiding behind Eira's placid blue eyes. She had seen that look enough times on Eira's face.

"What happened?" Feya asked, taking Eira into her arms.

"Nothing—it's just, everything. We're getting so close now, and I still don't know how to feel about all of this."

"I know. In two days you'll be heading out again. I don't know what will happen by the end of this journey, but I know that you're strong enough to face anything that comes your way."

Eira pushed back from her embrace, "Why are you guys all like this? Having so much faith that I'll just defeat a dragon and bring the snow back? Why can't any of you recognize that there is serious risk involved here?"

"Eira, don't take our happiness for your return as blissful ignorance to the fact that there is danger in your destiny. We know this—believe me. But unfortunately, it is something that has to be done."

Eira didn't say anything. She was sick of everyone telling her it was what needed to be done. She brushed off Feya and shook her head as if to say, *yeah, keep telling yourselves that.* And then she headed down the hall to her bedroom.


No one came knocking on her door for the remainder of the night. She could hear the party still at its full force, raging outside her bedroom windows in the brief moments where she regained some semblance of composure until the balling took over again and she heaved and shook herself, tears streaming down her pale skin. She was eventually able to find sleep, but only for a while. When she awoke again, eyes heavy and red with the effects of crying, she realized she had been asleep for only two hours, and the festivities were still happening outside. She headed to the bathroom, ran a warm shower, and tried to wash off any lingering emotions within. Refreshed, she looked at herself in the mirror, her hair hitting the top of her breasts being weighed down with the weight of the water. It looked almost brown, darkened by the water and soaking the top of the towel wrapped around her. She had to pull herself together again, to not start crying. Slowly she worked to dry her hair with a towel and then proceeded to braid it. She slipped back into her nightgown and crawled back into the warm serenity of her massive bed. She let her mind be blank. She had done enough for one night.

It was the last day of Myrrvintrel. Eira and Clea were already eating breakfast with Thomas and Boreas. Leon and Killian were making their way into the dining hall. Theo was still sleeping off his choices from the previous night. Apparently, he had hit the wine a little too hard—even for Killian's standards. There were more festival events scheduled for that day, but none knew what they wanted to partake in. It was alright partying for the first couple of days, but even Killian and Boreas were having enough of it. All were glad the Myrrvintrel festival was on its last day, and it was scheduled to conclude that evening with the finale celebration. A grand feast and ball was taking place that night, and they were all looking forward to it.

Leon sat down beside Eira and a plate was brought over to him by one of the barbegazi servants. He carried it high above his head with one hand. They were surprisingly coordinated even with their gnome-like statures. Killian sat down on the other side of Leon and a plate was quickly brought for him as well. Killian and Leon enjoyed their breakfast as Eira passed her plate off and sipped a cup of tea, elaborately poured for her by one of the Wintren-elf waiters. They chatted while the guys were finishing up their meals, mostly about Killian and his suspicious victory over Boreas in axe throwing; an event Eira didn't even know the Myrrvintrel festival had. It hardly seemed like something elves would partake in. She was sure the festival didn't, and that Killian and Boreas took it upon themselves to create their own event. She just hoped nothing was damaged while doing so and that they weren't about to be kicked out of the Valley of the Ethereal with a lifetime ban. That would be a great start to her reign as queen.

When all the plates had been cleared, Killian stood from his chair and looked across the table at Thomas, "Come on Thomas," he started. "You're hanging with me today, buddy."

"Why?" he asked hesitantly as he was making his way around the table to where Killian was standing.

"Two words little buddy," Killian placed an arm around Thomas, "elf chicks."

Eira and Clea grimaced at him, and Leon didn't seem too thrilled either. Thomas seemed happy enough with the answer though, and went with Killian out to the festival grounds.

"Should we do something about that?" asked Clea.

"It'll be okay. This isn't the first time Killian has chosen a questionable wingman, and I'm sure Thomas will survive," replied Leon.

Theo had wandered in at some point and was now sitting in Killian's empty chair, his head in his hands and groaning.

"Don't let me drink that much again," he moaned.

"I thought the elvish wine was enchanted somehow to not give you a hangover?" asked Clea.

"Apparently, not if you drink a whole *barrel* of it," mocked Leon.

"It wasn't a whole barrel," added Theo. A server appeared beside him with a rather unappetizing-looking concoction and informed him it was an elvish hangover cure, sure to do the trick within a few minutes. Theo unpleasantly contorted his face at the sight, and smell of it, but downed it anyway. The group watched as he tried not to puke, but he handled it well.

"So, what's everyone up to today?" asked Leon.

"I don't really know," replied Eira. "I was kind of thinking of taking it easy before getting ready for the ball tonight. I'm not going to lie, I'm kind of excited. I've never been to a ball before, let alone an elvish one. And these guys really seem like they know how to throw a party."

"That's for sure," Boreas agreed.

"Taking it easy sounds nice, though. I was thinking the same. Four days of partying tends to catch up on you," smiled Leon.

"Anyway, I was going to head down to the hot springs, so that's where I'll be if anyone needs me." Eira smiled and walked off.

Eira only got about an hour to herself until she was joined in the hot springs.

"Mind if I join you?" asked Leon looking down at her floating in the pool.

She opened one eye and gazed up at him, "No, go away," she joked. He didn't and instead hopped into the pool right next to her. They sat for an awkward moment in silence until Eira finally got the courage to ask,

"So, what's the story behind the tattoo?" she motioned to his arm.

He looked at it too as if he had to check that he did, in fact, have a tattoo. "Nothing, really. Just got it as a reminder of what we're fighting for. What we've been through and everything to come. That we won't truly be whole again until the rightful ruler sits on the throne and that I'll bow to none other than the true queen."

Wow. Dramatic much? Eira gave a flirtatious grin, "So, you'll bow before me?"

"Believe me, Princess, I'll do much more than just bow." Eira's heart kicked into freight train mode again and she could tell that Leon was doing everything in his power not to pull her onto his lap and kiss her with all that pent-up passion he'd been saving for her. She didn't know whether she desperately wanted it also or not.

Then Clea walked in—damn it.

"Leon, I think you'd better go save Thomas from Killian before he teaches him too much about the ways of women than a fourteen-year-old should know. Also, Killian knows nothing about the ways of women." Leon simply grinned at Eira—that stupidly charming grin—and hopped out of the pool leaving Clea and Eira alone.

"Oh, was I interrupting something?" Clea sat down next to Eira.

"No." The two chuckled, "Sorry about last night, I didn't mean to get mad at you. I wasn't really mad at you anyway, just this place—this five days of partying as if I'm not being sent to my death after it."

"You're not going to die, don't be dramatic," Clea nudged her shoulder to shoulder.

"Really? It's a dragon. I might."

"Believe me—none of those guys will let that happen."

"I hope so."


"What's wrong?" asked Eira as she and Clea made their way back to their rooms after the hot springs.

"Nothing," replied Killian, sauntering down the hallway. "Just Leon ruining the plan before we could even execute it."

"You know, you don't actually need a plan to get a girl," said Clea. "You could just try talking to them."

Killian looked positively taken aback, "Don't be ridiculous, Clea." And with that, he walked off to get ready for the party.

Eira found her room all ready for the ball that evening. Everything she would need, including a beautiful elf-made gown, was in her room. She showered and spent the next couple of hours getting ready with the help of some Wintren-elves.

When Eira came down to dinner, all eyes in the room fixated upon her, unable to pry their gaze from the being that stood before them. The gown the elves had given her was fit for a queen. She had never in her life worn anything as silky and rich. It simply melted over her body as if it was made just for her. It was the colour of the sky on winter mornings when the light was flat and everything looked blue. The silk flowed over every curve coming off her shoulders and down the length of her arms, cutting low in the back and coming to a point just above her hips with a slit high on her left leg. It looked as if it was made from dawn snow, shimmering in the new day's light.

The feast was wonderful, full of stories and elven music sweetly playing in the background as all the food was enjoyed to its fullest; each course more delectable than the last, especially dessert. Eira was sitting by herself next to the dance floor, watching as the elves swayed and twirled to the music, glowing under a star-filled sky. Killian sat down next to her, putting an arm around her and outstretching his legs and crossing them. He leaned over and kissed her on the side of the head.

"Having fun, darling?" he smiled.

"Yes, just strangely sad that we'll be leaving tomorrow."

He nodded and took a sip of the drink in his other hand. Leon was now standing in front of them as well. She looked up at him. He looked dangerously good in the elven formal wear. It might have been a simple dark navy suit, but it was cut perfectly to his features and the jacket had beautiful elvish detailing in silver thread along the cuffs and lapels.

"Would you like to dance?" Leon asked.

"No thanks, buddy." Killian took another sip of his drink as Leon scowled at him.

Eira pursed her lips and gave her head a slight shake, "Um, I don't think so." The response wasn't entirely because she couldn't dance, but more because she didn't know if she could control herself being that intimately close to him.

"Come on, Princess. It'll be fun." Killian removed his arm from around her and gave her a slight push upward off of her seat—right into Leon's arms. He took her hand and led her to the dance floor. Killian had somehow beat them there and was already doing who knows what with his arms and legs, mimicking some sort of large bird's ritual mating dance, while everyone around him just fell in time with the soft melody of the music. The elvish music was rather enchanting and easy to glide along with.

"I'm afraid I don't really know how to dance to this," said Eira.

"What—elvish dancing wasn't part of your training?" he grinned.

"Oh, and it was part of yours?"

"Just follow me." Evidentially it was. Leon placed a hand on her waist and pulled her in close, taking her somewhat by surprise. She was now extremely aware of the feeling of his hand on her bare skin. She had never really danced with a man before—not this way. There were few men left in the world, Eira had always thought, that truly knew how to dance with a girl, and she had always been waiting for the one who did. And Leon did—of course he did. He led her around in circles, keeping in time with the music perfectly like he had heard the song hundreds of times before and knew every twist and turn of the notes as they played together in a sweet melody. She had to admit that he had been right and she was starting to forget about everything that had been weighing on her mind for the last few days.

He suddenly picked her up with one arm around her waist and turned her around with the music, finally putting her down after a couple of twirls and dipping her low. She was surprised at how easy it was to follow his lead, like they were meant to move together like that. When the last few notes were played by the band, she did not want it to end. She hoped for the song to continue so she could have an excuse to be that close to him for just a little while longer. But sadly, the song had ended and the night's festivities would have to come to an end eventually too.

"See, that wasn't so bad now, was it?" Leon whispered into her ear, his warm breath causing her skin to tingle. Killian cut in at that moment and whisked her away for another song. Leon winked a goodbye to her as if to say, *I'll come find you later*, and walked off the dance floor.


It was Eira who went to go find Leon later, however. He hadn't been around for a while now and she was getting tired of being thrown around the dance floor by Killian and then Theo. She traded with Clea, much to Clea's dismay, and headed out into the walkways leading back to Lord Evian's palace. As she drew closer to the veranda doors, she could hear Lord Evian's voice,

"I've told you, it cannot be done. I'm sorry, I truly am. But there is nothing I can do."

Eira halted her steps a moment and then she was face to face with an angry-looking Leon rushing out of the doorway. "Oh," he paused before nearly taking her out.

"Are you okay?" she asked placing a hand on his arm.

He sighed and looked down at her as if he was ridding himself of the unpleasantness of the conversation he had just had, "Yeah...I was just coming to find you actually."

"Somehow I don't believe that." She knew. She knew he was probably having one last conversation with Lord Evian in the hopes that he had found some way to rid her of her destiny. She almost couldn't bear to see the distress mixed with worry on his face, knowing there was nothing that could be done.

"Don't worry about it, Princess," he smiled and took her hand in his. "Let's just enjoy the rest of the night. It's a new year tomorrow, after all."

"There you guys are," Feya walked over to them. "The best part of Myrrvintrel is about to start."

She led them out into the courtyard where everyone was gathered, drinks in hand and looking toward the deep sea of star-freckled sky above. They found where Killian, Clea, Theo, Boreas, and Thomas were all standing together. They walked up behind them, joining the group.

"What are we waiting for?" asked Eira.

"You'll see," smiled Feya turning her attention toward the sky. She breathed a few silent breaths, the warm air from her visible before her eyes. Then it began. The sky burst into a choreography of bright white, shimmering across the sky in various swirls, climbing hills and dipping into valleys, cascading above them, and then bursting into the finest shimmering powdered snow Eira had ever seen. It rained down on top of them, covering the crowd with dust that then disappeared, melting into oblivion. Her clothes were not wet or damaged however, the snow had just vanished as if it was never there in the first place. The fireworks of snow went on for a while, the crowd cheering, laughing, and dancing beneath it. That was it, this was the New Year.

"Happy New Year," smiled Feya pulling Eira into a warm embrace. She couldn't help but think about all the New Year's Eve parties they had celebrated back when they were living together, and how Feya must have missed this. How could she not? And everything she had given up to protect Eira.

She simply tightened her grip against her aunt and looked up to her, "Happy New Year."


The party was far from over, but Eira wasn't sure she had any more energy to continue. She bid her friends goodnight and was heading back to her room when she found the one person she hadn't been able to say goodnight to yet. He was leaning against the wall, hands in his pockets as if waiting for her.

"You're not going to keep partying?" she asked walking up to him.

He shook his head, "No, I think I've had enough for one night. Although we are definitely going to have to make this an annual tradition—maybe not for the full five days though," Leon smiled.

"Agreed."

They walked in silence to the threshold of Eira's bedroom. There they were, standing on the border of will they, won't they? She walked slowly into her room, leaving the door open behind her. He took a few steps in after her, but remained mostly in the entryway. Eira turned back to look at him, not being able to shake the words Theo had said that night—that Leon had tried everything to rid her of her fate.

"You okay?" he asked, noticing the sudden sadness plastered across her face. He moved closer to her.

"Theo told me—where you were that last time we were supposed to train together. The time you didn't show up."

His posture shifted as if he was trying to hide some sort of embarrassment, then smiled as if to say, *damn it, Theo.*

"Why would you do that?"

"What do you mean, *why?*" He turned and took the three strides back toward the door and closed it knowing the conversation they were about to have should stay just between the two of them.

"I don't think I can be more clear, Leon. Why would you do that?"

"I don't know, Eira. Because you shouldn't have to go up against a dragon! It's utter insanity that everyone thinks you'll be fine just because it's your *destiny* or whatever." He was getting increasingly agitated, and so was she.

"Well, you could have at least told me. You left me there waiting for you, without telling anyone you weren't coming. Especially after what happened at the last training session. I think I deserved more."

"That's what you're mad at me about? That's why you've been so cold to me for the last few days? Seriously?"

"Don't, *seriously*, me. You kissed me and then left and then never showed up again until three years later."

"You had me pinned, what was I supposed to do?"

"Not kiss me and then leave."

"It was barely a kiss."

"Yeah—well, it was *my* first kiss and you took it from me."

"What?" He calmed slightly for a moment, the heat dissipating from him. "Well, just don't think of it as your first kiss. It wasn't really even a kiss to begin with— nothing like a first kiss should be."

"Yeah, well you would know. I'm sure you've had a lot of practice." Eira folded her arms against her chest.

"Don't do that," he moved closer to her, bridging the gap between them in a few strides. He was now an arm's length away and she could feel the heat rising off of him, "What do you want me to say, Eira? You want me to say that for the last three years, I've spent every damn day thinking about that kiss and how I screwed it up and should have kissed you properly because you deserve it? That kiss changed my life, as brief as it was—is that what you want to hear? It shattered me knowing that you'd have to go face that dragon and most likely not survive. People don't just walk away after coming face to face with a dragon."

She could almost see the tears forming in his eyes, the tears being brought on by knowing that he might not have as much time with her as he had hoped. Her own eyes were also beginning to well up. She went to wipe them with the back of her hand but Leon had already closed the gap between them. He cupped her face in his hands, wiping away her tears with his thumb. She smiled up at him, gazing into his deep hazel eyes.

"If you don't kiss me right now—" But she didn't need to finish that sentence. His mouth covered hers with all the passion he'd been saving for the last three years. It was a kiss like none other. The kind that you feel in your whole body and the only thing keeping her from collapsing under the weight of it, was his arms around her. He scooped her up into his arms, never once breaking the bond of their lips, and walked slowly over to the bed. He sat her down on the edge of it, finally breaking free from the kiss, and looked down at her, her sapphire eyes beaming up at him. "What?" she finally asked, not wanting any of it to end.

"It's nothing. I don't want to think about anything other than this tonight." He leaned down and ran a hand through her hair holding the back of her head and then moved to her neck, pulling her close into him again. His lips crashed against hers and she couldn't hold back. She slid her hands under his jacket, up to his shoulders and it fell softly to the floor. He carefully guided her back onto the bed, crawling over her while she unbuttoned his shirt, pulling the bottom of it free from the waist of his pants revealing his taught muscles. She wanted him. More than anything. She couldn't believe how much she wanted him, and that feeling was certainly shared.

Eira had never felt so utterly comfortable than when she awoke in Leon's arms the next morning. His warm body pressed against hers. She listened to his soft rhythmic breathing for a moment then closed her eyes to try to savour a few more minutes before they had to leave the sanctuary of her bed. He awoke soon after and pulled her into him trailing soft kisses down her neck. "Good morning, Princess. Sleep well?" She nodded as he leaned down to capture her lips in another kiss.

"I don't want to leave this bed," she said when finally breaking free of him for a moment.

"Well, we don't have to. For a bit anyway." He pulled her on top of him, making his desire for her known. Then he sat up against the headboard and kissed her again. It was like every kiss was the first—earth-shattering and leaving Eira craving more. He eventually laid her down on her back, placing more kisses on every inch of exposed skin as he carefully removed her nightgown.


When they finally made it down to breakfast—after one more round in bed and a steamy shower—the rest of the group was already there enjoying their food. When Eira and Leon walked into the dining room together—they had discussed going separately but figured it wouldn't matter as long as they acted like their usual selves—Theo and Killian looked up from their plates and Killian dropped the bite that was headed for his mouth.

"What's with you two?" he asked.

"What are you talking about?" replied Leon.

"Something's up. Something happened."

"Nothing happened," Leon answered casually as he sat down across from them.

"No, something's different. She's not looking at you like she wants you to die anymore—it's weird."

Leon rolled his eyes, "I don't know what you're talking about."

They all went back to enjoying their breakfasts until Eira caved because Theo wouldn't stop staring at her and mouthed to him that she told Leon what he said.

Theo dropped his fork and it clattered on his plate, "What! I told you not to tell," he stated, more in the general direction of Eira and Leon and not to Eira specifically.

"Tell her what? Tell her what?" Killian begged to know.

"You already know," snapped Theo.

Killian's eyes widened, "Oh—you told her you're betrothed." And...that would be why they sent Leon to train with her once a month—real original. "Dude. I mean, a bit of weird timing, not going to lie. Maybe wait until after she defeats the drag—" He caught of glimpse of Eira's expression and realized he may have fucked up. "That's not what you were talking about was it? Well, you know. Who said betrothal—not me? I don't even know what that word means."

Eira glowered at Leon and then stormed off. "I'm going to kill both of you," Leon stated then turned to follow Eira.

"Fair. Fair." Theo and Killian nodded in agreement.

Eira was headed back upstairs when Leon caught her, "Eira, wait," he called reaching for her shoulders and sliding in front of her. "Look, I can explain everything."

"Yeah, you'd better."

"Okay, yes, we are *technically* betrothed. Our parents decided it when you were born, but I don't expect you to marry me if you don't want to. No one is forcing this on you. I want you to know that."

"Oh good, so this doesn't get forced on me, but saving the entire world does—great. How long have you known about this?"

He paused, searching her eyes for the right response, "A while," he finally said.

"Did you know about it when you kissed me that day in training?"

"Yes. I've known since I was eighteen. You were also going to be told when you turned eighteen, but you ran away."

"Oh, so it's my fault I didn't know?"

"That's not what I said. And look—this doesn't change anything. None of this has any effect on how I feel about you."

"Really? Because I don't know if you actually feel these things for me, or if you just think you have to because we're supposed to be together?"

"Eira, that's ridiculous—of course I have feelings for you. With or without this betrothal."

Eira sighed, "Okay, look. I don't really want to talk about this right now. I'm just going to go start packing."

"I hate to interrupt this," they turned to see Clea standing behind them, "but Lord Evian wants to see us."

The group felt as if they had been summoned to the principal's office—standing there, all annoyed with each other and not wanting to admit who started the fight. Lord Evian didn't bother asking what was going on and simply stated his reason for the meeting. He finally explained what had happened when the dragon came and destroyed the Wintren-elves' homeland. The elves, fairies, and other winter animals had no choice but to retreat into the depths of the forest.

"Long ago, we joined our magic with that of the fairies to protect our borders. When the snow left, so did most of our magic and it has been dying more and more ever since. The fairies' realm is across the valley on the other side of the river. They look after the animals that cannot survive without the cold of the snow, and neither will they for much longer. For years, my kind have remained in solitude, never leaving the safety of the valley until it was absolutely necessary; the day Eira needed to leave for her safety. The magic protecting our borders is fading. Soon the animals and us fae folk will be exposed. And, unless the snow comes back, they will not survive. We will not survive."

When the group was ready to head out, the elves were kind enough to provide them with horses for the journey. Eira and Leon walked out with Lord Evian.

"I believe I have someone here who would love to continue on this journey with you," Lord Evian said turning to Leon and then shifting his gaze to the white stallion happily stuffing his face with hay.

"Hey, buddy!" called Leon with open arms, walking over to his friend. Eira was not quite ready to leave just yet. She hung back for a moment with Lord Evian.

"Lord Evian?" she asked. "When we were in the forest before we came here, it seemed I was led here by a great white bear. He kept appearing and then disappearing. I saw him again during the festival."

"Yes, that was the great Guardian of the Forest. He wanders these lands watching out for all that dwells within. I suspect he knew you were someone special. There are only a remarkable few who have ever had the pleasure of seeing him with their own eyes." Then he continued, "Before you go, may I ask you a question?" Eira turned to him and smiled in reply. "Why didn't you go through the door?"

"Sorry?" asked Eira confused by the question.

"The first night you were here. The door you encountered in my study. It's an Almaluna door," he said so casually, as if she just knew what that meant. "Why didn't you go through it? You could have gone back, ran from this world, from your destiny? Why didn't you?"

"I honestly don't know," Eira replied.

"I think you do. You're just not ready to admit it to yourself."

"But—it was real then, I could have gone back? It was right on the other side of that door?"

He nodded and then smiled, "I'm glad you chose to stay."

"What about Thomas?" she asked. "You'll make sure he gets home like I asked?"

"Of course. In fact, he has already been sent home through the door. He was very grateful to us and wished for me to thank you again for saving him." She smiled.

Eira walked over to the elf waiting with her horse. Leon was already on Harwin, waiting for her. "This is Eivissa," said the elf handing the reins to Eira. Eivissa was a beautiful grey thoroughbred. Her coat was so silky she almost looked silver. "She is a good horse and I trust she will serve you well."

"Thank you," she said taking the reins.


The group headed out in the direction of the Hoarfrost Mountains.

"Alright," started Killian, "Now, I know we've been busy partying for the last few days, but it's time we address the elephant, or rather *dragon*, in the room." He looked at Eira, "Dragons can be tricky creatures. You never know what they are thinking. You'll be fine, fine, fine, and then *bam*—on fire."

Eira chuckled, "Huh, kind of like cooking with a broiler."

"Exactly," nodded Killian.

"You have about as much of an idea of what a broiler is as I do," said Boreas to him.

"Shhh, she doesn't need to know that. I want her to think I'm cool."

"Believe me, chatty one, she will never think that."

He was taken aback, "Chatty? Am I chatty?" he asked to no one in particular.

"You're not, not chatty," added Theo.

"You do like the sound of your own voice," said Clea.

"Well if your voice was as angelic and sexy as mine, you'd be talking all the time too."

Killian was right though—about the dragon. For beyond the eastern borders of Evervell, there was a dragon asleep in his cave and Eira was meant to conquer him.

# 12

"You're certain of this?" she asked Lord Evian as she walked into the great hall of the Wintren-elves kingdom. She was poised as always, gliding across the floor in a long alabaster gown that melted over her figure as if placed upon her by some sort of magic, built to fit her and no other.

"There is no doubt in my mind," Evian responded.

"How can you be so sure? We have no room for error."

"I have foreseen the war as well, my lady. We will finally have to fight the war we have been putting off for so long."

"But will she win the war, Evian? I will not risk the lives of my kin any more than you would risk yours. Our powers are dying and we cannot waste them on an unwinnable war."

"It is not unwinnable. I have foreseen war, but I have also foreseen victory."

"You know as well as I do that we foresee the possible outcomes, and there are always many. She will either succeed or fail. You have foreseen what will come of our world if she should succeed, but I have seen what should come of it if she does not. Her bloodline does not guarantee a victory," urged the woman.

"I am aware of that. It is not her that will win the war. She will merely help us defeat what has been controlling our lands for centuries. She alone cannot defeat the dragon and bring the snow back. We must all be ready to fight for our kind—fight for what was once here, and fight for our queen like we promised we would long ago. She is fighting for a world she does not know purely because she sees that those who dwell within this land deserve a right to survive. The least we can do is show her that we believe so too."

****

An hour had passed since the group set out from the Wintren-elves' kingdom. They were approaching a large ravine that had a rushing river below. The water was ice cold with small islands of ice floating along and the branches of the trees along the shore dripped with icicles. Leon pulled up alongside the edge of the ravine and peered at the waters below. It would be a long drop down if any of them were to fall off the edge. He could see a bridge ahead of them that connected the two sides of the valley.

"There it is. See that bridge over there?" Leon said to Eira. "Its name is Leth, after the great elven warrior that once fought a battle right here defending the borders of the valley from outsiders. Once we cross, we will no longer be under the protection of the Wintren-elves. We will be on our own from there."

"So," Eira began, changing the topic. They hadn't talked much since the fact that they were betrothed came out this morning. She was honestly still upset and was doing everything to try to avoid it being brought up again. "How did you and Harwin become a pair? I mean, I'm not from around here but I'm guessing unicorns aren't that common when you're looking to stock your stables. Also...he's the only one I've seen so far."

Leon seemed a bit taken aback by her sudden out-of-place question, but he took it as a good sign that she was talking to him again and replied casually, "Yeah, they're not that common. There aren't many of them left actually. It's a typical story though: found him as a foal and rescued him from a hunter's trap. He's been by my side ever since."

"Awe," Eira couldn't stifle the smile, however, Leon didn't seem too pleased with her girly reaction to his tale. "I mean, anyone can ride a boring old horse, this makes you look like a total badass." He seemed more pleased with that response.

"Honestly, I always thought it was kind of girly," Killian chimed in.

"Hey, you were not invited to this conversation," Leon snapped back.

Theo, Killian, Leon, and Eira were all still a little on edge with each other which had made the last hour a bit awkward for Clea and Boreas.

The group approached the beginning of the bridge. This was no rickety old bridge made of wood and vine, this was a bridge made of magic long ago which connected the Wintren-elves' kingdom to the rest of the Valley of the Ethereal. The group had no choice but to cross. They nudged their horses forward, but Eira's seemed unwilling to move.

"Come on," she said, squeezing Eivissa's sides harder and urging her forward. The horse seemed a bit spooked, by the bridge or something else, Eira did not know. She tried one more time to kick the horse forward, but it seemed to have the opposite effect. The horse took a few steps backward and then reared up, coming down hard on her front hooves. The motion was so quick that it sent Eira right over the front of the horse. Leon jumped from Harwin as quickly as he could and knelt down next to her.

"Are you alright?" he asked, staring down at her. "Where are you right now?"

"In an insane magical land, unfortunately," responded Eira.

"Yep, you're okay," said Leon reaching out a hand for her after getting to his feet. He pulled her up and brushed some of the snow off her shoulders, then went to get Eivissa who was watching the whole thing a few steps away, looking sorry for what she had done. He walked the horse slowly back to Eira, "The bridge must have spooked her. Horses can get that way sometimes. She can probably feel the elves' magic fading."

"Not the first time I've been thrown from a horse. Thanks," responded Eira taking the reins and pulling them back over the horse's head. She then proceeded to get back on. Leon took the reins and stood right by the horse's mouth, leading her over to Harwin who was waiting patiently at the beginning of the bridge. "What are you doing?" Eira asked when Leon didn't let the reins go and get back on Harwin.

"I'm leading you over the bridge."

"I feel like that's unnecessary. I'm fine, and she seems fine now too."

"I feel like it *is* necessary. I can't have you falling off a bridge, Princess. Then who will defeat the dragon?" he winked.

She scoffed, "Yeah, then who would you marry?" Leon grumbled at her reply. She rolled her eyes, "Fine," and proceeded to let him have his way—this time.

They made it across the bridge and continued their journey into the rest of the forest. Eventually, they came across a small lake, nestled amidst the mountains towering around them. The horses strode slowly over to the shore of the lake and Leon looked across it.

"I think crossing it would be our best option," he stated. "If we try to go around, we'll lose a lot of time."

"Are you sure it's safe to cross?" asked Clea. "Are you sure the ice is solid enough?"

"Yep," smiled Leon, "look." He pointed out to the lake and the group took a closer look. Until this point, Eira had merely seen a typical lake before her. There was a small amount of snow covering the surface which made it difficult for her to tell if it was frozen solid enough for them to cross. Just as Leon pointed out to the lake, a gust of wind came along and swept all the snow out of her view and cleared the lake to reveal the ice beneath.

"It's full of...bubbles!" exclaimed Eira as she stared down at the indigo ice with a giant white bubble trapped inside. The entire lake had bubbles scattered across it. It looked like the entire lake was polka-dotted. It was as if the bubbles surfacing were instantly frozen and trapped in the ice. Some looked like they were stacked on top of each other, creating these underwater irregular towers. They varied in size, but as Eira looked deep into the depths of the lake, she could see just how far down the bubbles were trapped; a couple of meters, at least.

"See, those bubbles travel far down and they're all trapped in the ice. I think we're safe to cross," assured Leon.

"Just when I thought this place couldn't possibly get more magical," Eira said in awe, still staring outward.

When they finally made it to the other side of the lake, they travelled inward for a while until they came to a small clearing where they decided it was the perfect place for a rest. The horses were in need of it, and Killian was beginning to get hangry—although he'd never admit it.

While Theo and Killian were setting up a small ring of rocks for a fire pit, Eira and Clea headed into the forest to look for some kindling. She didn't know where they would be able to find anything of that nature seeing as the ground was covered in snow and any brush would certainly be too moist to use for the fire. They searched anyway and did manage to find some twigs that seemed as though they would work.

"So," started Clea as they were heading back to the clearing, "I know I don't really know much about your situation with Leon, but coming from someone who was almost forced into an arranged marriage, I can honestly tell you that Leon didn't mean any harm by it. It's clear that he does have real feelings for you and this was just a weird coincidence that you guys are *supposed* to be together."

"I know." Eira hated to admit it, but she did know. She knew that Leon cared for her and the fact that she was supposed to be his future wife didn't have any sway over the feelings that were growing inside him—and her for that matter. "I just think he could have told me sooner."

"When would he have told you? As dense as Killian is sometimes, he was right. How would you have reacted if you showed up here after resisting for so long and, oh by the way...here's this guy you're supposed to marry."

"Not well."

"Exactly. He probably wasn't even going to tell you because why should it matter? That agreement was made long before you even left this place. How were your parents to know you would be forced to grow up somewhere else, away from this life and its customs?"

"True. I guess it's just another thing this world seems to have planned for me. These people seem to be in control of my entire future and—"

"Only you're in control of your future, Eira. It took me a long time and an asshole I was supposed to marry to help me see that. Don't let some destiny define you. It's supposed to be the other way around."


They were back at the clearing now and the guys were waiting by the fire pit they had created. Soon a roaring fire was filling the sky with smoke and a delicious lunch was cooking. The aroma of the roasting meat was filling the air and Eira's stomach started to growl. She hadn't realized how hungry she was, but then she remembered she had never gone back to have breakfast that morning. She was sitting on a boulder by the edge of the clearing waiting for the food to be done.

"Mind if I join you?" It was more of a rhetorical question as Leon took the seat next to her anyway without waiting for her response. She just stared at the ground. She couldn't bring herself to look up and see his face—that stupidly perfect face that she knew she couldn't stay mad at. Sure it was easy being mad when he wasn't around, but she already felt her anger dissipating the moment he walked over to her.

"Why did they pick you?" Eira finally asked. "My parents—and yours, I guess. Why did they think we'd be good together?"

"I don't know if it was so much as they thought we'd be good together as they figured it was a good way to keep the alliance between our lands. Most arranged marriages have everything to do with politics rather than love. I'm half Syysian and they're one of Talvia's allies. Very few get to marry for love when you're royalty. Your parents were an arranged marriage too, and it turned out well for the both of them." He caught a glimpse of Eira's expression, "Well, in the love department anyway. Your parents were madly in love with each other, and that doesn't often happen."

She looked up at him and gave a half-hearted smile, "No...it probably doesn't."

"Food's ready," Theo called from the fire.

Leon motioned his hand toward the fire as if to say, *you first.*

After lunch, an elven bow was brought out. No one was quite sure how it started, but at some point during lunch, Killian was challenged to a shooting contest by Theo and he was not one to turn down a challenge. The rules were simple enough: first to hit all five targets wins. The targets were the random things around the clearing the rest of the group told them to hit: that specific tree branch, the centre of the knot in that tree trunk, the apple placed on a boulder about twenty yards into the forest. Eira was going to be pretty impressed if either of them hit that one.

"This is stupid guys—we should really be going," Clea said with her arms folded across her chest as Theo and Killian were eyeing up their first targets.

"Oh relax, it'll only take a few minutes for me to beat him," assured Killian.

"Well, we all know it only takes you a few minutes," jeered Theo.

They were both tied—four to four. The last shot was a difficult one. Leon had chosen the highest branch in a tree at the end of the clearing. It was a good fifty yards away and then about fifty feet vertical.

"Okay...we're looking at the same branch, right?" Killian asked as he and Leon stared upward into the distance.

"Yes, the one to the left. It's the very last one."

"Alright, just checking. Don't want to lose because of a technicality." Killian fired—and missed. Defeated, he handed the bow to Theo who was about to take aim when they heard a terrible cry coming from the direction Killian's arrow had sailed.

"That doesn't sound good," said Theo.

They all ran in the direction of the cries, each one getting louder and more pain-filled as they drew closer.

"Great, I hope you didn't hit some sort of sacred magical creature or something," said Clea.

Killian sneered at her.

When they arrived at the scene, there was a large white stag lying on the ground. Luckily, the arrow had landed in its hindquarters and if they could get it out, there was a good chance the stag would survive. The arrow wasn't even that deep, just deep enough to cause pain.

There was more movement in the bushes surrounding the group and the stag. It sounded as if something was running through the woods toward them. Eira saw what looked like a blue wolf staring at them from behind the bushes and she had flashbacks of the one she had encountered in the Wintren-elves' land. She hoped it hadn't heard the cry and came for an easy meal.

Suddenly the wolf soared from the bushes landing between them and the stag, appearing to be no wolf at all— but a fox. No, not a fox—a woman, no taller than Eira herself. Drawing a bow and pointing it at them, it was clear that she wore a blue and white mask carved to look like a fox embellished with silver. Her long white hair was braided behind her and she was dressed in a deep cobalt and ash coat with white fur on the collar. Something glistened in a beam of sunlight behind her but Eira could not make out what it was. The girl quickly turned to the stag and removed the arrow from his haunch. She pressed her hand on the wound and when she removed it, the wound was healed. Her hands had what looked like white snowflakes tattooed all over them and her fingers, although still warm, faded into an ice-blue colour at the tips. It was almost as if she was wearing sheer lace gloves that blended into her skin. When the girl had turned around to help the stag, it appeared that the thing dazzling in the sunbeam was a pair of wings.

The stag quickly got up and bowed to her in a motion of thanks and leapt away. As soon as the stag had left, the girl turned her bow on the group again.

"What brings you here?" she demanded.

"I'm sorry," Eira replied, "we didn't mean to hit him."

"What brings you here?" the girl demanded again drawing her bow closer to Eira. Leon stepped in front of Eira in an attempt to calm the girl as Theo, Killian, and Clea drew their swords. Leon put down his sword and motioned for the rest to do the same as a sign of peace, and raised both hands in front of him.

"Please," he began, "we just came from the kingdom of the Wintren-elves. This is Eira, Queen of Talvia. She is on her way to the Hoarfrost Mountains."

"There is no queen of Talvia anymore," replied the fairy. "Talvia has not seen a queen for years."

"This is the rightful Queen of Talvia. She has returned to bring back the snow," continued Leon. The fairy did not seem to believe him. Fairies were creatures that you want on your side. They are very trustworthy once you gain their trust, however they do not trust easily. The fairy looked at them for a moment. She had noticed a change in the winds and that some magic was returning to the land. After a moment, she put down her weapon and raised the mask off her face. When she removed the mask, her eyes were the brightest blue—almost aquamarine—ever seen in any mortal or immortal creature. Her alabaster skin shone with the essence of pearl dust and her eyelashes glistened with frost as she blinked in the sunlight.

"My name is Alvara," she said. "I am one of the fairies who take care of all the winter animals protected by this enchanted land."

"Dude, I thought fairies were more..." Killian whispered to Theo as he pulled his thumb and index finger closer together in a shrinking fashion, "you know...compact?"

Alvara scowled at him—their hearing being impeccable. "Our magic has been slowly disappearing over the last hundred years. We used up most of it to create the valley to protect ourselves. When our magic is gone, we can no longer go between our fairy form and this one. Our wings can no longer fly and we remain in this form until our full magic returns with the snow. The amount of magic it requires to remain in fairy form takes a toll on our weakened selves. We still have some magic, but it will eventually run out." The group stared in silence. "Come, my High Lady will want to meet you."


They led the horses across the stream and into the forest where Alvara had come from. It was a long walk to the Realm of the Fairies. When they finally arrived they made their way through a monolithic tree. Its branches and roots had formed a long tunnel where at the end a light could be seen. The branches were covered with ice and blocked the sunlight from above. When they reached the end of the tunnel, there before them, stood a large tree twisted to form a walkway through the realm. It too was ice-covered and the snow packed in around it making it look as though it rose from a pillow of soft white powder. They walked the stone path leading to the tree and when they approached, the doors made of carved ice swung open as if they had anticipated their arrival. There were stairs that led up the tree trunks with balconies built into them in the various boughs. The group remained on the ground and walked into an opening. Once behind the doors, another fairy approached the group.

"Who have you brought here?" he questioned Alvara. He was a guard of the realm. The fairy men looked much like the men of Talvia—with the defining characteristic of wings. Not unlike the Wintren-elves, they had ears coming to a point at the top. However, elf ears featured a much less predominant point.

"I found them in the forest. She says she is the Queen of Talvia and is here to bring the snow back."

The male fairy looked at them for a moment, "I don't believe her," he said with disdain. "Besides, she does not wish to have any visitors now."

Alvara leaned in and whispered to him, "I know, it seemed strange to me too, but you have to agree that things have been changing lately. There has been talk of cold air returning to the mainland." He simply looked at her and then walked away. Alvara turned to the group, "Wait here," she said. She then walked away and did not return for a while.

When Alvara finally did return she led them to the courtyard. It was now evening and the stars were out looking upon the world below. There were torches lit that surrounded the great circle of the courtyard and various ice globes and flowers that glowed blue by some sort of fairy magic. They saw many more fairies and Eira was surprised to see so many animals that she was told may be extinct sitting mixed amongst them. There were badgers and snowshoe hairs, along with caribou, lynx, and a couple of snow leopards and glacier bears—both of which were rarely seen by human eyes.

In rode the High Lady of the Winter Fairies astride the great polar bear of the forest. She glided across the room with all the elegance and grace Eira would have expected from the highest of fairy nobility. Her gown was made from evergreen boughs and her long dark hair dusted with snowflakes and frosted at the tips draped over her shoulders, twisting into curls at the ends. She also shared the brilliant blue eyes that seemed to be a theme amongst the fairies. The crowd silenced and bowed as the High Lady walked into the centre of the court to greet Eira.

"I have met with Lord Evian in the kingdom of the Wintren-elves. From this point forward, we will trust and welcome her—we are now allies of the great Talvian Queen." The High Lady turned back to Eira, "I am Olwen," she greeted.

Olwen took Eira for a walk that evening around her kingdom. She was silent as she led Eira up a winding staircase into the tree's canopy. Eira simply followed in silence, unsure if she should break the silence, but knowing herself, she feared she would say the wrong thing and chose to keep quiet. They finally reached a platform where the tree branches formed a dome around them. The moonlight was creeping through the openings between the branches and there was a soft glow coming from the fairy lights bordering the dome. A flickering blue fire was dancing at the heart of the domed room. Finally, Olwen spoke,

"Lord Evian informs me that you pushed against this world for a long time. Why is that?"

Getting right into it—okay. "Well, I guess I just didn't want my life planned out for me. I was trained from a young age to be this person: a warrior, a queen. None of it was my choosing."

"And you discovered the risk associated with all of this."

"Well, yes. I mean...I didn't truly understand the risk until I was here. I was more just trying to defy what everyone wanted me to be. But I do know there is risk. I do know that facing a dragon—that going to war often doesn't end well."

"There are always two outcomes in life, and you should live your life aware of them."

"I know there is a possibility I might fail. I have always known that."

"The possibility of failure should not stop you—it is the possibility of success that one must be careful of. Are you ready to take on all that will come to you if you should succeed? This is not just a mere adventure, child. This is the rest of your life. I have always believed that when you see what will happen if the outcome is failure, it simply pushes you to defeat that outcome even more. If you are not ready to embrace all that will come with the end, then perhaps, as the old saying goes, you should let sleeping dragons lie, for now at least."

Eira stood there, unable to speak. She always knew that failure was a possibility, however, she had not put much thought into what would happen if she succeeded. She spent most of her life trying to run from it. She would be queen, she would have a kingdom, and Leon—was that truly what she wanted now? If she survives the dragon, could she just walk away? Could she just go back to her old life and someone else would rule this land?

Eira looked at Olwen, "But then this land won't survive. Don't you want your home back? How can you tell me to just give up?"

"I am not telling you to give up. I am telling you to be well aware of the outcomes. This land doesn't just need the snow back—it also needs its queen. Do not wake that beast unless you are completely and utterly prepared to deal with the repercussions."

Naturally, sleep did not come easily to Eira that night. She kept replaying every word that came from Olwen's mouth. The air around her was soft and still, and the pale blue glow of the moonlight hitting the white frosty trees was making it difficult for her to get the rest she needed. She got out of bed and wandered aimlessly around the tree's canopy, up and down the various bridges until she came to a gazebo nestled amongst the branches. In the centre was a small fountain, trickling over with some sort of silver liquid. It looked like mercury but flowed with the ease and grace of water. Just like a child who cannot keep their hands in their pockets when in a toy store, she wanted to touch the shimmery liquid, and reached a hand toward it.

"Don't touch that," came a voice from behind her. Eira jumped and pulled her hand away. She turned to see Leon standing in the doorway of the gazebo. "Unless, of course, you want magical fairy powers," he added moving closer to where she stood.

"Well...that could be kind of cool," she grinned.

He smiled, "I'm just kidding. It's purely decorative. What are you doing here though?"

"I couldn't sleep. Something about slaying a dragon was weighing on me," she joked.

"Yeah, we seem to share that sentiment." Eira looked up at him pulling her brow lower. "Haven't you noticed that anytime you can't sleep, I also seem to be awake?" She honestly hadn't noticed. She just figured he was a night owl. "Princess, I haven't been able to get a good night's sleep since you got here—longer, if I'm being completely honest. There were so many nights that I'd lay awake in bed, searching for the answer to save you from all of this. The only time I've actually slept was after Myrrvintrel because you were right there with me and I didn't let go of you all night." She moved closer to him. "I'm sorry you had to find out about us the way you did. I'm sorry about you having to even be here in the first place. I'm sorry about everything." She put a hand to his warm cheek and he slid his over hers, fitting her hand perfectly within.

"None of this was your doing," she said. "None of this is your fault. It was always going to be this way. There's nothing anyone can do."

"I wish there was."

"I know, but sometimes we just have to face the future and everything it brings. And when that dragon is gone and the snow is back, we can figure everything out after because we'll have our whole lives ahead of us to do it." She kissed him, long and gently, wanting to savour this moment and live in it forever—the feeling of his lips on hers and his body pressed close, wishing he could protect her from everything coming her way.

# 13

Daylight was washing the inside of Eira's closed eyes with a warm orange glow much sooner than she had hoped. By the time she and Leon fell asleep, there were only a few more hours of darkness left in the sky. They were both awake when he found her by the fountain, so may as well make the most of it. She rolled over in bed and it swayed gently from the ropes holding it to the ceiling. It wasn't a large bed, honestly only big enough for one, but they were perfectly content sleeping pressed against each other for the few hours they managed to get. Breakfast was already laid out for them on the small desk in the corner of the room.

"Whoa, you two look exhausted," greeted Killian as Eira and Leon made their way to the entrance of the Realm of the Fairies. The rest of the group was already waiting for them. "I don't want to know why, but I'm going to assume you two made up." Neither dignified Killian with a response. Leon walked over to Harwin and rubbed a hand up and down his neck.

Alvara led the group out of the Realm of the Fairies. It was not long before they would reach the eastern edge of Evervell forest. Alvara stood beside an ice-covered tree marking the entrance to her home and bid them goodbye. The moment the group turned to continue their journey, they found themselves back in Evervell looking upon a sunny green forest. Eira looked back and simply saw more of the same forest that was ahead of her. There was no trace of the direction they had come from or that the snow was ever there. Although the sun was still beating down in the days they were in the Valley of the Ethereal, the mainland began growing significantly colder. There was no snow returning yet, but the air had that same aroma that embraced the atmosphere in early winter. Eira knew and loved that time of year passionately. As they walked through the forest she thought to herself, *it smells like snow.*

Time passed steadily as they journeyed through the forest. They knew they were getting closer to the border of Evervell and should reach it by dusk. The town just past its border would be their resting place for the night.

"Alright, I don't know about anyone else, but I could use a break," started Theo when the sun was far past its midpoint in the sky. They had been travelling for hours at this point. "I think these horses deserve one too."

"Yeah, that's probably a good idea," Eira agreed.

"There should be a stream not too far from here. We can rest and give the horses a chance to get some water," added Leon.

The stream was a welcomed sight when they finally reached it. They were all long overdue for some refreshment and a break. They removed the horse's saddles and let them graze and drink freely for a while. Killian and Theo were sparring off to the side while Eira and Clea sat on a fallen tree by the river.

"How are you feeling?" Clea asked. "In only a couple of days, we'll be in the mountains."

Eira sighed, "I know. And it's weird, but I'm not really scared anymore. I guess I was never really scared, more just angry that this was something I had to do. It honestly felt like a major inconvenience for most of my life."

"I can get that," Clea smiled. "But for what it's worth, those two idiots over there seem to really have your back, and Leon definitely does. Boreas, I'm not too sure about. I honestly forget he's here most of the time."

Eira chuckled, "Yeah, I'm really glad I have you guys."

"Hey," called Leon, "you guys almost ready to leave?" The girls nodded in reply.

Everyone regrouped and while they were getting the horses ready, Theo asked, "So, we haven't really discussed what will happen when we get to the mountains. Is Eira going into that cave herself?"

"Absolutely not!" interjected Leon.

"Excuse me?" Eira looked at him.

"There's no way I'm letting you go in there alone."

"Letting me? I didn't realize I needed your permission." There was a sudden silence amongst the group.

"That's not what I meant."

"Well, what did you mean then?" Eira crossed her arms against her chest.

"I just meant that it's better if I go with you. For protection."

"You know damn well I can protect myself."

"Eira, you're overreacting." Bad choice of words.

"Um, no I'm not."

"Yes—you are."

"No—I'm not!"

"It is my job to be worried about you. And to protect you."

"Look, you're not my boyfriend and you're certainly not my fiancé, so just because we slept together doesn't mean you have the right to tell me what to do."

"I *knew* it!" interjected Killian. "Sorry...continue."

"In fact, I have a boyfriend and I really don't need another one always telling me what to do."

"What?" The group shared the same puzzled expression that Leon had plastered across his face.

"Okay, well he's not exactly my boyfriend. And, yes, I know I probably should have told you about him before all of this, but we're not even really together. He cheated on me, so we broke up and we just talked about getting back together last week."

"What?" Leon repeated.

"Ugh, never mind."

"No, no, no—we're going back to that."

"Look, I'm sorry, I shouldn't have even brought it up. Trey and I aren't a thing." A smile grew on Leon's face. "What?"

"Nothing," Leon smirked. "It's just, his name's Trey."

"What's that supposed to mean?"

"Come on," Leon looked to Killian and Theo for support. "I think I know everything I need to about him. He sounds like a tool." Eira looked taken aback and turned to see where Killian and Theo were nodding in agreement with Leon. "And he cheated on you, so clearly he is a tool."

Eira let out an exasperated sigh, "You know what, I'm done with you." She stormed off into the forest beyond the river with Leon trailing behind pleading with her to come back.

Killian spoke first, "I'm so glad they got together in the middle of this journey—this is so much fun now."


Eira was still stomping through the forest ignoring Leon's inane rambling when something bright caught her eye. She pushed her way through the brush to get a closer look. When she finally got closer, she saw what seemed to be a glass bead hanging from a branch catching the sun's light. It was strange what a hypnotic effect this simple little object had on Eira as if it was calling her closer and she wanted this precious jewel for her own. She could not control herself as she was drawn to it, watching the game of catch-and-release the bead was playing with the sun's warm light. As she got closer to it, she stretched a hand out to touch the bead but before she could touch it, Leon called out to her,

"Eira—no!" He tried to pull her back but it was too late, the ground fell from beneath them and the pair tumbled down into the underworld.

"Well...this complicates things a bit. What happened?" Eira asked as she sat up in the darkness. There was not an ounce of light around them. The two had tumbled down a rather large and deep hole with a steep drop at the end letting out into a small cave. There was no way they would be able to exit the same way they came in as the tunnel was now above their heads and out of reach. All Eira could feel around her was the cold damp earth, and if she could see better, she was sure her clothes were now covered in mud. The cave smelled of mud and earth, not entirely unpleasant but there was the faint aroma of the creatures that lived there too.

"It was a mole trap," replied Leon.

"A mole? You mean the little creatures that live underground and hardly set traps for prey as large as us—or prey at all? I think they're herbivores, or maybe insectivores?"

"The moles we have here are not the same creatures you may be used to. They are giant and vicious and will eat us if we don't get out of here soon. They set up those lovely glass beads, which you just couldn't resist, to catch prey. The moles are really the only creatures that can find them because they are constantly tunnelling into the deep underground where the beads reside. They hoard them for their hypnotic properties. It's the only way these creatures can catch a meal large enough to satisfy them."

"Oh...well, great."

Leon stood up and helped Eira to her feet. "Follow close behind me and try not to make a sound." He rifled through his jacket and pulled out a small lighter. He rummaged around in the dark for a second or two finally finding what he was looking for. He held up a stick and wrapped a small piece of cloth around it then lit it to make a torch. The two wandered the tunnels for what seemed like hours. It was pitch black save the small light emanating from the torch, but even that was burning down and would soon be extinguished.

"This is ridiculous," Eira began, "do you even know where we are going or how to find a way out? The things that live in this darkness have surely discovered by now that they trapped a meal and will probably not be too happy to find it has wandered off, which also means they're most likely tracking us."

"Yes, Eira! I realize that, but we have to find a way out somehow. The moles leave the underground at night to set traps for the animals during the day, which means if they have a way out, then so do we."

The last flicker of light from the torch burned out just as the pair made their way into a large opening among the tunnels. There were several additional tunnels leading out of the room and no way to know which to take. Leon lit the torch one more time, but the light was not as strong as it had been.

"I can smell them. We're getting closer," came a raspy voice from within one of the tunnels.

"Oh, great—they can talk too," Eira mocked.

Eira and Leon looked at each other. It was slightly lighter in this room and there was a small puddle of water to reflect any light creeping in from above. Leon rummaged through his coat again, pulled out a small object, and handed it to Eira.

"Take this. It will protect us...hopefully." Eira looked at what was in her hand. It was a small stone, just large enough to fit nicely in a pocket or the palm of your hand. It was smooth and a perfectly symmetrical oval shape in a deep indigo blue; the colour of the ocean when it meets the night's sky and you cannot tell where one begins and the other ends. Although it was fairly dark where Eira was, she could tell it was polished and had a nice gleam to it.

"Pretty," she exclaimed. "How is this supposed to help us? This is a rock."

"It's not a rock, it's called a Monarch Stone and it will help us. These moles live underground because daylight harms them, that stone—" but before he could finish his sentence he was ambushed by a mole jumping from above and landing atop him. He managed to free his sword from its sheath and kill the beast but there were three more moles entering from the tunnels and Eira and Leon were surrounded. The two were hiding behind a boulder as the moles crept closer and cornered them.

"Take out the stone," called Leon.

"Oh, right." Eira pulled the stone from her pocket and climbed atop the boulder they were crouched behind. Feeling confident that they had the moles beat now, she swiftly threw it at the middle mole and watched as it hit him square in the face and bounced off hitting the ground clattering against other rocks, and finally silencing itself by resting who knows where. With a sense of panic and urgency, Eira turned back to Leon, "That did nothing!" she yelled.

"You weren't supposed to throw it at them!" yelled Leon back.

"Well, you didn't exactly give me the instruction manual that comes with your special rock. What was I supposed to do with it?" The moles advanced as Leon was fighting them off with his sword.

"Just go get that stone and hold it tight in your hand."

Eira did as she was asked all the while muttering to herself about how ridiculous it was that rather than trying to fight off the moles she was crawling around on her hands and knees looking for a rock. *He really needs to get his priorities straight.* Finally, she found the stone and clasped it tightly in her hands. Within a few seconds, a glow emanated from her fist and she opened her hand to see the stone glowing a bright blue. As she held the stone longer, the light grew brighter and brighter until finally a burst of white light radiated from the stone. She had to shield her eyes from the light with her arm. A cry let out, echoing through the cave while the light burned the moles' eyes and they retreated into the tunnels. The stone kept emanating this white light highlighting every aspect of the tunnels. Finally, Leon saw what he was looking for—a tunnel leading toward the world above. He grabbed Eira by the hand and the two ran toward the tunnel as the stone's light faded out of sight.

Bursting through the tunnel they came to a small cave and saw the orange and pink hues as the light of day was fading into evening. They were still in Evervell, but they had lost their horses and the rest of the group with no clue as to their present location. Leon climbed up the outside of the cave until he was high enough to view the surroundings below. He soon spotted the path they were travelling on and the two made their way to it.

"We're going to have to just meet the others outside of Glasera. It'll take too long for us to try to go back and find them. Hopefully, they'll also think to meet us there."

"What is this thing?" questioned Eira as she handed the stone back to Leon.

"I told you, it's called a Monarch Stone," replied Leon as he placed the stone back into his pocket. "It glows a bright white light when held by someone of royal blood. It is used sometimes to make sure someone is, in fact, royal."

"And why did you have it? You're the ones that have been telling me I'm a princess my whole life. What— you needed to be sure?"

"No, but I figured it might come in handy, and clearly I was right."

"I can't believe you," she said shoving him away from her when he moved closer in an apologetic fashion.

"Eira, stop overreacting."

She clearly wasn't talking about the stone anymore and was back to being upset with him about before. "I'm," she shoved him again—harder. "Not," and again. "Over," one last time. "Reacting!" She went to hit him again but he grabbed her arms before she could and held them above her head.

"Eira, will you just listen to me?" They stared at each other a moment, the rage in Eira's eyes turning to lust. He pushed her against the tree at her back and kissed her ravenously, his body pressed firmly against hers. He took a breath and brushed a gentle hand on her cheek, "Look, you're clearly on edge these last couple of days and I get it. We're about to enter into a fight with a dragon, but you can't just keep trying to push me away. I'm not going anywhere."

"I'm not trying to push you away."

"You literally just were," he grinned.

When Leon and Eira arrived at the city's gates, dusk had fallen upon them. The glow of the lights marking the entrance to the city of Glasera was all that could be seen for miles around. The gatekeeper was not so willing to let them through though. The gates were so large that it was difficult to see into the city even from far away. The weatherworn logs stood upright, side by side, protecting all that dwelled within their mighty barrier. All that could be seen over the top, was a clock tower, its face illuminated telling Eira that they had been in the forest for hours.

"State your business here," demanded the gatekeeper.

"We wish to pass through to make our way to the Hoarfrost Mountains," replied Leon.

"Wait here." The gatekeeper left for a moment and then returned to open the gates for them. Leon and Eira entered the city.

Glasera was a pleasant city nestled in the foothills of the mountains, well maintained for the current predicament that was plaguing Talvia. The streets were cobblestone and most of the buildings were stone as well. There was a beautiful fountain in the centre of town and the streets were decorated with various flower pots and trees to add some greenery and life against the stone. The street lamps and shops made the city seem impenetrable to the night. The people of the town seemed happy enough, and there were vendors and shopkeepers in the streets giving their evening greetings to one another. They found a hotel pretty quickly and got a room for the night. They were also in desperate need of some new clothes as theirs had taken quite a beating underground. They stopped at a local boutique and managed to find something fitting for the evening. Eira chose a casual yet beautiful emerald green dress that would work for dinner later, even though it was highly impractical for the journey they were on. She hoped they would be able to meet up with the rest of the group in the morning and she could get her clothes back. There was no sign of their friends anywhere and the hotel said that no others had checked in that evening.

"Well," began Leon coming out of the bathroom after a well-deserved shower, "I guess we should get some dinner. There's no use wandering around here tonight looking for everyone. If they're here, we'll find them in the morning."

Eira had already showered and changed into the dress, her hair twisted neatly atop her head in a messy bun. She agreed and they soon found a nice-looking restaurant. It felt weird eating just with Leon as if it were a date. In fact—it was a date. They hadn't been alone like this together before. Sure, they had been alone together, but never for a meal. All her meals up until this point were shared with everyone.

Dinner was lovely, though. It was as if they had done this every week for the past few years. There was no awkwardness or trying to impress one another. It was simply them. They took a stroll through the streets after dinner, but their exhaustion soon caught up with them and it was time to head in for the night.

Their room was nothing special. Nothing like the rooms at Lord Evian's palace or in the Realm of the Fairies, but it was cozy and clean and that's all they needed. It had a bathroom with a tub just big enough for the two of them, so Eira dragged Leon into a hot bath in an effort to keep the night they were having alive. She knew as soon as she went to sleep and awoke the next morning, the reality of everything would hit again and just like how the mountains loomed over the city, they had been looming over her since she got here.

She leaned against Leon and traced a finger up and down the peaks and valleys of the tattooed mountains on his arm. He leaned down and placed a kiss on her neck just below her ear.

"What do you think tomorrow will be like?" Eira asked. "When we get to the mountains?"

"I don't know," he replied quietly. "I honestly can't say. I just know that every moment like this with you is the greatest pleasure I've ever known, but it's also this unbearable torture knowing that any of these moments might be the last."

She turned in his arms to face him, the water filling the gap now between them. "Don't say that, don't think that way. It's going to be alright."

"You don't know that."

"No, I don't. And at the beginning of all of this, I would have agreed with you that this is ridiculous and I can't just put my life on the line. But, now I feel strangely alright with it. Like somewhere deep down I know that everything will work out the way it's meant to."

He reached out and pulled her back toward him, "I hope you're right because I can't bear the thought of losing you—of never being able to hold you again, or kiss you again." He pulled her into his embrace and kissed her while the waters washed over them.

The next morning, as luck would have it, they found Killian, Theo, Clea, and Boreas at breakfast. Killian ran up behind Leon, wrapped his arms around him and scooped him up into a hug, then proceeded to give Eira a kiss on the cheek. Eira smiled and they ate breakfast together, just like they had every other day before this one. After breakfast, the group headed into town. They were going to gather a few supplies before heading out to the mountains later that afternoon. It would be about an hour's ride to the foothills and then they were unsure of how long it would take them to reach the dragon. They knew they were going to have to camp in the mountains that night as there were no traveller's cabins once in the mountains.

"Alright," started Leon as they walked out the doors of the hotel, "let's try to get out of here as soon as possible and make our way into the mountains before nightfall." They were in agreement: Killian and Boreas were going to get the tents, Clea and Eira would get some food while Leon and Theo were going to ready the horses at the hotel stables. They were about to separate when the gatekeeper came up to them.

"The master would like a presence with you this morning," he stated, more to Eira than anyone else. It wasn't a question. They picked up on the fact that they were not allowed to decline. The gatekeeper led them through the city until he stopped at a large building with massive columns climbing two stories high and grand stone steps leading up to the front doors. "Come with me," said the gatekeeper. "Wait," he put a hand to everyone except Eira and Leon, "just these two. You lot can wait here."

He led them through the hallways of the building until they reached the last door. He opened the door for the two of them and stepped aside to let them through. Inside it appeared to be an office, but whose? Eira did not know. At the moment they were the only ones standing there until a man came out from behind one of the doors in the office.

"Welcome, Your Majesty," he bowed to Eira. "I was told you were coming to our humble little city. I am Kane, ruler of this city. Welcome to the city of Glasera," he announced cupping Eira's hands in his and shaking them slightly.

"Thank you," said Eira taking her hands back. "But how did you know who I am?" She did not know why, but she had a feeling this man was not normally as nice as he was being to her currently. It seemed forced or fake. Either way, her gut was telling her something seemed off about this place.

"Do you really think I don't know who is coming into *my* city? I've heard that the rightful heir was back. Some farther from the mountains may have forgotten the prophecy, but I have not, seeing as that dragon has forbidden my people from travelling into those mountains for a hundred years."

"Well, I suppose it's a good thing we're here then. We are just making our way through, if that is alright? We don't plan on staying, though your city seems lovely."

"Thank you, my dear," said Kane walking over to his desk, "but I'm afraid you cannot simply pass through my city." Eira and Leon looked at him needing more of an explanation. "I don't let anyone into my city without knowing exactly who they are and what they are doing here. You say you just want to pass through to head to the Hoarfrost Mountains, but I am not so sure. I am also not so sure you are who you say you are. You may pass through my city on one condition. You must defeat me in a tournament first."

*Oh, great.*

# 14

The unmistakable footsteps at a running pace came up the street toward the large old estate house, splashing through the puddles that had formed from the night's rain. The man climbed the stairs and rang the large brass bell, indicating to all inside there was a caller at the door. A small man answered with his long cloak draped off his shoulders and fastened at the waist with a large gilded belt. He was not the owner of the estate, but his confidant. His name was Horace and he was the owner's trusted advisor. The owner was the master of this small hamlet.

"What are you doing here?" Horace asked the man outside the house. He was standing in the doorway preventing the man from stepping foot inside the master's house. The master did not like strange people stepping foot inside his sanctuary.

"I have news for you," answered the man.

"It's about time. It is your job to bring news from beyond the mountains and not be seen by anyone. I can only assume your tardiness is due to the fact that you were caught. Master Florian will not be pleased that you have been gone this long."

"I think Master Florian will forgive my tardiness in this instance."

"And why would he do that? He has no patience for people like you."

"She is here," said the man.

"Who is?"

"You know who. The very person we have been trying to keep out for years. The very person who will be Florian's undoing."

"How do you know this?"

"Because I met her."

"How could you have possibly met the heir to the Talvian throne? She would hardly deal with scum like you."

"I met her when I was on my way through Evervell after I saw her in a pub in Huurre."

"You mean you kidnapped her when you were dealing in people trading." Horace grabbed the carriage driver by the collar and forced him against the wall, "How many times have we told you to stop that nonsense, Errol? You are a spy, not a trader. Do we not pay you enough for that? Perhaps you would like to see what it is like without Master Florian's fortune?"

"He won't care," Errol said pushing Horace off of him. "The point is that she is back and she is heading to the mountains now."

"Who's to say she will succeed even if she makes it to the mountain?"

"She will succeed. She has help, and I have seen her. There is no doubt in my mind that she is the heir and the one the prophecy spoke of."

Horace glared into his eyes and then stepped back, "You can leave now."

Errol left through the large wooden door and the sound of it shutting bellowed through the empty foyer.

"She has arrived, Master," said Horace. "We received word from beyond the mountains. Spies in the cities say that the rightful heir to the Talvian throne has arrived in Talvia and is in Glasera as we speak."

Florian pursed his lips as he sucked on the remains of the chicken he had just devoured. He was at the head of his large dining table spread with a feast large enough to feed an entire army. The town of Innis lay just behind the Hoarfrost Mountains. There were some who would never pledge to be allies of the queen; people who had benefitted from her absence and would continue to benefit if she were to die trying to defeat the dragon. Florian was a powerful man and did not like being disturbed during his dinner. He had long been master of the town of Innis and his people adored him, not knowing any better.

"No!" Master Florian slammed a fist on the table. He then tucked a piece of auburn hair behind his ear. "And what of Kane? What has that bastard done to our deal?"

"Word is that there is...doubt amongst his people. The fear-mongering can only last for so long until someone decides to fight against it."

Gold is a powerful thing in the eyes of mankind. It can cause the total destruction of a world. Florian had long ago made a deal with Kane to claim part of the riches he earns off the people in turn for not revealing his voracity to the people of Glasera.

"Call together our troops, we must march on the people of Glasera and stop any attempt to overthrow Kane and defeat that dragon," ordered Florian.

Under the influence of Master Florian for so long, the people had been corrupted and this once kind mountain settlement turned into a place of greed and war amongst neighbours and friends. The only thing the people of the mountain now coveted was their gold. Every member of the town was rich from Kane and the dragon, and they were not about to give it up. There was more gold than there was a need for in this small outpost and Master Florian had the most.

The men readied themselves for war.

# 15

"What?" replied Eira.

"You are in my city, you abide by my rules. Tournament, or go around. It is up to you. Archery will be the game," answered Kane.

"Fine, we'll go around," Eira stated, but Leon was already shaking his head at her. "So, if we want to pass through your city, I must beat you at an archery tournament?" She turned Leon around with her and whispered to him, "Is it just me, or is this kind of strange?"

"Well, it's his city and we must obey his rules. We can't go around, it'll add a few days to our journey and we don't have time for that."

"Oh, but we had time to hang out with the Wintren-elves for five days?"

He didn't respond to that. "Not being crowned queen yet means you have no real authority over him. Many people still don't even believe the rightful heir will ever come back. If this is what you have to do, then we're just going to have to do it. However, if you're not sure, we can just go around. It'll be a longer journey, but..." sighed Leon.

This all seemed very strange to Eira but she agreed, "Deal!" she said shaking Kane's hand after a moment of reflection.

"Are you sure about this?" Leon whispered in her ear, but she didn't respond to him, just kept smiling at Kane.

"Wonderful!" exclaimed Kane clapping his hands together. You will have the finest rooms in the city for the night. Tomorrow will be the tournament."

The gatekeeper escorted Eira and Leon out of Kane's office and out of the building where their friends were waiting.

"So, what was that about?" asked Theo.

"He's not letting us through his city until Eira beats him in an archery tournament," Leon informed them.

"What?"

"So, we're stuck here for another night. He did upgrade our rooms though."

"Oh," Killian perked up.


They settled into their rooms nicely and Kane was right, they did seem to be the nicest rooms in the city. A massive four-post bed and furnishings fit for a queen, all of which made the strange feeling Eira had about this place grow more and more pronounced.

"Don't you think it's a bit odd how lavish this city is?" she asked Leon walking out of the bathroom.

"What do you mean?"

"Well, you said that Talvia was suffering since the dragon came, and I've seen the poverty with my own eyes. How is this place surviving, or rather—thriving?"

"I don't know, but that's really nothing we should concern ourselves with right now. Let's just make the most of the rest of the day and get out of here as soon as you beat him tomorrow," he gave her a devilish grin.

"Oh yeah, and what were you thinking we do to pass the time?"

"I have a couple of ideas," he pulled her close. "I'm just trying to decide if I'd rather make use of this bed or the wall." He reached his hands under her hips and pulled her legs up around his waist.

He chose the wall.


Later that evening, the group retired to a local eatery in the city centre. It was as if Kane had informed the entire city of her presence and for some reason, no one seemed happy for her to be there. The whole time Eira felt as though she was on display.

"Are you alright," Eira asked Clea who looked as if she was trying to hide while they were at dinner.

"Yeah, it's just...I'm actually from here. I don't want anyone to recognize me and know that I'm back."

"What?" started Killian. "Well, that was dumb of you. You had to know we'd be going through this city?" She glared at him.

"I'm sure you'll be fine. It's a big city. I doubt you'll run into anyone you know." Eira assured her.

"Clea," called a female voice. Clea looked up to see the face of a younger woman who looked like her. You could tell instantly that they had familial ties.

"Bianca." She practically leapt from her seat and gave the woman a hug. Then she turned to the rest of the group, "This is my sister, Bianca." The group all gave a round of smiles and hellos. "What are you doing here?"

"I was out with some friends when I saw you. What are you doing here? If Mom and Dad find out."

"Don't tell them. And please tell your friends not to mention it to anyone either."

"I won't say anything, I promise. But why are you here?"

"I joined up with Eira, the future queen. She's the heir we've all been waiting for. We're here to finally defeat the dragon."

"Of course you are. Only you would defeat one dragon," she said referring to Clea's former fiancé, "and then sign up to battle another. And a *real* one this time. But look," her voice got quiet and she pulled an empty chair to the table and motioned Clea to sit with her, "you have to leave. This city isn't what you think it is. Kane isn't going to let you just go into those mountains and take away his only leverage over the people here."

"What are you talking about?" asked Leon.

"Have you heard of the Day of the Dragon? Once a year the dragon emerges from its lair to take the riches the people leave him and in return, he doesn't destroy our city. Well, I don't think that's true." The group looked at her for more answers. "The guards Kane sends into the mountains are sworn to never tell of what happens on the Day of the Dragon or they'll be killed. Kane pays off spies everywhere and if anyone talks ill of him, they are taken away. But I heard that the dragon hasn't left its cave since the day it came a hundred years ago. No one has ever seen it."

"What are you talking about?" asked Clea. "We grew up participating in the Day of the Dragon ceremonies. We learned all about it."

"It's all a lie."

"How did you find this out?" asked Leon.

"My boyfriend works in the city offices, and that gatekeeper—Kane's crony, let's just say he doesn't exactly reek of intelligence. Kane is hoarding those riches for himself and if you finally get rid of that dragon—his way of life is gone with it. The people here believe it too, they just won't admit it out of fear. Not while Kane rules and the dragon sleeps above them. Kane has made them all believe he's their saviour, but I looked into it. There was no Day of the Dragon until Kane came into power. He's been spinning this lie ever since he got here to siphon the riches from the people. The people are under his control and convinced that there is no heir to Talvia that would ever return. They're slaves to the dragon, and Kane came to save them. I don't know how he convinced everyone of this, but somehow he did. While this city may look like it's thriving, it's all an act. The people are just barely getting by and Kane puts all the money into keeping up the ruse and convincing the people that without him, the city wouldn't thrive and everyone would be homeless and starving. He keeps anything extra for himself."

"We have to stop him," said Eira.

"Well, you getting rid of the dragon would do it, but he's not going to let you out of the city. That little tournament you're supposed to have tomorrow is a trap. He intends to make it look like you're cheating and have you thrown in jail. All of you."

"Oh goody, back to jail," added Killian. "At least this one's not on a ship."

"Okay, we have to get out of the city tonight," said Leon. "We'll leave at midnight and hopefully no one will spot us."

"I wouldn't be too sure of that. Kane has his guards watching you guys. They're all over the city," said Bianca.

"Well, what are we supposed to do then?" asked Theo.

A new voice joined the conversation, "I think I can help you with that." The group looked toward the man standing behind Bianca's chair, resting his hands on her shoulders.

"Oren?" gasped Leon. "What are you doing here?"

Eira recognized him immediately, for he looked exactly like a younger version of the portrait she had seen at Trillium Nivale. He was tall with the same eyes as Eira's only he had the dark hair of their father. "Oren?" she asked.

"Hey, sis," he smiled.

"Well isn't this city just full of surprises," nodded Killian taking a sip of his drink.

Eira didn't know what came over her, but she felt compelled to hug him. Just as Clea did a few minutes before, Eira leapt from her seat and grabbed Oren into a hug.

"What are you doing here?" asked Leon.

"I didn't know where I was going when I left last year, but while I was figuring it out, I met Bianca and she told me where she was from. I realized that coming here with her might be the best place for me to be, seeing as you'd probably end up here soon enough."

Eira smiled, "You're her boyfriend who works for the city." He nodded.

"Oh, Mom and Dad will sure be pleased about this match. Have they planned the wedding yet?" Clea rolled her eyes but her sister just sneered at her.

"For your information, I left too." Clea's eyes widened. "When they disowned you I decided I also wanted nothing to do with a family that would force their daughter into a brutal marriage, and I knew I'd probably be next. They don't know about Oren. Joke's on them, right?"

"Okay, so how are we going to get out of this city unnoticed?" Theo asked.

Oren sat down with them and began, "Look, Kane's already moved your horses from the hotel stables to his personal ones. You're going to have to get them back first, and that won't be easy."

"We're going to have to break in?" asked Leon.

"Yes," nodded Killian with a gleam of excitement in his eye.

"Your best bet is early in the morning. Get some rest tonight and meet me there an hour before sunrise. With any luck, you'll be out of the city and into the mountains before the sun is over them."

"And what about Kane? We can't just let him get away with this," added Eira.

"He'll get what's coming to him eventually, especially if that dragon is gone. Plus, I happen to know where he's been keeping all the siphoned riches, and intend to send them back to the people," added Oren.

"We'll help with that," said Killian and Clea.

"Eira, Theo, and I will get the horses back. Boreas will be our lookout," Leon said. They all nodded in agreement and the plan was set.

"Well, well, well. Look what the cat dragged in," a tall man came swaggering over to the table. "Couldn't stay away from me could you, sweetheart?" he said to Clea.

"Get lost, Dorian. I think I made myself perfectly clear last time I saw you I want nothing to do with you."

"Is that what happened? I thought you humiliated me in front of my whole family with your little display of independence. You think I liked having my woman act like that?"

"I'm *not* your woman," she kept her composure calm but her words certainly had bite, "I *never* have been. And I certainly hope that no woman ever has to have the displeasure of marrying you." She stood and confronted him. He didn't take too kindly to her words and motioned toward her.

"Hey," jumped Killian from his seat, "I'd think twice if I were you. You want to be humiliated a second time when I kick your ass out of this bar and back to whatever hole you crawled out of? No woman should have to deal with a lowlife useless asshole like you, especially Clea. She's more woman than you could ever handle, and I think you just got scared."

Dorian assessed the situation and agreed that it would most likely not end well for him if he decided to take Killian in a fight, so he simply looked to Clea and growled, "You're not worth my time anymore," and left. Everyone, especially Clea, was slightly shocked at the fact that it was Killian who decided to stand up for her.

"Thanks, Kil," said Clea. "I didn't think we were that good of friends already."

"Friendship has nothing to do with it. He's a chauvinistic prick who needed to be put in his place. But sure, we can be friends."


Eira was walking out of the restroom when she bumped into Clea.

"Hey, Eira," she started. "Look, I kind of feel like I need to tell you something." Eira looked at her with confusion in her eyes. Clea took a breath, "Look—that night we met in Huurre wasn't exactly by coincidence. I had been talking to my sister for a bit and she mentioned this guy she was seeing. I pried and learned he was your brother. That's where the whole thing started. I learned the prophecy was real and you were here to *save* us. Your brother begged me to find you and go along with you guys to help keep you safe. I've been keeping him updated as best I could this whole time."

Eira smiled, "Clea, did you honestly think I'd be upset about this? This does make more sense now, though. It was a bit odd that you just happened to be in that pub, and what? Just thought to yourself, 'you know what I could go for right now—fighting a dragon with the future queen'." She leaned in for a hug, "I'm glad you came along."

The group finished their meal and made plans to meet Oren early the next morning. They headed back to their rooms at the hotel for the night, knowing they were in for a big day tomorrow. If they could escape this city—they had a dragon to conquer. If they didn't—there was still a different dragon that needed slaying.

# 16

Eira, Leon, and Theo met Oren early the next morning, just outside of Kane's stables. Sneaking out to the stables was no easy feat. It seemed as though Kane was just as paranoid as Oren and Bianca had warned. There were guards patrolling everywhere, including the front doors of the hotel. Eira, Leon, and Theo had to sneak off of the balcony of Eira's room, something Leon and Theo were surprisingly good at. A little too good.

"So, sneak off many balconies?" Eira asked as Leon was helping her down onto the street.

"Um, no. Why?"

"You guys are just a little too good at it."

"Alright, fine. We snuck out of the castle all the time as kids—you happy now?"

When they finally made it to the stables under the cover of the early morning darkness, Oren was there waiting behind a tree.

"Over here," he called in a hushed tone. Surprisingly, there weren't any guards around the stables. Or none that they could spot anyway. A little suspicious, but they had no time to overthink it. Oren and Theo kept watch.

Ever so carefully, Leon tried the door, "It's locked," he said.

"Well of course it is. Do you think he would just leave it unlocked?" said Eira.

"No. It's just been a long time since I've broken into someplace," he winked at Eira expecting a response of utter shock from her.

"Well it's my first time, so I'm pretty pumped," she grinned.

"Okay, well we're going to have to figure out another way in." They looked around and saw a window that was open high on the second floor of the barn.

"There's no way we can reach that," concluded Leon.

"It's not that high up. If you had something to stand on, you probably could. You're pretty tall."

"There's nothing here to stand on," said Leon looking around.

Then Eira spotted something, "Or," she nodded upward, "something to climb."

"No way, I'm not climbing a tree for you."

"Come on, it's not for me, it's for Harwin. Think of how lonely he must be in there."

"He's fine, I'm sure of it," Leon assured her.

"Look, it's our only option. We didn't come all this way for nothing," Eira pushed.

With a deep breath and a heavy sigh to follow, Leon walked over to the tree that was beside the barn and started to climb. He managed to do it rather quickly and efficiently, though.

"So, do you climb trees in your spare time?" she joked. "You did that really quickly."

"No, I just want to get this over with," he said making his way across the branch that was almost connecting the tree to the window. It bowed a bit under his weight, but it seemed strong enough to not actually break. When he made it to the end he reached for the window, pushed it open to its full extent and swung a leg over it until he was straddling the windowsill. Then he was out of sight. Eira wandered around to the barn doors to make sure there was still no one there and soon the door was opening from the other side. Leon opened it only enough for Eira to slip in.

"See, that wasn't so hard, now was it?" she smiled.

"Easy for you to say," he said picking a leaf out of his hair. "Anyway, let's get them and get out of here." They walked over to where Harwin and Eivissa's stalls were. When Harwin saw them he let out a little whinny and padded the ground with his hoof. "Shhh," said Leon rubbing Harwin's nose. They soon found the rest of the horses. Eira opened the stalls while Leon found their saddles and bridles. They tacked the horses faster than Eira thought was possible and they led them out the back door of the barn. They handed them off to Oren and Theo one by one, finally leaving Harwin last. Just as they were about to lead him through, they heard a voice.

"Hey."

Eira's and Leon's hearts stopped. They were sure they were caught, but the call came again a little too casual to be a guard. "Hey—over here." They turned to see where the voice was coming from, but all they could see were horse stalls. Some were empty and some had horses poking their heads out to see what was going on. They both stared down the long hallway of stalls and tried to narrow down where the voice was coming from. "Last stall," they heard the voice call. Finally, they reached the last stall and pulled the door open, only to find that it was no stall at all, but the entrance to a staircase. The voice grew louder as it continued to call to them. They looked at each other and mutually decided, without words, that they were going in.

Leon headed down first and Eira followed only a step behind. When they reached the bottom, all they could see were a few glowing lamps and a small bit of moonlight trailing in from a ground-level window above.

"What is this place?" Eira asked.

"It looks like a dungeon."

"Of course, he has his own personal dungeon. What's wrong with this guy?"

"Over here," the voice called again. When they finally reached the cell where the voice was coming from, they were greeted by a man sitting solemnly on his cell bed. "Thank goodness I heard you guys upstairs. I knew right away you weren't guards." He said walking to the bars to be face-to-face with Eira and Leon on the other side.

"Who are you?" asked Leon.

"My name is Neil. I'm just someone who doesn't believe in Kane's rule, so he put me in here."

"Why?" asked Eira. "It can't be just because you disagree with him."

"All anyone has to do is disagree with him and they end up in here for a bit. But, it is a bit more complex than that." Neil smiled and then sighed, "Pirates took my boy. I've been trying to find him ever since. Many times I've attempted to escape the city walls and go after him, but Kane's guards drag me back every time. He can't have anyone finding out the real reason my boy is a pirate now; Kane sold him to them."

"What? He can't do that!" Eira gasped.

"Unfortunately, he can, and he did. No one is going to go against him because he keeps this town thriving. What's one boy's life when the money he got from the pirates can contribute far more to this town than my family ever would? We're just farmers and the crops have not been great lately. My family was never meant to be farmers. Nothing really grows in the snow, but since the dragon came, times had to change. My family used to be the best woodcarvers in town, making wonderful sleighs and anything else you needed. But people don't have the money to spend on such extravagancies anymore."

"I'm so sorry about all of this," consoled Eira.

"Why? It's not your fault," replied Neil. Eira knew this was true, but she couldn't help but feel a bit responsible, although she couldn't quite explain why. "But when I heard the two of you talking upstairs, I knew it was you. My boy, Thomas, came back to us a few days ago and you're to thank for that."

"What? Thomas is your son? So he got home safely?" asked Eira.

"Yes. And all thanks to you, Your Majesty." Neil bowed slightly.

"Well, it was the least we could do. I'm glad you have him home."

"Do you think you guys can do one more thing for me and get me out of here?" asked Neil.

Leon and Eira looked at each other. "Alright, but we really can't waste any more time. We need to get to the mountains by sunrise," said Leon grabbing the keys from the hook by the door. He clicked the key in the lock and the door swung open.

"Thank you," smiled Neil. "I owe you two more than you could ever know. Not just for this." His sincerity hit Eira. If she still had any doubt in her mind, she knew that she was on the right path now.

They hurried up the stairs and back out the stable doors to find Theo and Oren still waiting with the horses.

"Who's he?" asked Theo.

"Don't worry about it," assured Leon. "He's on our side."

"Thank you again," Neil took Leon's hand in his. "I will be sure to do everything in my power to aid you. Whatever you need, don't hesitate to ask." Eira hugged him and they bid him farewell.

They met the others at the rear of the city. There was no wall bordering this side, for it was nestled against the forest that bordered the base of the mountains.

"Did you guys find the people's money?" Eira asked as Killian, Clea, and Boreas met up with them.

"Oh, yeah—and then some," said Killian. "This Kane guy sure is a greedy son-of-a-bitch. Man, if I had that much money—" Eira's facial expression cut him off. "Anyway, we left it in the city square just as you instructed, with a little note so they know who to thank," he winked.

"Good, now let's get out of this place."

Killian was standing beside Leon, leaning slightly against Harwin, smiling at him with a peculiar look on his face while Leon made sure Harwin's saddle was tight enough.

"What?" asked Leon as he brushed past Killian and made his way over to Harwin's bridle to check that too.

"Don't *what* me, you know what."

"Um, not really," Leon replied.

"Dude, come on. Have you told her yet?"

"What are you talking about?" Leon leaned in and lowered his voice a bit looking over to Eira to ensure she couldn't hear them.

"Oh, come on. Sure you guys are hooking up or whatever, but have you actually told her how you really feel?"

"Excuse me?"

"Well, we're about to head into those mountains and who knows what will happen. You may think she knows, but have you actually said those three little words?"

"Dude, this is not something we talk about," Leon made a motion with his hand between them as the words came out.

"Well, maybe we should." He put a hand on Leon's shoulder, "Tell her. Who knows how this dragon thing will turn out? My advice—do it now before it's too late." Leon let out a sigh of frustration, then Killian left him with some final words to urge his old friend in the right direction, "Trey would," he smiled.

Leon clenched his jaw and took a deep breath, using every fibre of his being not to punch Killian. Killian simply grabbed the reins of Eira's horse and started walking toward where she and the rest of the group were. Leon grabbed hold of Harwin's reins and did the same.

"What was that about?" asked Eira as the two got closer.

"Nothing. Just giving Leon advice about something. It's not important."

"Okay. Well, let's get going then." Eira took the reins from Killian and he helped her onto her horse.

The rest of the group mounted their horses also and headed off in the direction of the mountains. They had not been walking for long when Eira had something on her mind she wanted to ask.

"Alright, I know I probably should have asked this earlier but, what exactly is it that I am supposed to do?" she turned to Leon. "I know I am supposed to find the dragon's weakness, but how is that done?"

"Every dragon has something secret about them that if revealed, will weaken their armour. Each is different. Tales of old tell that sometimes it is a prized possession of the dragon's you have to steal, or it may be a guessing game. No one knows until they come face to face with the dragon itself." Well, that sounds easy enough—not! Eira was really beginning to love Talvia more than she ever thought she would, and the friends—family she had made. It would be a shame to die.

They had made it to the other side of the forest bordering the mountains when they heard something behind them. Leon turned around quickly and saw Kane's guards galloping toward them. There were six on horseback charging them. The thunderous beat of their horse's hooves echoed through the valley.

"Eira, get off now!" Leon yelled at her. She turned to see he was already standing on the ground beside her horse. "Now!" he yelled again, slightly startling her. She quickly dismounted Eivissa. "Get on Harwin and get out of here," he ordered. "Eivissa's fast, but you can't outrun them on her I'm afraid. I'll hold them off for as long as I can. Get to the mountains."

"What? I'm not going up there by myself!" she said now sitting atop Harwin.

"You have to."

"No, I'll stay and fight with you, and then we'll go up there together."

"You don't have a choice!" He stared at her with his eyes wide and she could see the desperation behind them and she knew the truth of what he had said. She didn't have a choice. She never had a choice. This was always going to be the outcome—just her and that dragon. She looked behind her to see Killian, Theo, and Clea already fighting against the guards that had caught up to them. Boreas was being chased by another through the forest. She looked down at Leon again and shook her head, tears beginning to form in the corners of her eyes. She kicked at Harwin's sides and headed toward the mountains while Leon charged the guards. She pushed Harwin faster and faster hoping that she would not be caught. One of Kane's guards was on her tail shortly, but the forest was dense and Harwin moved as if the trees bowed and waned to him, avoiding them like they weren't even there. When she was in the safety of the mountains she rode to a small cliff overlooking the forest below. She could see her friends in the clutches of Kane's guards, being led back through the fields and into the city. It was just her now—and whatever beast lay within these mountains.

The people of Glasera started to awake that morning. Some were already out starting their work for the day, but most were still enjoying their slumber until something awoke them.

"Come outside! Come outside!" someone was calling in the streets. "Everyone, wake up!"

People opened their windows and looked out at a boy running through the streets making quite a racket.

"Boy! Be quiet!" yelled a woman from her window. "Don't you know what hour it is?"

"You have to come see this," replied the boy. "It's all here, it's all back!"

One by one, the people emerged from their houses and followed the boy to the centre of town. Their eyes widened at the sight of the baskets sitting in front of the fountain.

"There's more too. A trail leading right to all of our baskets," said the boy.

"What is going on out there?" called Kane as he made his way over to his window overlooking the square. When his eyes gazed upon the sight of his gold being displayed for all to see he called his guards, "Guard! Guard!" A man rushed into his room and over to the window. "What is the meaning of this? Where did that gold come from?"

"I'm—I'm not sure," replied the guard.

Another guard rushed into his room, "Kane! We have just received word that, *your guests*, have escaped. Neil too."

"Go find them!" ordered Kane. "I will deal with the people." He made his way into the square, "My people," he called with open arms, "this truly is a wondrous morning. The dragon has returned our riches."

"No, he hasn't," called the boy. "I followed the trail and it led to all of our baskets being hidden in a secret cave."

"You must be mistaken, boy. I assure you all that gold went to the dragon," argued Kane.

One of the townspeople spoke up, "The rumours were right. You were lying to us and keeping the gold for yourself."

"How preposterous!" defended Kane. "I did no such thing!"

"Then what's that note about?" asked the boy pointing to a small piece of paper resting on one of the baskets. Kane turned around and looked at the basket: *You seemed to have misplaced this,* read the note and it was signed: *The Future Queen.*

"You pathetic fool," Kane said to the boy, grabbing his arm and pulling him close.

"I'd let go of him if I were you," said Oren standing behind him with Neil and Thomas at his side. "You foul creature. These people suffer in poverty while you sit on a throne of riches. What right do you have to call yourself a ruler over these people? What right do you have to tell them lies?"

"What right do I have? What right do you have to come to my city and spin my words against them? What right does that so-called queen have to come in here and change all the rules?" retorted Kane.

"She has the only right," smiled Oren. At that moment, the guards Kane sent to find Leon, Eira, and the rest of them marched back into the square dragging everyone except Eira along with them.

"What's going on here?" Leon asked Oren as the guards stopped beside Kane.

"He's a traitor!" yelled one of the townspeople.

"And a liar!" called out another.

"Lock him up!" another shouted. Kane's guards looked around and realized what had happened. They were no match for the entire town coming for them and realized that not even Kane could save them now. They were better off to side with their people.

"Unhand me!" called Kane to the guard who promptly cuffed him. "What is the meaning of this? I am your leader. You cannot do this!"

"Ahem," coughed Leon holding his cuffs up to one of the guards.

"Where's Eira?" asked Oren when the commotion was over.

"In the mountains by now," replied Leon. "She got away with Harwin."

"What? I can't believe you left my sister to face a dragon by herself!"

"She'll be fine." He was more reassuring himself at this point. He knew she was trained well, and more than capable, but the aching in his heart was not making his decision to leave any better.

"I knew I should have stopped her from going. I thought at least with you there she might be okay, but now. How could you do that?"

"How could I?" snapped Leon. "I stayed back to fight Kane's guards who came after us. I gave her her only chance to not be dragged back here. You don't seriously think I would leave her in any real danger? That dragon is not going to harm her."

"You don't know that! If I were that dragon, I wouldn't hesitate to kill her while I had the chance."

"That's not going to happen!" retorted Leon.

"How do you know?"

"Because it told me." Leon took a breath, "I've been here before. I've been up that mountain and into that cave to try to find some way to spare your sister from this fate of hers. That dragon is not interested in a fight. It abides by its own laws and is bound to let her have a chance to defeat it before any fire will rain down. I tried—I tried to solve the riddle for her, but I couldn't do it. I've played the words of it over and over in my head for months and I can't solve it. It is meant for her and only her. "

Theo and Killian came up behind Leon and each placed a hand on one of his shoulders, "What are you going to do now?" asked Theo.

"I'm going to go find her. She couldn't have made it that far up the mountain. The rest of you should get ready for when that dragon comes down from the mountain," replied Leon. "We'll need all the help we can get."

There was a joyous celebration in the streets and bars that day, for Kane had met his downfall. Killian, Clea, Boreas, and Theo needed to help the people prepare for the battle they were facing and they knew that battle was coming sooner rather than later. The distance between the city and the Hoarfrost Mountains was not far—especially for a dragon to fly.

\*\*\*\*

There were many mountains that made up the collection named the Hoarfrost Mountains and Eira had no idea if she was even on the right path up them. She hoped that Harwin had some idea of where they were going, but he seemed to just be heading in an upward direction, which she supposed was a start. It was getting colder by the day and the dragon had too felt it. Harwin led Eira slowly up the side of the dense tree-covered mountain. There was a narrow path just wide enough for someone on horseback that could be followed. They continued their ascension for a couple of hours until it was clear that they needed a rest. Eira found a suitable spot to stretch her legs and let Harwin rest his. In the late morning light, the sun was starting to get into position above her head. This day was the coldest she had encountered by far. Eira made a small fire after finding some matches in the bags Leon had packed. She wished he was there with her—if only for the fact that he was far better at making fires than she was. She hoped he and the others were alright, but she knew she had to keep going. Thinking that way was not going to help the situation.

Eira looked over and noticed frost on the grass beneath her feet. She could not help but imagine how beautiful the mountains must look all snow covered with the sharp green of the fir trees contrasting the white canvas. She could not wait to see Talvia in its former glory. She grabbed the blanket tied to the back of Harwin's saddle and wrapped herself in it. Thinking of what Talvia would be when all of this was over was one of the only things getting her through what she was facing.

Harwin walked slowly over to her and gave her a nudge indicating he was ready to keep going. She got to her feet and placed his saddle on his back again and secured it, then kicked out the fire and mounted the unicorn's back. She had no idea how long it would take to get to the dragon's cave or if she would even be able to find it. Then again, she didn't know if Leon would have been able to find it either. She rifled through the saddlebags looking for some water when she came across a map. She pulled it out and looked over it. It was of Talvia and the Hoarfrost Mountains. There was a route directly to the dragon's cave marked out. The only problem was, she had no idea where she was on the map.

"Great," she said to Harwin, "I have a map and no idea how to read it. I don't suppose you know where we are on this mountain?"

Harwin bounced his head up and down as if to respond, *yes*. She smiled at this and hoped he was right.

For parts of the journey up the mountainside, Eira gave Harwin a rest and walked along beside him. It was difficult work for a horse to walk so much more vertically than they were used to, and all the while carrying packs and a person in his saddle. They were walking slowly when Harwin's ears started to twitch in the direction of something. A rustling came from the distance and the two looked into the trees. They could see grass and bushes moving, along with the occasional tree branch high in the canopy. Whatever was moving toward them was leaping from ground to treetop. Eira stood there as the noise grew louder and the surrounding greenery continued to be disturbed.

From the bush directly in front of her, appeared a small white ermine. He stopped in his tracks as if not expecting to run into any human, or unicorn for that matter. The ermine looked at her and Harwin, wide-eyed and curious.

"Awe, you're cute!" exclaimed Eira.

"Well, thank you," blushed the weasel.

"Oh...um...you're welcome," Eira was stunned. As most would be. She was not expecting the little animal to respond.

The ermine and Eira continued to stare at each other in silence. Finally, the ermine broke the silence, "Can I help you?" he asked.

Harwin looked a little taken aback and huffed at the thought of asking a rodent for directions, but Eira cheerfully responded, "Actually, maybe you can. We are trying to find our way to the path that leads to the dragon's cave. Do you know where that is?"

"Of course. Follow me," and off he ran.

Eira followed with gratitude but Harwin took a moment to get started. She had to tug at the reins a couple of times to convince him to follow. He still didn't like the idea of taking directions from anyone, let alone a small critter. The little ermine jumped up into a nearby tree and as Harwin walked past, he leaped landing on Harwin's shoulders and was now eye level with Eira.

"My name is Tuque, by the way. What's yours?"

"I'm Eira, and this is Harwin. It is very nice to meet you, Tuque."

"The pleasure is all mine," Tuque responded with a little bow.

They had only been walking for about half an hour when Eira got the feeling they were not going in the direction they should be.

"Are you sure you know where we are going? There are probably lots of paths that lead up the mountain, not necessarily leading to the dragon's cave," Eira asked. Tuque did not answer. He simply pointed to the side of the path and Eira looked in the direction of his paw. There was a small road marker in the shape of an arrow that read:

*Dragon's Cave,* pointing in the direction they were headed. "Oh," Eira exclaimed, "well that's convenient."

"Well, there you go," said Tuque.

"Thank you so much," replied Eira as she pulled Harwin to a halt.

"Why are you going up the mountain anyway?" questioned Tuque.

"Well, I'm going to defeat the dragon," replied Eira. The little ermine stared at her a moment and then burst out laughing and rolled around on Harwin's back. "Why is this so funny to you?" she asked Tuque with a smile.

"Well, it's just you don't look much like a dragon slayer."

"Well, maybe I should introduce myself properly. I'm Eira, the future Queen of Talvia. The one who is supposed to free these lands from the dragon's clutches."

The ermine silenced himself immediately after hearing these words, "Your Majesty," he bowed. "I am sorry, I did not know."

"It's alright, and thank you again for helping us."

"You're very welcome. Good luck with the dragon. She's not as bad as everyone says," he called leaping from Harwin's back and scurrying back into the woods.

*She?*


The sun was hitting its highest point in the sky and in no time they had reached their final ascent up to the dragon's cave. Eira had to take this last part by herself for Harwin could not make it through the narrow path and dense forest. Harwin waited below as Eira made her way through the boulders and into the forest. Luckily for her, there were still small markings leading the way to the dragon's cave, otherwise she would have surely been lost.

Eira looked upon the mouth of the dragon's home. It was dark inside and there was no sound, not even of the dragon's breath, coming from inside. She stood there, staring into the darkness, wishing she was not alone. She was frozen in place and as hard as she tried, it was as though she could not lift her feet from the rocky ground and make that first step into the cave.

"Okay, just be cool," she said to herself. "Cool— cool, cool, cool. I can do this!" she said jumping on the spot and shaking her hands in an effort to psych herself up. She finally stood still and swallowed the lump in her throat. Then, taking a deep breath, she turned toward the cave and took her first few steps inside. However, her confidence was short-lived, and just as quickly as she had ventured in, she turned and walked right out again, *Nope, can't do it.*

She turned to face the cave one more time and took another breath. The trees and the mountain itself were her only witnesses as no one was there to watch as the future Queen of Talvia vanished out of sight into the darkness of the cave.

# 18

The dragon's cave was rather tight. Eira slithered through the damp darkness, her back and front constantly brushing against hard cold stone. *How could a dragon possibly get in here?* When she finally made it farther into where the narrow passageway began to widen, she could start to see the flickering of light and as she made her way farther and farther in, the light grew until she could see every detail of the cave around her. The light was coming from overhead when she reached a dead end in the cave. That can't be right? There was daylight streaming in through the top and the smell of fresh air was trickling through. She had no choice but to climb. Placing her hands on the cold rock, she found a footing and began her ascent. It was not an easy climb. She stumbled and her feet slipped a couple of times, but eventually, she found her rhythm and was climbing the ten-foot stone mound in front of her.

When she finally reached the top, the cave let out into a massive hidden valley. The lake in the middle was glistening in the midday sun and the vegetation around was blooming with life. It was not at all what Eira had expected to see. For one: she had thought the dragon lived in a cave, and secondly, she didn't think anything grew so abundantly in Talvia, especially high up in the mountains. How was it that this valley looked as if it was the picture of summer? The heat overtook her. It was like she had walked into an oven. Her face was blasted with the humidity of the valley only causing more confusion in her mind. She took note of her surroundings. There was no dragon to be seen—no treasure either. None. The valley was completely empty. This dragon had never taken a single coin or jewel from anyone. Unless it was hidden somewhere else? Eira knew deep down that was not the case. Kane had used the dragon as an excuse to get rich—that was all.

Eira assessed her footing and was trying to find the best way down into the valley when she heard the unmistakable sound of rocks tumbling above her head. She quickly jumped back into the opening of the cave and watched as a few rocks no bigger than her fist and then some larger boulders tumbled down past the entrance and continued on into the valley below. She had a strange feeling, but against her better judgement, she peeked her head out of the cave and looked upward.

There he was. The sheer size of this monolithic beast was overwhelming. The dragon made its way atop the sheer rock face above the cave where Eira lay hidden. Or at least, she thought she was hidden.

"I can smell you, you know," bellowed a mighty voice. "I can sense your presence." Eira's eyes widened as she backed into the cave. She could hear the rocks falling all around her again as the dragon continued moving on the cliff face. He was stalking her. "So, you are the one who has come to try to defeat me?" The dragon shook the valley with his bellowing voice. When he began to speak, Eira pressed her back against the side of the cave wall and cupped her ears with her hands. The echoing of the dragon's voice in the cave was deafening. "No one has ever been able to defeat me, and many have tried. Come into the light so I can see the face of my next victim," continued the dragon slithering its way closer and closer to the cave.

Eira's heart was pounding. She was sure she was going to pass out from fear. But something stopped the fear from taking over and told her to get a grip. She moved her hands from her head and tightened her hands into fists as if to tell herself, *You've got this. You've trained for this. It was always your destiny and you can't let your fear win.* Eira stepped out onto the cave ledge. She held her breath, listening and looking for the dragon, but it was gone. Not a good sign.

The thunderous sound of wings beating nearly pushed her to the ground. The stories did not do the creature justice for he was a dragon like none other—not that Eira had many firsthand experiences with dragons. His tail hung low, almost touching the valley below and his wings blocked out the mountains behind him. His crimson scales shone with iridescent gold in the sunlight as the impressive beast flew down overhead, soaring into the valley. He had spikes all the way down from head to tail, embossing his body like knives. The dragon raised its head toward the cave where Eira waited when it reached the bottom of the valley. She would have to move closer to it if it had any hope of hearing her.

"What makes you think you can defeat me?" The dragon shook the rock face again with his bellowing voice as Eira slid down the side carefully. The dragon prowled closer to Eira.

"Well maybe it's just a feeling I have, but I think I'll give it a try," Eira called out as she slipped down the mountain rather impressively.

"You are the one I have been waiting for. I can smell the royal blood that runs through your veins. Tell me, heir of Talvia, what makes you think you will finally be the one to defeat me?" Well maybe the fact that there was a prophecy about her? The dragon knew of the prophecy and this girl standing before him. Of course, he knew. And he knew that this girl could very well be his undoing.

"I don't know, but I'm willing to give it a try." Eira made her way to an outcropping of stone that jutted over the valley. She stumbled as her feet slid to the flat earth and she ran a couple of steps to the edge of the ledge, only to be blown backward by the dragon as his mighty head became eye level with hers. She lurched and stumbled back a few steps.

"Very well," he began again. "I am bound by the laws of my kind to let you have a try at my riddle." Then to regain his authority over her he said in a placid voice, "I suppose I can humour you for a bit. I have travelled to many lands and lived for hundreds of years. I have seen many things, but none have ever bested me." The dragon circled and tucked his mighty wings in beside him, preparing to settle himself down for a game.

The dragon began to speak his riddle, "'X', 'I', 'X' is where we start, another 'V' and we must end. I reside by sulphur springs, to embrace what the healing water brings.

Snakes you'll often find with me, a vision to cure I can see. I boiled the sky with the notion in my mind, to take a home you will never reclaim. Unless, of course, you should guess my name."

Eira stood in wonder. She looked at the dragon and paused for a moment pondering the riddle in her mind. Pacing back and forth she had no notion of where to start. Minutes passed and the dragon waited patiently. Dragons love to play games when they know they will win, and this dragon was committed to giving Eira as much time as she needed until he won.

****

Leon raced back toward the city centre. The horse's hooves crashed against the pavement as it made its way to where the others would be. He could see Theo, Killian, and Neil outside of the city's main building—the former offices of Kane.

"What is it?" asked Killian when he saw Leon racing back toward them. He dismounted his horse and ran over to the group. "I thought you were going after Eira?"

"Change of plans," huffed Leon as if he was the one who had just run through the fields and the city, not the horse. "We have a problem."

"What sort of problem?" asked Killian.

"There's an army marching through the fields toward us, and they certainly don't look like they come in peace."

"Are there any other towns in the mountains? Any that would want to wage war on Glasera?" Theo asked Neil.

"Innis," answered Neil. "But why would they be waging war on us?"

"I don't know, but they are coming. They are a few hours out of town still. But I saw them when I was headed up the mountain, so I made the decision to turn around," said Leon.

"Well, we will meet them at the gates and try to reason with them," said Killian.


Florian flanked by Horace and backed by an army of hundreds was met at the entrance of the city.

"Why have you brought your army here?" asked Neil.

"Where is Kane? I only deal with him," responded Florian.

"Where he should be—in his own dungeon," responded Theo. "His reign of terror is over."

"Well, that simply doesn't work for me. You have one hour to reinstate him as ruler of this city or my armies will invade."

"You can't be serious?" added Neil.

"We have a mutually beneficial relationship going on and we don't need you to ruin our way of life! If Kane and that dragon are gone, it won't end well for this city."

"That's not up to you! Talvia needs to be restored to a land of winter, and Kane and that dragon need to go!" argued Leon.

"Well, I guess it is settled then. One hour, or we will see you on the battlefield. And you better hope that little princess doesn't throw a dragon into the mix. I can only imagine what battling dragon fire and my armies will do to this place." Florian turned his horse to head back to his army where they were preparing to wait for one hour and one hour only until they would invade.

"Why don't you stop him?" asked Neil as the gates closed cutting off his last glimpse of the army.

"What are we going to do? Imprison the head of their army? Either way, we're going to have them as our enemy," said Leon. "How is this city's army? Do we have soldiers to fight?"

"Not many. There hasn't been a war here in...ever, I think," answered Neil.

"Well, we have an hour to gather any capable and willing to fight."


Word had spread about the oncoming battle. The city of Glasera was readying itself for a fight against the army of Innis. Killian, Boreas, and Theo were signing up anyone willing to fight. There weren't many, but some were better than none. Killian, Theo, and Leon were valiant soldiers, but the three of them were no match against hundreds. While the Innis army was small, they knew that Glasera's was basically nonexistent.

"What's going on?" asked Oren as he, Bianca, and Clea met the guys outside of Kane's old office.

"Kane made some shady bargains is all, and now we have to deal with it," informed Killian.

"There's an army waiting at our doorstep if we don't reinstate Kane as ruler in one hour. Obviously, we're not going to do that, so we're going to have to fight, but few are willing to sign their lives away—I don't blame them," said Leon. He then turned to Killian and Boreas, "Raid the city's armoury and get every weapon in this place."

*On it*, Killian's hand gesture indicated.

"What can we do to help?" Bianca asked.

"Get the children and the ones not wanting to fight out of the city. If we can drain it and even the playing field a bit, we may stand a chance."

"And what if that guy is right?" asked Theo. "What if Eira does piss off that reptile and it heads for us looking for some outlet for its rage?"

"That's what I'm banking on," replied Leon. Theo's brows rose. "If we can get that dragon to divert its attention to Innis's army, we can wipe them out with one blow."

"That's a big, *if*?"

"Yeah, but it's the only plan I've got."

As Leon led the group that had recently signed up for battle to where others were getting a briefing, and seriously—brief, about swords and fighting from Killian, Boreas, and now Clea, he noticed Oren looked a little perplexed.

"Hey, are you alright?" he asked in a brotherly manner.

"No," he looked at Leon, "no, I'm not. All of this...everything that's happening. I didn't think I would feel this way. My sister is somewhere up a mountain with a dragon right now and I'm just expected to give my attention to this city down here?"

"Look, you think I'm not going crazy in my mind thinking about what's going on in that mountain? I'm only putting my focus into this because if I don't—I don't know what I'd do. But she's been trained for this. I told you, I tried to find a way out of the prophecy but—"

"There is no prophecy!" yelled Oren. The surrounding crowd's noise was enough to drown out his yelling and not draw any attention to himself. "Can't you see that? I left because all I heard growing up was that my sister was going to return and save us all. It's too much pressure to put on one person. You can't expect her to just be a saviour because some ancient piece of paper told you so. She's a twenty-one-year-old girl, and you expect her to fight a dragon."

"Oren, none of this is your fault. You couldn't have protected her even if you tried—I would know. We're all here to fight and we're ready to. Whether the prophecy is true or not, we all knew that this day would eventually come and she was raised to be ready for it. No one was going to live under the dragon's rule forever. It was going to go down one way or another. No matter what happened in the past, this is what is happening now and all we can do is be ready for whatever comes. If you're not up for that, you can go with the children and wait it out with them." Leon didn't mean that as an insult, he was simply giving him the option to not fight. Oren was trained growing up, just as Eira was, but he shouldn't have to fight in a war he doesn't believe in.

"I can't watch another member of my family die over some stupid prophecy." He turned to walk away but the people packed into every corner and crevice of the square made it difficult for a quick getaway. He pushed his way through the crowd with Bianca trying her best to follow his movements, having caught the tail end of his and Leon's conversation, calling after him to wait but it was no use. He finally disappeared behind some large men walking toward her and Bianca could no longer see the familiar movements of his figure as he walked away from her.

A hand touched her shoulder, "He'll be okay," reassured Clea. "Just give him time."

"We don't have time. We have an hour, right? Less than that now."

Clea turned to see Boreas's large figure in front of her. The crowd was beginning to dissipate. Everyone moved in different directions like herds of cattle being shuffled into various lines based on what their plan was for the next hour: fight, or get out of here.

"We have to keep training these people as best we can," said Boreas. Clea nodded and gave her sister a small side hug and headed back to training.

Workers were starting on the city walls, reinforcing them against Florian's battering rams. The wall was more meant as a deterrent—it wasn't as sturdy as it was foreboding. Clea was helping a young boy with his sword fighting, teaching him proper stance and balance to ensure a win when someone caught her eye.

"That's not the stance I taught you," he said walking over to Clea.

"Well, I've made some improvements," she smiled.

He twirled his sword in his hand and took a stance against Clea, "Care to show me?" Their swords clanged together. "I heard you were back, but I had to come see it for myself. Missed me that much?" he grinned.

"Don't flatter yourself. I came to help the heir to the throne."

He squinted as if to say, *you're going to have to explain more about that after we're done.*

"And I stayed because these people never asked for what is coming, and they don't have enough resources to win this battle. Whether I like it or not, this is my home and maybe it's time I make my peace with that."

"Good for you."

"That doesn't mean I'm staying after all of this though. As soon as this is over, I'm leaving again. I'm just here to lend a hand as long as they need it."

"Well, I guess that's better than just deserting them."

Boreas and Theo soon made their way over to where Clea and the man were finishing up their battle.

"Nice one, Clea," Theo called as she knocked him to the ground and his sword went bouncing out of his hand. Clea reached a hand out and he climbed to his feet.

"You still have it—just like the first time we met," he smiled.

"Who's this?" asked Theo to Clea when the four were standing beside one another.

"This is Nevin," responded Clea. "He's not from around here originally, but he's lived here for the past few years."

"Nice to meet you," said Theo. "It's good to have another man who knows what he's doing on our side."

"Except he just got beat by a girl," added Killian who suddenly appeared beside them.

"Well, not many can beat this one," said Nevin. "My pride can handle being beaten by her."

"So, Nevin, you're going to fight with us?" asked Boreas. He nodded in reply.

"So where are you from?" asked Theo.

"Kesa originally, but I haven't lived there in years. I make my way around, never staying in one place too long."

"You know, it's funny," began Theo, "you have the same name as the prince—kind of look like him too. I heard he's dead though."

"Is he now?" he looked to Clea. "So that's what they're saying nowadays. I guess that's not so bad, easier to fly under the radar that way. I suppose it could be worse, I could be known as a fugitive or something." Nevin glanced over the expressions of shock on the men's faces, especially Killian whose mouth was almost hitting the ground. Nevin smiled at them and shrugged his shoulders.

Suddenly Killian dropped to his knee, "Your Majesty," he stated as he bowed before him.

"Get up," forced Clea with a kick to Killian's side. He stood and cleared his throat, adjusting his shirt and brushing off the dirt from the ground.

"Well then," Killian started, "now that that's sorted, we should probably get back to work." He nodded his head to Nevin and turned, leaning into Clea, "I'm going to need more of *this* story later."

He brushed past Oren who was sauntering over to where Clea and the rest stood. Leon was suddenly behind him also, "I see you decided to stay," said Leon joining the group.

"Yeah, I couldn't just leave and let you screw up my sister's life too much."

"You're unbelievable you know that? You should have just stayed away."

"Okay guys, enough," interjected Clea. "Look, Leon cares more about Eira than any of us. He would never do anything to harm her. And Oren, you may be her brother, but so far Leon has spent more time with her than you have her entire life. Put all of this aside and focus on what we're here for. Arguing isn't going to help Eira."

"Alright fine," said Oren turning to Leon. "You have done a pretty good job taking care of her up until now. I'm here to help, so what do you need?"

"Who's this?" asked Leon looking at Nevin.

"Oh, Prince of Kesa," Theo informed casually.

"What? What the hell is he doing here? Also, I thought he was dead."

"I can hear you guys," interrupted Nevin. "Also...you want my help or not?"

They both shrugged. It didn't matter why Nevin was here, his help was needed. "Your father's going to kill you if he finds out you helped Talvia," said Leon.

Nevin shrugged, "I'm already dead to him."

The group took over the Glasera city hall and made their plans for the attack there. The great hall was equipped with a table and maps of the immediate surroundings of the city.

"The Innis army will start breaking down those walls in less than thirty minutes, but the full force of Florian's army is at the back of the city. The forest is dense enough there that if we can keep them in it, we might be able to sneak up on them with a few archers strategically placed. If we can push the battle into the foothills of the mountains we can hopefully keep it away from the city."

"And what about the dragon?" asked Killian.

"The dragon is going to be more difficult. Assuming that Eira has discovered his secret and weakened his armour, all we need is a few clear shots at him and he'll fall. If she hasn't weakened his armour—that's another story entirely," added Leon.

"Then we're just holding off dragon fire until he tires and returns to the mountains," added Clea.

"Right," said Nevin, "which is a lot more difficult." He pulled out another map, this one of the city itself. "We're going to need water cannons and a lot of them."

"We can prepare those," said Killian as he gestured to himself, Theo, and Boreas.

"Good. We'll have to place as many as we can on the outer walls of the city, and some on top of the highest buildings within the city. We can tap into the main water supply and feed the cannons that way."

Theo, Killian, Boreas, and Leon headed out of the hall to ready the cannons, leaving Nevin and Clea behind.

"Do you think this plan is really going to work?" asked Clea.

"I don't know. But, I hope so," Nevin answered still hunched over the table looking at the various maps. He looked up at Clea and moved toward her taking her hands in his. "I hope this princess of yours is smart enough to pull one over on that dragon. I hope that she will live to know Talvia like it used to be. I hope we'll all live to see the snow return. I hope I'll live to see you again." He pulled her close and kissed her the way he used to. "No one in the other countries will admit it, and especially my father, but this world is dying without Talvia."


"Do you trust this guy?" asked Boreas when he, Leon, Killian, and Theo were standing on the steps outside.

"Yeah, why shouldn't we?" responded Theo. "He is the Prince of Kesa, after all."

"That's just it," continued Boreas. "None of you think it's strange that this character just suddenly shows up out of the blue? He's the prince, yet he deserted his duties and family to wander around the land. Up until today, all of you thought he was dead. Why is he suddenly fighting for *Talvia* now?"

"Kesa isn't exactly on good terms with us," added Killian.

"You mean *us*, or Talvia," Leon chuckled.

"Both, I guess."

"I don't know, but if you ask me, I'm glad he's here," said Leon.

The children and anyone unfit or unwilling to fight were led underneath the city and were to remain there until word was sent that it was safe to return to above ground. For years they had lived in the shadow of the great beast, giving up their riches to satisfy his thirst for gold and the time had come to give in no longer. The citizens of this city in the foothills were of a different breed—brave and steadfast toward their goal of reclaiming their earnings and home for their own, and giving into Kane's lust for treasure no more.

# 19

In the valley of the dragon, Eira continued to talk to herself trying to work out the riddle and the dragon continued to scoff at her attempts to decipher his clues.

"You dimwitted royal. You insolent child. You cannot beat me at my own game. No one with think less of you if you just give up now. Save yourself the humiliation you pompous princess and run back to your castle."

"Okay, I get it," sneered Eira. Time went on and at one point she simply called out every name she could think to suit a dragon, "Dudley? Mushu?" A clever grin grew on her face, "Smaug?"

But each time the dragon yelled out, "Wrong!"

He was gaining more and more pleasure with each of Eira's incorrect guesses. Finally, Eira attempted again from the beginning and talking mostly to herself she began,

"Okay, 'X', 'I', 'X'. What could that mean?" She tried sounding out what that combination of letters might produce, but no luck. She could not think of any names that would start with the phonics she was producing. She started again, "Okay, maybe it's not a sound, maybe a number? Roman numerals!" she shouted looking at the dragon. The expression on his face indicated she may be on the right track. "Who uses Roman numerals anymore? Also, how does a dragon know about them and the alphabet from— you know what, never mind. If I poke too many holes in this, it'll ruin it. Okay, think. 'X' is ten, and 'I' is one." Eira tried adding the digits and came out with, "Twenty-one!" she called out with joy. The dragon laughed again leading Eira to the conclusion she was yet again wrong. "Okay, maybe not twenty-one. 'X' is still ten, but maybe the next is 'I X'. What is 'I X'? One and ten, ten minus one is nine. 'I X' is nine so 'X I X' is nineteen!" She went through the alphabet in her head and came up with the nineteenth letter to be, "S!" she shouted out with confidence. The dragon was taken aback as if she was beginning to solve the riddle. "Your name starts with an 'S', doesn't it?" Eira asked in a boastful tone very pleased with herself.

"Maybe so, heir. But you will still never solve the rest of the riddle," said the dragon. The dragon's annoyance with Eira was increasing monumentally at the fact that she was getting closer and closer to solving his riddle. It was time for him to switch the attention off of him and onto her. "Let's talk more about secrets," started the dragon. "It is hardly fair that you are revealing my secret, yet I know none of yours."

Dragons are very ancient and magical beings. They can feed off of a person's deepest emotions and feelings to distract from the task at hand. Dragons work underhandedly; they have no remorse or empathy for tormenting their victims into submission. They will draw out a person's deepest secrets to toy with their mind.

The dragon continued, "There is something that tickles in the back of your mind, isn't there? Oh yes, something indeed. Perhaps, it's a...boy? That prince who journeyed with you?"

"How do you know about him?" queried Eira. "And, he's not actually a prince," she added.

"I can smell him on you. You too are close. Very close. He may not be a real prince, but the feelings you possess for him certainly are. And he certainly shares those feelings."

"How do you know that?"

"He didn't tell you? He paid me a little visit a few months ago. Trying to make a new bargain with me to spare your life—assuming of course, that I wouldn't. We'll see about that though. If I deem you worthy of living or not."

*What? Leon had been here and faced the dragon. Why didn't he tell me?*

"Oh, you're upset now. I can see it on your face. Your precious man hasn't been truthful with you," the dragon clicked through his teeth.

The dragon could see he was getting through to her—through to her deepest feelings and secrets. Suddenly the dragon puffed a ring of fire around her and instinctively she crouched for cover. Once realizing she was not on fire, she slowly stood to look at her surroundings. The flames danced with images of her and Leon, hypnotically terrorizing her mind. The dragon was attempting to lure Eira into submission and cause her to lose focus on the riddle. Eira was drawn into the images and as she reached out a hand to the flaming image of Leon standing before her, the fire went out. The dragon sneered with pleasure as emotion filled Eira's eyes.

"Oh, that is not all though, I suspect. There are more secrets you are hiding, yes? The lost princess returns to an empty home. No family there to greet you." Another ring of fire grew around Eira with the images of her parents and herself as a baby and a toddler: taking her first steps and laughing, meeting her baby brother. As the fiery scene unfolded, the dragon continued to speak, "Your parents gave up on you. They could not even hold on long enough to see this day, to fight with you. That must torture you every day, the knowledge that your parents did not love you enough to hold on to the hope they would see this world restored by your hand."

"That's not true!" Eira called out.

"Isn't it though? And what about your brother? The recently discovered prince who didn't care enough to remain in his home long enough to see his sister return. He abandoned you and your cause." The fire continued to play out scenes of Oren and Leon playing together as children. A joyful occasion she never had the chance to take part in.

With that, the fire went out again. Eira was brought to her knees, her eyes filling with tears, "No," she said in a calm voice. She took to her feet and slowly raised her head to the dragon, "No, my parents were clinging to the hope that I would survive and bring peace to this land again— and destroy you. They had the most hope in the world, and you cannot make me submit that easily." She stood before the dragon with pride in her eyes and the dragon knew at once there was no emotion buried deep within her heart that he could feed off of anymore.

Eira continued thinking of the riddle. The next bit was difficult as well and she repeated the riddle aloud,

"'I reside by sulphur springs'," Eira paused and thought a moment then continued talking to herself every once and a while blurting out ideas loud enough for the dragon to hear and judge her place in solving his riddle. "Sulphur springs? Like hot springs? But what about the 'V'? The first was Roman numerals, so maybe 'V' is actually five? We start at nineteen and end with five. The fifth letter of the alphabet is, 'E', so maybe your name ends with 'E'? No, you said, *'Another five and we must end'*. Another five is twenty-four, that letter would be 'X'. Ugh, I could really use Google right now." Then Eira turned to the dragon who continued to mock her attempts and declared, "This is impossible." Frustrated and running out of time, she sat on a rock and thought out loud again, "'Another 'V' and we must end'," reciting the riddle. "Maybe, start with nineteen and then five more letters?"

She smiled deviously and looked up at the dragon, "Your name has six letters, doesn't it?" The dragon let out a loud roar and a snort of fire. Eira ran for cover behind a boulder. The dragon was pacing around the valley frustrated that Eira had got that far. He decided she was getting too close to the answer and took to the skies, sending a blaze of fire into the atmosphere. Eira wondered if it could be seen from Glasera, like a volcano erupting over the mountain. He calmed himself and landed in the valley again.

Eira sat down, "You know, it's already so damn hot in here, you didn't have to add to it." The dragon scoffed at her. "Why *is* it so hot?"

"I think you know the answer to that, princess."

Eira rolled her eyes, "Well, yes, but this valley is hotter than outside the mountain. Like there's some sort of magic here."

"There is. My magic was just enough to create this valley after I destroyed your precious snow."

Eira watched the dragon staring at her for a while. "So why did you come here anyway? Why did you choose Talvia?" she asked. Did it matter why he chose to destroy this land? Would the answer change anything?

"No one has ever asked for my story before. Why do you want to know?"

"Why not?"

\*\*\*\*

An unexpected sight was embracing the people of Glasera. The Wintren-elves had emerged from the protection of the Valley of the Ethereal and were ready to fight. They were ready to fulfill their pledge to remain allies of the Queen of Talvia. If this was it, they may as well fight to the end. Their magic was weakening and they were going to go down fighting with the heir of Talvia and her people rather than sitting in hiding. Lord Evian led his troops to the city walls.

"There's someone at the gates," Neil said to Leon.

"What? It hasn't been an hour yet. We still have more time."

"It's not Florian."

Soon after the Wintren-elves had arrived, some of the fairies came to lend aid to Talvia as well. Not all of the fairies had come, but Alvara was there along with Olwen and some of the other warriors of their kin. Fairies were not known to fight battles but the last of their species would soon be wiped out if the snow did not return. They may not fight battles, but that is not because they cannot. It is for the simple reason that no one dares scorn a fairy.

****

Eira sat on the ledge above where the dragon was lounging in the valley. "Alright, princess, I'll give you my story," the dragon began. "Dragons don't normally leave our country, and if we do, it is only out of dire need to do so. Long ago, your ancestors and those from the other countries made their way into my country. We made each other our allies and the leaders of the armies were given a dragon scale as a token of friendship and peace between our lands. A dragon scale is not something someone would ever just come across. It has to be given and there is no substance harder in this world. The only thing that can scratch or pierce it is a dragon scale itself. My kind thought that was that—that the time of hunting dragons and war was over. But we were wrong. Your kings took those scales and forged them into blades, then returned and ransacked my country, killing every dragon in their wake. They turned their backs on our alliance and double-crossed us. They came in the night and slaughtered every dragon they could. I was the last of my kind, so I fled."

Eira had noticed that the dragon would every so often glance toward a pile of rocks behind him. She didn't think much of it until this time, when the sun hit them at the right angle and a glint of light bounced off of one. *Weird.*

Rocks don't normally reflect the sun. Eira fixed her gaze on it and upon closer inspection, to her shock, there sitting right in the middle was an egg.

"Tuque was right. You are a girl. And you just needed a safe place to protect your baby."

"Very clever, little princess," the dragon called. "But your ancestors stole my land from me, so I did the same to them. Dragon eggs take a hundred years to hatch, and that time is coming soon. We are the last of our kind, and I have spent the last century protecting my child from the people who live beyond the mountains."

"If my ancestors had these blades that could kill you, why did they never come after you here?"

"The blades were broken and destroyed in battle and the men who did return from the war were not in any shape to fight."

Eira was saddened by the dragon's tale. "Why were we never told this?"

"You think mankind would have admitted to this treachery? Of course, they would spin the tale. I seethed with all the rage I had left in me the night I made my way here. I destroyed those snow gods and claimed this land for my own. Your ancestor was the leader of all of this. *He* convinced the countries to make a deal with us. *He* convinced them to deceive us."

"I'm sorry," was all Eira could say, "I had nothing to do with that." The dragon's rage churned within her and Eira could see a fire boiling within. Back to the riddle. She thought again, *Sulphur springs and healing. Snakes. Healing.* Then it hit her, "Wait—I know your name." *Huh, I guess I was paying attention in that class.* The dragon was taken aback. "I'm not going to weaken you. Take your egg and leave this land. Find somewhere else to call your home."

"I'm sorry, princess. But I don't trust humans that easily. You are made from the same blood that ran through your ancestors."

"I'm not my ancestors."

"I think I have had enough of this game," began the dragon. She rose to her feet and stretched her wings. "Maybe, you're right. Maybe it is time I pay the people a visit again."

"No!" Eira yelled. "No!" But it was too late. The dragon was airborne and heading for the city.


Eira scrambled up the side of the cliff, back to the cave's entrance. She shuffled her way through the narrow path so quickly that she had a few tears in her shirt and pants when she arrived back where Harwin was waiting. Harwin reared as he watched the dragon flying higher and higher into the skies above. When he saw Eira coming he raced over to her and she quickly got onto his back. He galloped down the side of the mountain as fast as he could, which was far faster than Eira had ever known. Leon had said unicorns were fast, but she had no idea how fast they could truly be when the need arose. It was almost as if Harwin was flying down the mountain, so sure of his footing and not skipping a beat.

The dragon was ready for another battle. The dragon did not like getting so close to having her home taken from her and her cries echoed through the sky like screeches of impending doom directed at the city below.

The warriors from Glasera that had been gathered by Leon and the others along with the Wintren-elves were already locked in a battle with the Innis army in the fields below the mountain. Many remained within the walls of the city to protect its borders from the dragon's anger.

As Eira and Harwin made their way down from the dragon's cave, Eira stopped at the sight of a battle unfolding below her.

"Who are they? What's happening?" she wondered, but of course, Harwin didn't answer her. She looked toward the sky and watched as the dragon got closer and closer to the city. There was not much she could do from where she was. She hoped that the city was ready for a battle because even though Leon and the others had done their best to prepare her for this outcome, she had never truly considered the fact that innocent people would end up in dragon fire. She watched as the dragon let out her first fiery breath across the sky. *Shit!*

# 20

There was silence all around and within the city of Glasera. The howling echo of the dragon's wings beating against the sky like drums of war was all that was heard, and that drumming was mimicked in the heartbeats of the people of Glasera as the fighting ceased and they stood in the eerie silence. Eira's friends all stood in the square, heads turned toward the sky watching the dark figure grow bigger and bigger as it drew nearer. She soared right over the foothills and over the city, encircling it a couple of times deciding her point of attack.

The dragon made her descent upon the city of Glasera. In her anger, she tried to burn down their walls. The people readied the water cannons to ward off the dragon fire. Archers in the foothills aimed their arrows at her underbelly but with every hit, the arrows bounced back falling to the ground. Eira had refused to weaken her and until she could get there, the dragon could not be defeated.

When the dragon hovered close enough to the ground, snow leopards leaped onto her back and tried to claw the scales from her body. Giant snowy owls appeared, almost as big as the dragon, and began attacking her in the skies. The warriors in the foothills had no choice but to retreat inside the walls of the city. Everyone held off the dragon for as long as they could, but they were running out of water just as the sun was nearing the mountaintops. The dragon was as strong as ever and it seemed she would not tire. All the people could do was try to hold their defences in the city.

Harwin was racing down the mountain as fast as he could with Eira in tow, however it had taken them a couple of hours to reach the dragon's lair from the base. The people of Glasera along with the Wintren-elves had been holding off the dragon attacks for most of the late afternoon. The dragon would, every so often, get tired and run out of fire and take to the skies again circling the Hoarfrost Mountains until she reminded herself that Eira had almost guessed her name and if she returned to her valley she would surely be defeated. Once her fires reignited, she turned on the city again.

The dragon had noticed Eira racing through the fields and she now had her eyes set on the desolation of the future Queen of Talvia; the only one who held the key to her demise. She flew stealthily beside Eira.

"Run all you want little queen. You can't protect them from me."

"Please stop this—please! I promise I won't weaken you, I promise we will let you leave in peace."

"You are not the first royal who made promises to me," and she took to the skies again.

The people knew the dragon was playing with them. If she wanted them all dead, they would be. Men were firing arrows from crossbows atop the city walls when Eira was ushered into the city. As she was coming in, Oren, Clea, and the rest of the group were making their way out.

"Oren! Where's Leon?" Eira exclaimed as she brushed past him almost missing him entirely.

"Around here somewhere."

"Oren, come on!" called Clea.

"It's good to see that dragon didn't destroy you," he smiled.

"Well, not yet," answered Eira. "But, we have to stop. We have to stop attacking her."

"Are you crazy? That's a dragon and he's going to destroy us all."

"*She*, won't. Not if I can get to her."

"You're insane. I don't care what you say, that dragon is destroying these people's homes and I'm going to help fight it." Oren raced to meet Clea, and Eira watched as they headed out of the gates into the foothills. She felt a hand clasp hers and soon she was being pulled out of the way of dragon fire by Killian.

"Eira," he said, "we need to get you somewhere safe." He led her along the cobblestone side streets until they found a small spot in the corner of two stone walls, untouched by dragon fire.

"So, did you do it? Has the dragon been weakened?" Killian asked.

"Um," she replied.

"Well, did you figure out his weakness?"

"Yeah, *her* name."

"What? *Her*?" He shook his head, "Whatever. So, what is it?"

She looked at him with worry in her eyes and plainly stated, "I don't know yet. I figured out the first bit, but..." She looked at Killian, "We need to stop fighting her. We need to tell everyone to stop firing at her."

"Have you lost it?"

"Ugh," she screamed and ran in the other direction looking for Leon. No one was listening to her. Why would they? It is a dragon attack, after all. Maybe if she could find Leon, she could convince him to stop the attack.

She raced through the city, trying to make her way out of the walls and into the foothills. If she had any chance of saving that gargantuan reptile currently circling the skies around the city, she had to make it back to the mountain and gain a higher vantage point. All around her people were racing for shelter from the dragon fire and ducking out of the way of falling chunks of stone from the buildings and walls. She got closer to the city's gates and noticed a group of soldiers fighting off some of the people from Innis who made their way into the city. Amongst them was Leon, locked in a battle of swords with another man roughly the same size as him. She was about to rush past when she was forced to stop in her tracks at the sight of another man ambushing Leon from behind. His sword was raised ready to attack without his victim having the slightest idea his demise was approaching. The chaos was so loud any attempt to call out to Leon would not make it to him in time. Before she could stop herself by overthinking, she drew her bow and two arrows from her quiver. Running closer to them for a better shot she drew back her bow.

*Please don't miss, please don't miss.* She let the first arrow fly right into the assailant who was sneaking up on Leon. He fell to the ground as Leon pulled his sword from the man he was fighting and turned to see who had just saved his life. He stared at her stunned and wide-eyed for only a second then she started to move closer to him.

"Well," she said meeting him where he stood, "now that I've saved your life, we can call the whole wolf thing even." She looked past him at the war still going on around them, "We have to get back up that mountain." She pushed past him but suddenly her arm was caught just above her elbow by his hand. She was pulled back toward him. Before Eira could say anything, his lips covered hers. She could feel the warmth of his body against hers. Not exactly the best time for this, but she understood his need for it.

Beside her came a great whinny and the moment was broken. She turned to see a horse rearing and pacing looking for an escape from the commotion. She gave Leon a quick look and ran over to it. She was almost knocked to the ground by its great hooves sailing into the air. Leon was soon beside her, calming the horse. When the horse seemed itself again, Eira grabbed the reins, gently moving them over the horse's head to its neck.

"Eira, stay here where it's safe," pleaded Leon.

"I think you know me better than that by now. Besides, I figured it out." She looked to the sky at the circling dragon. The dragon caught her sight and began to lower herself to the ground. Eira grabbed the saddle and threw herself atop the horse. Scanning her surroundings trying to find the safest route out of the city, she noticed her best point of exit; a clear path to the city's gates. She had to take it before it was too late. She moved her legs to kick the horse, signalling her to move forward, when there was a tug at the reins, halting the horse's motion.

"Eira, don't!" ordered Leon as he grabbed the horse's reins. "You'll get yourself killed, and then what?"

"We have to stop her, and I'm the only one who can convince her to leave this place." She forced the horse forward and the reins were ripped from Leon's hand.

"Eira! Get back here!" He called after her, but it was too late. Harwin appeared beside him at that moment and he jumped atop the stallion and raced after her.

All around her, the fighting subsided as everyone brought their sights to the mammoth beast landing in the middle of the field. She stood on all fours, staring right at Eira. A lull made its way across the fields and into the city. It was as if everyone was frozen in time, waiting to see the outcome of the awaiting standoff. Eira reached the middle of the valley where the dragon was waiting for her. She slowed the horse and walked slowly toward the dragon feeling her warm breath as she exhaled heavily. Rearing her head, she spoke,

"You dare come back for more?" she began. "Be wary, heir. I will burn you to a crisp if you do not tread lightly."

"I told you to leave. I told you I wouldn't harm you," Eira replied.

"I cannot trust you." The dragon waved her mighty wings and took off again hovering a few feet off the ground. "This battle is between you and me, princess. Let's say we take it somewhere else." And she shot into the sky again heading back for the mountains.

Lord Evian raced over to Eira, "Take this," and he thrust a sword into her hands. The blade looked as if it was made from ruby and Eira knew immediately what it was. "It's the only thing that can penetrate the dragon's armour."

The final battle against the dragon was upon her. Arrows continued to fly through the air but made no mark on the dragon's exterior. Circling high above the city she blasted her breath into the foothills creating circling fires surrounding the soldiers still fighting. Water was fired from cannons as fast as could be done, but the fire was strong. Eira turned her horse ready to race back up into the mountains. There was a ledge that jutted out over the foothills below which would be the perfect place to strike. Leon glanced at her and watched as her gaze moved from the surrounding battle to the mountain ledge. He knew all too well what she was about to do.

"No, Eira. It's too dangerous," he shouted at her as he cut her off with Harwin.

"I have to. We need a better vantage point and the mountains are the only place we're going to get it."

"Let me go. You can't risk your life any more than you already have. You need to rule this land after. No one will care if I'm gone."

"I will," she smiled. "Then I'll have to find a new fiancé, and dating is really exhausting. I'm kind of over it." He smiled and turned his gaze to Killian and Theo who were riding up beside them.

"After you, darling," Killian said to Eira. She thrust her horse forward and Harwin reared racing after her.

Eira jumped over the flames and raced toward the mountain. The horse was swift and brave, reaching the ridge in no time. Eira leapt from the horse and ran to the edge. She could see the dragon circling low in the foothills below and as the dragon caught sight of her, she turned and headed toward the mountain soaring up the mountainside right before Eira's eyes showing her underbelly. She was so close Eira could have reached out a hand and touched her. She backed up on the ledge as the force of the dragon's great body pushed against hers. Leon, Killian, and Theo were at her back.

When the dragon reached her target height, she straightened herself in the sky, head aimed toward Eira. She stood there. Still. Not frozen from fear, but standing bravely facing the beast readying herself for any blow she would give her. She drew the sword that Lord Evian had given her, holding it at her side for the dragon to see. The dragon's eyes widened at the sight of it, and rage boiled within. She landed on the ledge in front of Eira.

"That's impossible! All those blades were destroyed."

"I guess not all of them," replied Eira.

"See, you people are all the same. You *lied* to me! I told you I could not trust you."

"I didn't lie to you. I'm not going to hurt you." Eira threw the sword toward the dragon. She watched as it clanked onto the rock and landed before her dagger-like talons. The dragon looked at Eira and back to the sword. She then lifted her foot and crushed the sword under it. The sword's blade vanished into dust.

"What are you doing?" Leon called to Eira, but she wasn't listening to anyone. It was just her and the dragon. They faced off for a moment, silence all around when it was suddenly broken by a cry. Florian and a couple of Innis soldiers had followed them up the mountain and were battling Killian and Theo. Leon was lying on the ground, blood pouring from his side.

"No!" screamed Eira rushing over to him. The Innis soldiers along with Florian were down and Killian and Theo were standing over Eira as she knelt down next to Leon's body. His breathing was shallow and he could barely form words. She looked into his hazel eyes and feverishly wiped the tears that would not stop flowing from hers.

He reached a hand to Eira's cheek, "Hey, you know," he coughed, "this was always your destiny—but you were always mine. I just wish we had more time together, Princess," he winced and grabbed his side.

"No. No," cried Eira. "You're going to be fine. We just need to get you off this mountain." She looked to Killian and Theo, "Help him up." They reached down and pulled him off the ground, Leon clenching his teeth through the pain, each under one of his arms. They knew it was hopeless, but wouldn't dare tell her. Even if they did manage to get him down the mountain in time, who was going to help him? Even Lord Evian's powers could only go so far without the snow, and a wound like that was something not many come back from.

"Put him down," said a calm voice from behind. Eira turned to see that the dragon was still there. She had not fled. She stayed and watched. She watched as Eira's heart was torn open at the sight of Leon bleeding on the cold, hard earth. Eira turned around and wiped more tears.

"Put him down," the dragon said again. There was something in her voice that told them to listen. Theo and Killian laid Leon back on the ground and he clutched the wound on his side, grunting through the pain. Eira ran immediately back to his side. "What is the answer to my riddle?" the dragon asked.

"What?" Eira turned her head to the mighty beast.

"What is the answer to my riddle?" she asked again calmly.

Eira looked into her great yellow eyes and saw remorse and compassion. She spoke, "Sirona," she whispered. Then looking back at Leon, "Your name is Sirona," she said again through her tears.

Then Sirona's body began to glow and a ruby dust emanated from it as if her armour was dissolving just like the blade of the sword had. It floated in the air and began to fall over Leon. Eira, Theo and Killian watched as the dust swirled around them, always landing on Leon. She had sacrificed her armour to save another. She had transferred it to Leon himself. Eira watched as the wound on Leon's side began to close.

"Thank you," she turned to Sirona and smiled.

"I should be the one thanking you," Sirona replied. And if dragons could smile, she would have. "We have no debt between us now. I will leave this land and let it be restored to how it should be." With that, the magnificent beast took to the skies once more and headed for her valley in the mountains. Eira watched as she rose into the sky. She watched as a tiny red spot joined her and they both soared over the mountains to their new home—wherever that may be.

Eira turned back to Leon who was now sitting upright, looking at where his wound used to be. There was no trace of the stab wound, only a scar in the shape of a dragon.

"Are you okay?" she asked kneeling down in front of him, tears still streaming down her face.

"Man I love you," he smiled and placed both hands on the side of her face and pulled her lips to his.

"Yeah you do," smiled Killian. They turned to see Theo and Killian now nodding their heads with a couple of smirks on their faces.


The soldiers from Innis were still battling in the valley below until a single snowflake landed on the tip of a sword. Then another. Then another. Soon the skies had filled and the battle ceased. The Innis army surrendered to the new Queen of Talvia. They had nothing to fight for any longer. Boreas along with the Wintren-elves and fairies had their full magic returned to them and in no time they had covered the trees with a layer of frost and snow. The blood-stained battlefield was covered with a sheet of white. Before long the fires in the foothills were extinguished and the vast landscape, the whole of Talvia, was returned to its rightful state as the Winter Country. Eira stood atop the mountain and watched as the snowflakes fell all around her. She turned to see Theo and Killian, bowing to her; to their queen.

"You know, I seem to remember you saying something about bowing to me, too," she looked at Leon standing beside her.

"Oh, I will later," he winked, "believe me. But right now, I'm still a little sore." She smiled. "Hey, so how did you solve the riddle anyway?"

"Oh, well I took a mythology course back in my world and that name always reminded me of this song, so I never forgot it."

"Huh."

"Yeah—it's convenient when it works out that way."


The city of Glasera was destroyed by the wrath of Sirona. The last few embers of fire-scorched buildings were put to rest. Eira, Leon, Theo and Killian sauntered through the city, taking in the ruin as people hugged them and thanked Eira profusely for what she had done for them and for Talvia. She made her way through the streets looking for familiar faces and assuring the injured they would be helped. They finally found Clea, Oren and Bianca outside the crumbled city hall.

"Whoa, dude," Oren said looking at Leon's bloodstained and mangled jacket, but also noticing that he was clearly fine. "What happened to you?"

Leon glanced at him and took a breath, "Long story."

"So," started Killian, "do you think you have cool dragon powers now?"

"I don't think so."

"Bummer."

Leon put an arm around Eira and pulled her close to him, kissing her on the head.

"You sure you're okay?" she asked again.

"I'll survive," he shrugged.

"Good, because I'd hate to actually be the death of you," she smiled.

"You might still be, Princess. You never know what our future holds," he smiled.

"Well, I know one thing," she said turning to face him and rising to her tippy-toes. She pulled him close. The kiss was just long enough and everything both of them needed after what they had just been through. She lowered back down to her feet, looked into his eyes and smiled, "I'm glad we get to find out together."

# 21

The days after the battle were long and filled with sorrow. Many had lost loved ones in the battle and the city would take a long time to heal. Eira promised the people that she would make sure that their city was built back to where it was before. The missing funds from Kane would provide more than enough to pay for the rebuilding of the city. The people of Glasera who lost their homes were relocated to Innis while they waited for their city to be habitable again. Innis welcomed them with open arms as if a spell had lifted from them the moment the dragon fled and the snow returned.

After a week of helping wherever they were needed, Eira and her friends knew it was time to go home.

"You know, darling," said Killian wrapping an arm around Eira as they were readying their horses to leave the city. "While I'm really glad you're back, it was nice not freezing my ass off every time I walked outside."

She chuckled, "So, you're going back to Syysia after this?"

"Nah, this has kind of become my second home. Plus I hear that castle of yours has lots of room."

"You know you're always welcome there, Killian."

Leon walked over to them, "You guys ready? It's a long way back to Lord Evian's and I have no idea what type of party we're going to be sucked into this time. We might end up having to stay longer than a night."

"I'm just looking forward to those hot springs again," added Killian.

"I'd tell you what I'm looking forward to," Leon's eyes darkened as he leaned into Eira, "but not in front of Killian."

"You guys are gross," and Killian walked away from them, just as Oren and Bianca were walking toward them.

"I really can't convince you to stay?" pleaded Eira.

He shook his head, "It's time for me to leave. I was stuck in that castle my whole life. There's a lot of this world I want to see, but I'll be back someday. Don't worry. I wouldn't miss getting to know my big sister." She hugged him and Bianca and watched with sorrowful eyes as they walked away into the snow-covered city.

"It's a lot to take in, isn't it?" asked Leon.

Eira looked at him, "Yeah, it's pretty weird. I mean...I'm a queen."

"Yeah, you are," he smiled.

"I have to live here now," she added talking herself through everything that was going to change in her life— not like it hasn't changed significantly already.

"Yes, but I think you'll like living in a castle."

"I mean, I'm sure I'll get used to it," she smiled and the two stared at each other for a moment.

"Look," began Leon, "I did want to still talk to you about before, about the whole betrothed thing. We never really got to discuss it properly."

"Oh yeah....so I guess we're supposed to get married now."

"No, that marriage alliance ended the moment I met you."

"Excuse me?"

"That's not what I meant," he assured her. "I just meant there is no way I would expect you to marry me or anyone you didn't want to. Even if you had grown up in Talvia and we had got to know each other more than just once a month, with you kicking my ass most of the time."

"Ha, so you do admit that I kicked your ass."

He rolled his eyes, "If you don't want to marry me, no one's going to make you."

"Good, because maybe I don't want to marry you. I mean you've basically ruined my life..." she paused and looked into his eyes lowering her voice and taking a breath, "since I met you." But what she meant was that he ruined her life in the best possible way, and he knew it.

He leaned in close and teased her with his lips hovering over hers and then whispered, "Well, I do prefer brunettes anyway," and before she could retort, he kissed her quickly and backed off.

"You are the most insufferable human being I have ever met!" Eira shoved Leon in a playful manner.

"Yeah, but you kind of like me," he smiled.

"Well, I suppose it could have been worse. You could be some ugly old fat dude with a receding hairline. At least you're not completely unfortunate looking."

"Oh, thank you. I'm glad I meet your standards, Princess."

"Hey, you two," called Theo. "If you're done with your unnecessary displays of affection, we have important stuff to do over here."


It was a cold winter afternoon when Eira, Leon, Killian and Theo set out for the Valley of the Ethereal. Clea had decided to stay back with her sister and help the city rebuild. While she did harbour a sense of animosity toward this place, it was her home and she also felt a responsibility to help the people rebuild. She never did run into her parents during the time spent there. She had no idea what had come of them. Boreas left too when the war was over and the snow was falling again. His debt to this land and the Queen of Talvia was paid.

The rest of the group would stay in the Valley of the Ethereal for the night and head out again in the morning. The journey back felt strange. Not a strange, strange. But a good strange. Their conversations and laughter as they walked were dampened by a silence that lay upon the land that had not been there for over a hundred years. The still air that only comes with newly fallen snow.

"So, when did you two finally, you know, embrace your feelings for one another?" Killian asked when they were nearing the Valley of the Ethereal. They could see the bridge ahead of them in the distance.

"Oh, um...well the last night of Myrrvintrel, I guess," answered Eira.

Killian smiled at Theo who grumbled and tossed him a coin.

"Seriously guys? You bet on us?" asked Leon.

"Oh, come on. You should have seen the look on your face when Eira showed up in that dress on the last night. I thought you were going to pass out. I knew it was going down then. There was no way you'd stay away from her," mocked Killian.


When they arrived back at Lord Evian's palace in the Valley of the Ethereal, it looked as if they had never left. While this place seemed not to have changed one bit— even Eira's room looked as if it hadn't been touched since she left, the group certainly had. They were not the same people they were when last they were guests of Lord Evian's.

"Well, back here again," Leon smirked from the doorway of Eira's room. Not in the doorway though, leaning against it. Of course he was. Eira had read enough romance novels to know what would happen next.

"I guess so," she said looking up at him.

"Either shut the door or come to the hot springs with us," said Killian as he and Theo walked past.

The two chuckled. "So...hot springs?" asked Leon. Eira nodded.

When the sun warmed her face the next morning, Eira felt a complete sense of calm over her. She didn't need to revel in the warmth of her bed or Leon beside her. She didn't need to try to go back to sleep to savour a few more moments before the real world and her destiny took over. She was now living the best dream of all—one that she had pushed away for so long but was now all she ever wanted. She couldn't wait to get up and see what the new day had in store for her, because whatever it was, it was worth fighting a dragon for.

The group stood before Lord Evian's Almaluna door, now placed nicely in the stables.

"It will take you back to the edge of Lake Isas and you can journey home from there," said Evian.

"Why didn't we just use this the first time we were here?" Killian whispered to Theo, "It would have saved us from having to hang out with those fairies."

Lord Evian cleared his throat. "You all had better get going. It is time for our queen to go home," he smiled. The men and horses walked through. Eira was about to when she remembered something.

"Lord Evian," she asked. "Why didn't you just give me, or Leon the sword when he asked you if there was another way to defeat the dragon? When he was trying to spare me? If that's what he wanted to do?"

"Because it is not his job to fight your battles for you." Well, it could be. It would have made her life a lot easier. "You needed to believe you had something worth fighting for. You were always meant to conquer the dragon, not necessarily slay her. If given the sword, your companions perhaps would have convinced you to simply go in there and be rid of the beast. Or they would have done it themselves. It was only when you learned of the true tale that you were ready for it. Anger can corrupt a lot of people, and it takes a strong person to stand against it and find the light in a dark world. It's the making of a true queen—compassion goes a long way."

She hugged him and stepped through the door.


They arrived at the edge of Lake Isas, just as Lord Evian had said they would. The world around looked as if everything suddenly belonged. The peaks of the roofs in Huurre were covered in a thick blanket of snow and the colours of the woods were popping against the white.

"Well, this is it," began Leon walking over to Eira, "last stop before we're home."

"Yeah, it's weird how different it all seems here. I mean, we were just here not too long ago and yet, everything seems to have changed." She was right. The air around was not only colder, but it had changed in another way. The people's spirits seemed higher and there were more people out in the streets, smiling and saying friendly greetings to those they passed. The absence of Sirona not only brought back the snow but a long-lost feeling in the hearts of the people of Talvia. It was the feeling of belonging and having their way of life brought back to them, even if they had long forgotten what exactly that was. People were starting to find their place in the world again.

"Hey, come with me for a second," said Leon taking Eira by the hand and leading her down to the shore of Lake Isas. They stopped before hitting the water that was now frozen. Eira looked to the west and gazed upon her kingdom rising above the lake and watched as the sun radiated off the turrets and glazed the snow-covered roofs in warm yellow.

"Wow." She turned to Leon, "do you really think I can do this?" she asked. "Do you really think I'm ready to rule a kingdom? I know nothing about being a political leader, or even if I truly want this job. I certainly want it more now than I did before, but still. I know that sounds bad, but—"

"You don't have to do anything you're not ready for," Leon interjected. "You don't have to take the crown until you feel like you are ready for it. But I know that despite all of the feelings you're having right now, and all the feelings you had before, you are more ready for this than any of the queens that came before you. And remember...you're not alone in this."

"Thanks," she placed a small kiss on his lips. "Well, I guess we should, wait—" she suddenly altered her train of thought, "how long have I been gone for—from my world I mean? People can't just up and leave without telling anyone where you're going. People have probably been looking for me, and school. I've missed so much school, and I'm not sure I can convince the university it's because I'm the ruler of a magical land. I'll lose my visa."

"Don't worry about any of it," chuckled Leon taking her by the shoulders and leaning down to kiss her. "Now, we should get back home."

Eira was exhausted and as soon as they made it back to Trillium Nivale and her head hit the plush pillow resting at the head of her bed, she fell asleep right away. It was almost as if something came over her, she didn't think she was that tired but the snugness of the bed knew otherwise. It was hopeless to think she could stay awake once she was in its warm covers. As soon as her mind drifted off into the land of dreams, the snow began falling at a familiar pace down from the heavens above; that same heavy snowfall that surrounded her a few weeks ago when she was walking home from work.

# 22

She felt like she had slept forever when Eira awoke from a most pleasant nap. She wandered down the hall—three doors to the right, to Leon's room and knocked, but there was no answer. The sun was setting in Talvia and the halls of the castle were washed with an orange glow. She tried the usual spots: the kitchen, the library, the study, but she couldn't find Leon anywhere. If only the castle wasn't so big. She eventually did find him in the open-air sitting room with a fire roaring in the fireplace and a drink in his hand as he read a book. She wandered over to him. He looked up and put his drink down and reached an arm out for her as she snuggled in beside him.

"Did you have a good nap?" he asked. She nodded and leaned her head on his shoulder, not saying anything. "So, you ready to go back? To the other world?"

"What?" her head shot up.

"Well you didn't think we'd just kidnap you and not let you sort things out there first before starting your new life, did you?"

She nodded, "Okay, makes sense."

They headed to the library and down behind some of the bookshelves. Way in the back, and practically hidden, there was a small door. Leon opened it and they walked inside where another familiar door was hidden from all unless you knew where to look.

"You guys have one of these too?" Eira asked as she looked at the Almaluna door; an exact copy of the one Lord Evian had.

Leon nodded, "How do you think I was able to go train with you every month?"

"Oh, yeah. I guess I never really thought about it. Wait. Why didn't we just use this for the journey to the mountains? It would have saved so much time."

"Where's the fun in that?"

She gave him a look as if to say, *you guys suck.*

He grinned and opened the door. On the other side, Eira could see a setting she was all too familiar with. Her living room looked the same as if she had never left. He motioned for her to go inside and she walked through. Almost instantly something in her pocket needed attention. She reached into her pocket and pulled out her phone. Plain as day and in big bold letters it said *December 23* with multiple unread notifications. Not even a day had passed since she had fallen into Talvia.

"That can't be right?" she said to Leon showing him the phone.

"See, I told you not to worry about it," he smiled. "No one will even have known you were gone."

Her phone was still exploding with texts incoming one after the other,

*Where are you?*

*Did you forget you're supposed to be at work right now? This isn't like you.*

*Seriously, Eira!*

*ANSWER ME!*

*If you've been kidnapped, can I have your apartment?* They were all from Nell.

They spent the afternoon packing the things she wanted to bring back to Talvia and honestly getting sidetracked a few times. Maybe Leon wasn't the best person to have with her if she actually wanted to get things done. They were just about ready to leave but Eira had one last stop to make.


"Ah, Eira, there you are," greeted Peter as she walked through the doors of the pub. "Hope you're feeling okay? Take these plates to the table by the window and then there are some dishes in the sink that need to be washed." Eira stood there for a moment, plates in hand, staring at them wondering how no time had passed and no one noticed she had been gone. "Eira, now!" urged the manager again breaking her trance.

She handed them back over to him, "Um, no. Actually, I came here to tell you that I quit."

"What?" gasped Nell coming over to her. "What are you talking about?"

"Look, I'll explain it all in a minute—hold on," she said raising her hand and looking out the window. Then she brushed past Leon and Nell and walked outside to a couple standing on the street waiting for the light to change. Leon looked out the window to where Eira had been staring and saw the couple.

"Who's that?" he asked Nell who had moved closer to him to get a better look at what Eira was doing.

She looked out the window, "That's...Trey. Wait— who are *you*?" she turned to him.

"That's Trey?" he replied looking at Nell, but before she could say any more he walked outside with great purpose.

"Hey, Trey," said Eira interrupting the couple's sidewalk make-out session.

"Oh, damn. Hey, Eira," Trey replied.

"Who's this?" asked the girl, but before Eira could answer Leon was beside her.

"Hi, Trey is it?" The question was rhetorical and followed by Leon decking him in the face.

"Don't worry about who I am," Eira said to the girl smiling, and then walked back into the bar with Leon who was shaking his fist. She sat him down at a table and Nell, having seen the whole thing, came out with a bag of ice for his hand. She handed it to him and stood beside Eira.

"I don't know who this guy is, but I like him," smiled Nell.

Eira turned to Leon and smiled, "You didn't have to do that. In case you haven't learned by now, I'm pretty capable of handling my own affairs."

"I know," he smiled, "but it felt good."

"Okay, can you please tell me what is going on?" asked Nell. "Who is this, and where have you been?"

"Oh, I'm Leon," he held his hand to Nell. "Her fiancé."

"What?" gasped Nell.

"Sort of," replied Eira. "I will explain it all later, after your shift. Meet me at my place." Then she turned to Peter who was now standing beside Nell. "Like I said, I'm going away," she began, "probably forever. So, I quit."

"Hold on, Eira, you are my best waitress, now where do you think you are going?" asked Peter.

"To a magical land with knights and castles and dragons to be slain." She turned to Nell, "I'll see you later." Then she grabbed Leon's hand and headed out of the pub.

"Eira, have you lost your mind?" called Nell running out onto the street after her. "Are you going back home or something?"

"Yeah, something like that."

She turned to Leon and smiled, "Oh, and just because we're betrothed from my birth, doesn't mean you can get away with not proposing." She turned and started to walk down the street. He quickly jumped to follow her.

"Um, yes it does. That's the whole point."

"Oh no, I still expect you down on one knee, the ring, all that jazz. It'll be great."

"Okay, we may have to talk about this."

"Hey...guys," called Nell running after them, "will someone please tell me exactly what is going on here?"

****

Months went by in Talvia while Eira was preparing for her coronation. She had a great deal more to learn about Talvia and its history that would ensure she would be a great ruler.

"I see you have settled into your new role here quite nicely," said Leon as he met Eira in one of the corridors after she met with the queens and kings of the Spring and Autumn Countries. Kesa would prove to be more difficult. They were not going to be allies that easily and did not wish to meet with Eira.

"Yes, I think I might actually be able to do this. And I've even gotten used to these elaborate gowns they keep dressing me in," she motioned to the a-line gold and cream number she was sporting for the meeting.

"You wear them well," smiled Leon pulling her close and kissing her.

Later that week, Eira was getting ready for her coronation when a familiar knock was at her door. It was the same loud rapping pattern that a friend always made outside of her apartment in Adelaide.

"Nell!" Eira exclaimed opening the door and taking in the girl standing before her. The last time she opened a door to Nell, she was greeted with a lit birthday cake. This time, she was holding a large box.

"This is so cool, Eira," Nell was beaming in the awe of it all.

"Right?"

"It's like *The Princess Diaries*—except you did know you were the heir to this throne. And I have to say, Leon is a pretty close second to Chris Pine."

"I know, right? I mean...he'll do." The girls smiled and laughed.

"Anyway," Nell shoved her arms containing the box forward, "I have a present for you."

"For *moi*?" questioned Eira placing a hand on her chest. She took the box and walked over to the coffee table and placed it down. Pix jumped up and started to sniff the wrapping paper.

"Think of it as a, *congratulations on being a queen,* present."

"You really didn't have to get me anything."

"Well, I didn't really. Just open it."

Eira moved to the box and pulled one of the ends of the purple ribbon until the bow came loose. She then proceeded to tear at the Disney Princess wrapping paper. She opened the box and looked inside to see her laptop and speakers. She looked up, puzzled at what was in the box.

"It's loaded with all of your favourite movies. I know you gave it to me seeing as there's no internet here, but I figured you might need it."

"I love you," said Eira pulling her laptop from the box. "I thought I was going to have to live without this."

"And I got you a solar-powered charger. I didn't know if they had electricity here or not."

"Of course they do, Nell. You think they have magic but they can't figure out electricity? But anyway, I don't think they sell Talvian adapters online."

"Yeah, probably not," agreed Nell. Then she took something small that looked like rolled-up fabric out from her sweater pocket, "Oh, I also got you this." She unrolled the fabric to reveal a t-shirt and held it out in front of her, "Bam!" Written on the shirt were the words: *Because I'm the Queen, that's why.*

Eira read it and smiled, "Awesome! I can wear this to my coronation right?"

"I don't see why not. It goes with everything."

"Can you help me with my dress?" she asked heading over to the closet.

"Of course, Your Majesty," Nell bowed.

A Moment later, Eira emerged wearing her coronation gown. "Holy crap!" gasped Nell. "You look amazing!"

"Thanks, but I need help with the buttons." She turned around to reveal the full back of her dress having to be done up with small buttons.

Nell proceeded to begin the tedious task, "Oh man, Leon's gonna have fun with this later."

"Nell!"

"What? Like you haven't thought of it?"

It was six months after Eira had gone on a journey, defeated a dragon and decided she was ready to be a queen. She was more than ready to take her place in Talvian history as the new queen. The Talvians rejoiced in crowning the first queen they had in years. Eira walked slowly down the aisle in the same great hall at her new home in Trillium Nivale that she had walked her first day there. She wore a gown fit for a queen of the Winter Country; a stunning deep royal blue ball gown completely embroidered in silver with vines, leaves and snowflakes that faded to a lighter blue around the bottom and at the tips of the ruffled layers all around the skirt. The Queen Anne neckline suited her frame perfectly.

This was her moment and she had to keep reminding herself to breathe. All eyes were on her as she made her way to the throne that Leon's father, Charles, stood beside holding her crown—the very one that Gideon had gifted to her on her first day in Talvia. It seemed so daunting then, the first time she held it in her hands. She could feel the weight of it, but now it seemed lighter, like she was born to wear it. The thought of hundreds of eyes fixated on her and her alone was something she would have to get used to in the coming months—years, her lifetime really, for it was she and she alone who was responsible for the wellbeing of this land. She knelt down and Charles began. She swore to rule over Talvia with all the grace, patience and undeniable judgement like her ancestors before her.

"I hereby crown you Eira, Queen of Talvia. May you rule a lifetime in the adoration of your people."

Charles placed the crown atop Eira's head. She stood and turned to her people cheering in the crowd. Everyone was there including Neil and his family who had travelled from Glasera for the coronation. Nell was cheering quite possibly the loudest of all and Eira hoped that she wasn't being judged too much by it. Eira was now queen and ruler of all the Winter Country. She would always have a home there and always be a queen of Talvia, for as long as she would reign.

The coronation ball was a night Eira would remember forever. It was still a strange thought to her that she was now responsible for the security of an entire land, but she was ready for whatever that responsibility might bring. She found Leon in the crowd standing with his mother and two other women she could only assume were his sisters. Eira now had a brother and she had Nell who was always like a sister to her, but she had always wondered what it would be like to actually have a sister. She walked slowly over to them and Leon caught her eye and smiled.

"Hey, Princess," he smiled, but Eira simply shook her head and pointed to her crown. "Oh, yeah. I guess I'm going to have to stop calling you that." He turned to the women beside him, "I'd like you to meet my sisters, Amelia and Gwen."

"It's very nice to finally meet the two of you," Eira smiled.

"And you too, Your Majesty," replied Amelia with a small curtsy. "We've been bugging Leon for information but he doesn't really share much."

"Sounds about right," laughed Eira.

When a moment came in the night for her to escape from the tireless questions and obligations that came with her new title, Eira made her way off toward the balcony that overlooked the entire winter gardens of the castle. There was a towering evergreen tree all lit up on the balcony. It was one of the most beautiful nights Eira had ever seen. The stars were glowing like tiny windows in the floor of heaven and there was not a cloud in the sky to disrupt the sheer majesty of the deepest blue she had ever witnessed. The snow atop the mountains was highlighted by the moonlight and they stood out as a shielding backdrop to the castle. Breathing in the cold winter's air was the only thing that calmed her nerves about being a good queen. It was better than any sedative that could be administered.

"You wear it quite well," began Gideon referring to her crown as he came up to Eira to congratulate her.

"Thank you," exclaimed Eira embracing him for a hug, remembering back to the first time she had met him and the words of wisdom he had bestowed upon her that day.

"This truly is a wonderful evening, isn't it?"

"Yes, it is," responded Eira as she looked out toward the crowd of people in the ballroom.

"Now, my dear, I do believe it is time for your first dance as queen."

"What?" Eira was never told anything about having to dance.

There was a tap on her shoulder and she turned to see Leon standing behind her, "May I have this dance?"

Eira smiled up into his calming brown-green eyes and took his hand. He led her ever so gracefully into the centre of the dance floor in the great hall. Glittering snowflakes hung from the ceiling and white, leafless trees bordered the hall creating the ambiance of a grand winter festival. The lights sparkled around them creating a golden glow on the scene and the deep blue of a winter's night sky radiated in through the windows. When their dance was over, Eira found Nell standing by herself in the corner of the ballroom.

"Hey," she started.

"Hey," answered Nell. "So...you're going to live here now right? I mean, I know you told me and I've been here a day now, but it still seems..."

"Not real?"

"Yeah."

"Yeah, well, you get used to it."

"But you can come back and visit right? I mean, you're not stuck here forever?"

"Yeah, I can go back. And you can come here anytime you want, too."

"Yeah, so...this place is like, *all* winter, *all* the time?"

"Yes," Eira rolled her eyes.

"Well, okay, maybe I'll come for a bit. You do have hot springs, right?"

"Yes," Eira nodded. "So, what are you doing standing here all by yourself?" Eira asked.

"Are you kidding me?" responded Nell. "Most of the guys here are princes, or lords, or something far out of my league. And is it just me, or is everyone in this world ridiculously attractive? I hardly fit in, and this dress you put me in is squishing parts on me I didn't even know I had," she said as she tried to adjust the bodice of her gown.

"Well, I guess you're just going to have to find some nice gentleman to help you with that." Eira turned to look at the room and then she caught someone's eye, "Killian," she called out and motioned for him to come over to her. "This is Nell," she said when Killian was standing in front of them.

Nell glanced at Eira, "Girl," she said with wide eyes as if to really say, *have you seen how gorgeous this guy is?* She blushed when Killian took her hand and led her onto the dance floor.

"What are you doing?" asked Leon appearing beside Eira.

"What do you mean?"

Leon nodded toward Nell and Killian in the centre of the dance floor and glanced back at Eira questioning her matchmaking abilities.

"Oh, come on. She's my friend and they would actually be perfect together."

"Oh, sure—except for the fact that he lives here in another world entirely. That's just taking long-distance relationships to the extreme."

"Oh please. Who says they'll even hit it off? I'm simply making her time here worthwhile until she has to go back to her boring mundane life because not everyone can be a queen and live in a palace."

"You're such a good friend," he stated with every ounce of sarcasm he could muster.

"I know, right?" she smiled and he smiled back.

"Anyway, it's time for a coronation tradition."

"And what's that?" she asked warily.

He led her out to the balcony. She could see people standing in the gardens below and atop the hill where her parent's monument stood, all with flickering lights lining the grounds. All the guests had made their way outside and were waiting.

"What's going on? Why is everyone outside?" she asked.

"You'll see—just look." Suddenly, the sky lit up with blasts of colour. She twirled around from the sound of the blasts and watched as drops of gold, silver, blue and purple rained down on them.

"Wow," she exclaimed in awe. They watched the fireworks in silence for a minute, but then it was broken.

"So, still happy I found you in the woods all that time ago?"

"Well, mostly because if you hadn't come along, I would probably have been eaten by wolves," she smiled.

"That would have been less than ideal," he joked.

"Well, things certainly got a lot more complicated since I met you, but that's not necessarily a bad thing. Plus, embracing where I come from kind of gave me a whole new perspective on everything. It's pretty good."

"Believe me, this right here, is as good as it gets," he smiled and pulled her close, then turned her around and embraced her from behind as they watched the last of the fireworks.

It was a night to be remembered by all and a new beginning for the people of Talvia. The snow glistened across the land once more under a starry sky just like it had done for many years when Eira's ancestors ruled.

In the months that followed her coronation, Eira was inundated with things that needed to be addressed regarding Talvia. The life of a queen was proving to be less fun than she had thought it would be. She was far too busy to even think about her old life in Adelaide and far too happy with her new one in Talvia to let herself be sad while reminiscing.

Eira sat on the lounge chair on the balcony overlooking the vast frozen waters of Lake Isas. Looking out to her kingdom, she thought of the first time she had gazed upon the same scene. She could not even think of what she had left behind from the world she once knew; the world she had grown up in. Talvia had certainly become her home, and she had a family and friends there like none she could have imagined.

"Ah, look at that. It's snowing," he said as he walked out onto the balcony. Eira turned to see Gideon walking up beside her. "It truly is amazing what a little snow can do, don't you think?" Gideon said to Eira with a wink and a sparkle in his eye. He looked out over her kingdom, covered in a blanket of snow and sparkling in the radiance of the afternoon sun over the mountains. "So pure and illustrious; the way it comes and covers all the troubles of the world and wipes it clean as if for a fresh start. It really is quite magical, the first snowfall of the year. You could almost say it brings with it the notion that something magical is about to happen." He then walked off with his hands behind his back, pausing at the door when Leon approached. "Ah Leon," he said patting him on his shoulder as he walked past.

"There you are," said Eira as she turned to look at him. He smiled and walked over to her.

"Aren't you cold out here?" he asked as he motioned for her to move forward and sat behind her, pulling her between his legs and wrapping his arms around her midsection.

"Not really," she replied. She was wearing a pair of cozy leggings and Leon's sweatshirt. "Look at how beautiful it is with the sun shining, making the snow all sparkly."

"It *is* nice," he replied. "How about we go on a little adventure?"

"With you—always. But I don't know," she continued, "the last adventure you dragged me on nearly killed me."

"I promise this one will be perfectly safe."

"I seem to remember you saying that about the first one too."

"It was supposed to be safe. It's not my fault *you* kept getting yourself into situations where you needed saving. And I seem to remember *I* was the one who almost died."

"My fault?" she drew her head back in shock. "I was just following you. If anyone got us into tricky situations, it was you."

"Alright fine—we'll blame Killian. Anyway, are you coming with me or not?" Leon smiled, "I can promise it will be magical."

# Epilogue

It had been a year since Eira was forced back into Talvia. Leon was just making his way back into the castle from the skating rink when Ceilidh came running up to him, "My lord, there you are. It is urgent. Gideon needs to see you right away!"

Leon ran into the castle to where Gideon was waiting for him. As soon as he made his way through the door, Gideon pulled him aside and shut the door.

"What is all of this about?" he asked calmly, but he could tell by the look on Gideon's face that this was not a situation for calm.

He looked at Leon and spoke closely to him to ensure none would be able to overhear what he was about to say.

"I am afraid we have just received word from our allies in the East. It is not good, Leon, and we must figure out a plan as to how to move forward with this information."

"What information?" pushed Leon. "You're not actually telling me anything? Should I go get Eira?"

"No!" shot Gideon, cutting him off. "We shouldn't burden her with this information just yet. Not until we have come up with a plan. Let her enjoy her time a little longer."

"A plan for what?" pushed Leon again, getting a bit annoyed with the fact that he was not actually being told anything of any importance.

Finally, Gideon felt it was time to let Leon in on what was happening, "Do you remember that conversation we had several months ago? I am afraid it is time to remember the man I told you to forget."

# About the Author

Alexandra Louise lives in Alberta, Canada with her husband and daughters. She spends most of her time writing and taking care of her littles because she enjoys being bossed around by tiny dictators, retreating to her own fictional worlds, and getting paid for neither. Her books are full of relatable characters, fun adventures, low spice/ fade to black for everyone to enjoy, swoony moments, and of course happily ever afters.